Guardian of the Gem

The reptilian creature facing him bolted forward, its enormous body swaying to and fro in its charge. Brewing with anger, Logan lashed out with his dagger. The blade skimmed off the creature's forearm, leaving a faint white streak across the grey scales. Gargling, it took three quick steps to one side, oval eyes flaring.

Logan stanced himself for battle, legs spread slightly apart for balance. His arm shook with fear as the iron-scaled creature shambled forward.

Hardly two feet separated the combatants. Ablaze with his hatred, the young man swung about, plunging Moknay's gift directly into a nostril. Blood spumed into the air as the monster howled, rearing back its head in pain. With a silver flash, the dagger thrust out again . . .

THE JEWEL OF EQUILIBRANT

STEVEN FRANKOS

ACE BOOKS, NEW YORK

This book is an Ace original edition,
and has never been previously published.

THE JEWEL OF EQUILIBRANT

An Ace Book / published by arrangement with
the author

PRINTING HSTORY
Ace edition / March 1993

All rights reserved.
Copyright © 1993 by Steven Frankos.
Cover art by Den Beauvais.
This book may not be reproduced in whole or in part,
by mimeograph or any other means, without permission.
For information address: The Berkley Publishing Group,
200 Madison Avenue, New York, NY 10016.

ISBN: 0-441-80243-5

Ace Books are published by The Berkley Publishing Group,
200 Madison Avenue, New York, NY 10016.
The name "ACE" and the "A" logo
are trademarks belonging to Charter Communications, Inc.

PRINTED IN THE UNITED STATES OF AMERICA

10   9   8   7   6   5   4   3   2   1

*Dedicated to the memory of my mother,
who taught me that not only is it okay to be weird,
slightly warped, and given to flights of fancy,
but more fun that way, too.*

N

SEA OF
HEDELVA

TRYSLENE

CLYNDAS

FRELARS

PRIFRANE

OHMMARBIOUS R.

PLESTENAH

LEPHAR R.

GELVANIMORE

WAILVYE

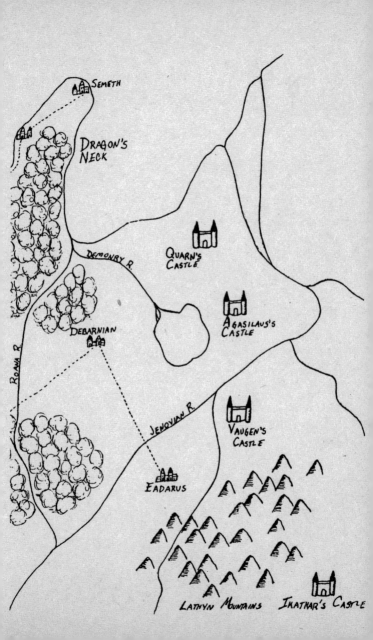

·1·

Dream

"*Have you no fear of dreams?*"

The voice arose from the eddying tidepools of red and silver light, piercing the stillness with its harsh, rasping tone.

"*Know you not that dreams have the powers to crush and to rend and to shred?*"

Matthew Logan blinked his eyes repeatedly, staring at the spiraling vortex of blood and metal that encircled him. A disorienting sensation of wrongness swelled up around the young man, and, frantically, he wondered where he was.

"*Most vivid during the REM stage of sleep, during what doctors call the paradoxical stage of sleep, do dreams descend upon the sleeper like lions upon their prey. There they lay bare your deepest fears, claw open your best-kept secrets, and feast upon your anguish with ghoulish delight. Can you not hear their laughter?*"

The wheezing, disembodied voice slowly sank into the vacuum of lights and colors, and Logan knew it would not be back in that form. Instead, another rattle began to reverberate through Logan's ears, and a faint, shuddering chuckle rose up out of the red and silver glare around him. Again the overpowering sense of mismatchment fluttered about Logan, causing a small voice in the back of his mind to tell him he did not belong.

A hazy figure took form within the blaze of red and silver; quick, brisk strides bringing it closer to where Logan stood.

The laughter began to recede, but the oddness of the area about him refused to depart.

The whirling gyration of the fluid colors quickened as the lean form stepped up to face Logan. Reflecting the red and silver illumination of the whirlpool, the gaunt figure peered down at the young man, and its frown was highlighted by the glare.

Trying to slough off the feeling of disharmony, Logan stared up at the form. Yellow-white hair, tinted with reds and silvers, dangled from the sides of the domed head, descending to the shoulder and beyond. The top of the stranger's head was bald, glistening as the spiraling colors danced upon its naked surface. Throughout the insistent gleam, Logan could make out the neat three-piece suit which garbed the newcomer.

The stranger's eyes reflected his frown.

"*Traverse not into folly,*" he told Logan in the same rasping wheeze as before. "*I am sorry.*"

The red and silver glow brightened as the long-haired businessman lowered his head solemnly. Unexpectedly, he jerked back up and his eyes were ablaze with fire.

"*Take heed,*" he snarled, eyes flickering, "*you who fears not dreams. Learn to decipher dreams from reality, unreality from falsehood, falsehood from truth, or doom shall fall upon your worlds!*"

Logan cringed as the wrongness that surrounded him seeped into his flesh and made him helpless.

The frown on the businessman's face had been replaced by a murderous smirk. "*Know you not that dreams have the power to kill?*"

Matthew Logan woke up. With a murmured curse, he looked about his cluttered bedroom as his eyes adjusted to the dim rays of early morning light that seeped between the shutters. His black hair was slick with sweat, and the covers of his bed lay twisted and coiled like serpents of fabric. Inhaling deeply, he gently settled back down, staring up at the dark ceiling. He feared if he closed his eyes the dream would return with all its vivid colors and sounds.

That was a damn interesting one, he told himself, wiping perspiration from his brow. A long-haired businessman? And what the hell was all that about dreams?

Muttering at the loss of sleep the nightmare cost him, Logan continued to stare at the ceiling until the sun crested the eastern mountains and sent brighter slivers of daylight into his apartment. Gradually he dressed, put in his contacts, shaved, ate something for breakfast, and started for the door. As he slipped into his dark blue sweat jacket and sweat pants and headed out of his apartment for his early morning jog, the scratchy, asthmatic voice went on taunting him:

"Have you no fear of dreams?"

Something filled with color darted past upon the wings of the wind. A cool breeze filled the morning sky, swirling into the fine, thin mist that hung above the street. The snowy haze drifted lazily along with the wind, hovering over the sidewalk. Again a shred of brilliance danced upon the breeze, sparkling like a misplaced moonstone.

Matthew Logan briskly jogged into view, his sight half-obscured by the curtain of fog dangling above his head. The morning breeze strengthened once more, ruffling Logan's black hair as it whipped the mist away. The crisp, cool air invigorated the young man, and Logan slowed to a halt, gazing out over the deserted street to his right. All thoughts of his troubled sleep were behind him, and, as dreams tended to do, his nightmare had faded from his conscious mind. Inhaling, Logan brushed his dark hair out of his face and began to resume his pace.

Something screamed past Logan's ear, flickering with eerie color. Eyes wide, the young man tried to follow the invisible blasts of air; confusion washed over him like a great wave of water, and, wonderingly, he scratched his chin.

"By the bubbling brew of Fraviar!" an accented, but understandable, voice boomed.

Logan wheeled about. The exclamation resounded about him, and his blue eyes narrowed as he glared at the empty field to his left. Someone was probably hiding in the tall grass, he confirmed to himself. Don't know why someone would be fool enough to be out here at six-thirty in the morning, though.

"Somebody there?" he called.

His answer was the moan of the wind.

As Logan took a cautious step into the field, the knee-high stalks of weeds bowed respectfully in his direction as another wave of wind swept over them. The abrasive clang of metal striking metal rang out across the empty field, and Logan ducked instinctively. An agonized scream pierced the breeze as the wind shifted.

"Jesus Christ!" Logan exclaimed, glancing about him. "What's going on here?"

Blinking his eyes, the young jogger peered at the weed-engulfed lot before him. He no longer suspected someone hiding amongst the brush—the noises he heard were too exact and came from everywhere at once. No, Logan stopped wondering if someone was playing a joke and feared for his sanity. Hearing things in the wind was impossible!

The desolation of the field and street surrounding him suddenly focused in on the young man, and Logan wished he was not alone. He was a determined loner—independent and self-assured—but, in certain circumstances, a companion could be handy.

The mist parted like a foggy curtain as the wind tore through it. The snort of a horse erupted from the breeze, and Logan jumped in fright, spun backwards, and leapt to one side.

"All right!" he yelled, confusion and fear combining to form an odd mixture within him. "That's it! Who the hell is there?"

"Who the what is where?" the same booming voice inquired from nowhere. "Don't bother me with blasted questions when I'm fighting for my life!"

Logan turned on his heel, eyeing the empty field. "Who said that?"

"I did!" the voice retorted.

This is too much! the young man concluded. I'm going to go home, take some extra-strength Tylenol, and go back to bed! Then I'm going to call the nearest mental institution with a vacant room!

A shrill shriek shattered the misty morning, spearing Logan's forehead and setting his mind afire. In agony, Logan clamped his hands to the sides of his head, trying to shut out the horrid screech that filled the street and his body. Unexpected pain wracked his nerves, and Logan crashed to his knees, gritting his teeth.

As the flaring pain diminished, Logan unsteadily raised his head. A gigantic serpentine coil of wind was rushing directly at him! The oddest manifestation he had ever seen! A miniature tornado spiraled straight for him, blood-red light flecked with silver sprouting forth from the funnel.

Crimson stabbed Logan's sight as the tunnel of wind screamed down upon him. Vertigo seized the young jogger, and bile rose in his throat as all sense of stability ceased. He was weightless, sightless, disembodied; suspended inside a whirlpool of red and silver. Agony wrenched his lean frame, and molten steel flowed through his veins rather than blood. The hideous screeching intensified as the strange and wondrous coil of wind swallowed Matthew Logan whole, and his world exploded about him.

The world pulled itself back into being with an electrifying jolt of blue and brown. Dazed and bewildered, Logan staggered forward blindly, once again feeling hard-packed earth beneath him. Hard-packed? His mind rebelled in its befuddled state. The ground of the field had been soft—almost muddy. How had it become hard-packed?

Fuzzy shapes and outlines began to form ahead of Logan as he tried to regain his balance and sanity. A dark blue sky loomed overhead, its clouds tinted pink by the rising sun. The barren earth below him was devoid of greenery and littered with broken stones and dust. Far off in the distance, backed by the brilliant sun, was a glossy black castle.

Logan jerked his head around. Castle? Naw . . . but, there it was! Situated atop a ridge was a midnight-black fortress, complete with battlements!

A snort caught Logan's attention and he swung about. A line of mounted men all clad in chestplates confronted the jogger, their weapons drawn and catching the rays of the rising sun. One lone figure a few feet from Logan faced the horsed warriors, his own drawn sword bloodied and swaddled in gore. The shaggy mane of hair turned toward Logan, and the enormous fighter smiled with yellowing teeth.

Logan stared back, gaping. Warriors? Castles? Swords? Screaming winds? Wake up, Matthew! You're only twenty-seven! You can't go insane!

The huge man near Logan leapt to one side as a mounted warrior charged. With agility surprising for someone that size, the large fighter dodged to his right, bringing up his sword and skewering the horse. Blood splashed across the man's vest of chainmail and spattered his reddish brown beard and mustache. The hair on his head was almost touching the fighter's massive shoulders, and portions hung down over the beady eyes that peered out at Logan.

"So!" the huge man exclaimed, and Logan recognized the booming voice. "You're the question-asker!" His sword ripped across the thigh of another chestplated man. "Where do you come from?"

Logan rubbed his eyes, lost in his confusion. Stunned, he faced the fighter. "What?" he said, quite stupidly.

"I asked you where you came from," repeated the fighter.

Logan shook his head in disbelief. This wasn't happening! It wasn't real—*couldn't* be real! I must have slipped and knocked myself cold. I'm dreaming . . . Yeah! That's it! I'm not really here at all.

"What's the matter?" the larger fighter shouted. "Are you deaf? Very well, then, WHERE DID YOU COME FROM?"

Logan stepped back, his ears ringing. "I'm not deaf!" he hollered.

"Well, neither am I, so stop yelling!" the fighter replied.

Logan blinked and blinked again. No, he told himself, I haven't gone insane. I'm sane. I'm mentally sound. I've never touched a drug in my life.

A frenzied cry pulled Logan away from his thoughts as the massive fighter knocked a rider from his horse and thrust his weapon into the warrior's armpit. Logan could hear metal grate against the rib cage, and he winced as if the steel had driven into his own breast.

"You must excuse me." The bearded fighter grinned at Logan. "I'm being very rude. Here!"

A bow and quiver dropped at Logan's feet, and his eyebrows shot up. It was a self bow, the young man noticed. A bow made of one single piece of wood, unlike the built or backed bow. The wood was no doubt yew, and the bowstring was cord. All in all, the bow was something found in early England; however, it, and the arrows, were enormous. The bow was some four to five feet in length, and the arrows, following close to what was an English rule, were half the length of the bow. Logan had used modern bows, and knew something of the history of such weaponry, but was amazed by the craftsmanship at his feet.

"He thinks he has gained a companion," a sudden voice cackled. "Quickly, you two! Dispose of him! Teach him his error in daring to defy the Reakthi!"

Two horses turned toward Logan, and a pair of chestplated men headed for him. Smirking down at Logan, one of the men slowed his mount, lowering his blade. Logan watched the pair, half-crouched, his fingers touching the bow and quiver.

"An easy task," one of the soldiers said with a grin. "You may have the pleasure."

His companion nodded. "Many thanks." His eyes narrowed as he gazed at Logan's sweat suit. "What strange garments he wears. Perhaps he comes from Droth?"

The other shrugged under his chestplate. "Ask him yourself, if the buffoon knows how to talk."

Logan snatched up the bow and nocked an arrow into place. "I know how to talk, you wimp," he gritted. "And I also know how to use one of these!"

As the bow was raised, the two Reakthi spurred their horses. Panic swept over Logan as he realized the primary release would not work on a bow of that size. He had instinctively held the arrow between his thumb and first finger and surrounded the string in that manner. In the lighter bows he was accustomed to, this maneuver would have pulled back the string by the pressure of the arrow. As the two Reakthi charged, Logan discovered this bow was too strong; another hold was necessary to pull back the string on this sucker!

The oncoming horses filled Logan with dread, and the hard-packed earth shuddered in sympathetic horror to Logan's situation. Fortunately, the terror subsided within Logan, and he switched to the Mediterranean release, a release he had been taught basically as a historical reference to the usage of bows in early England.

Logan's muscles tensed, and the bowstring "twanged." With a sharp retort, the two-foot-long missile rocketed from the bow, burying into the nearest Reakthi's neck. With a blood-garbled scream, the warrior pitched off the back of his horse, crashing to the ground and snapping the wooden shaft that protruded from his throat.

Something whistled beside Logan's ear, and the young man leapt to one side, narrowly avoiding the second Reakthi's sword. Knowing there was no time to reload, Logan arced the enormous bow about like a baseball bat, catching the Reakthi on the back of the head with the horn-crafted tip. With a grunt, the chestplated soldier careened out of his saddle, spilling into the dirt.

Sore rather than stunned, the Reakthi immediately got to his feet, sword still in hand. Snarling, the warrior lunged,

sword first, and Logan ducked to the right, bringing up a foot
and catching the Reakthi in the stomach. Both men yelled:
the Reakthi winded, and Logan clutching his Nike-encased
foot. Damn! the young man swore. Those chestplates are solid!

Silver flashed in the light of the rising sun, and Logan had
to ignore the pain in his toes. Clumsily, he lurched to safety,
escaping the downward sweep of the Reakthi blade. Logan
lashed out a hand and caught the Reakthi's wrist. With his left
hand, Logan threw himself into a final punch. Blood splattered
as the Reakthi's nose splintered under Logan's fingers, and the
chestplated warrior toppled to the arid soil.

"It seems I have good taste in my allies," the large fighter
declared, carelessly observing Logan's battle while he waged
his own.

Logan turned on the fighter, glaring. He was still confused
as to what was going on and had only acted to survive.
This couldn't be real, he told himself, but . . . why does my
fist hurt?

"Withdraw!" one of the chestplated men ordered. "Back to
Vaugen's fortress!"

The reduced band of Reakthi drew back their horses and
galloped for the glossy castle ringed by the rising sun. Logan
watched them diminish, staring into the fiery orb and squinting
as the red-orange light emblazoned itself upon his pupils.

"Well done," the fighter was chuckling, sheathing his blade.
"I could not have done better myself."

Logan glanced at him. "Sure, right. Look, I don't know
what the hell is going on, but I want some answers!" *Need*
some answers. "What is this? Some dream or something? I
mean, how else could I get here, right? For that matter, where
in God's name am I?"

"Which one?" the fighter asked.

"Which one what?" Logan asked back.

"Which god? Brolark? Harmeer? Imogen?"

Logan stared at the fighter before turning away. Questions
cluttered his brain as he scanned the alien horizon, and an
odd—yet familiar—twinge of unbelonging sparked within the
young man.

"By the way," the fighter started, "you never did answer my
question. Where did you come from?"

Logan kept his back to him. "Santa Monica," he sighed heavily. Then, abruptly, he faced the fighter. "Now answer me a question: Where the hell am I, and who are you?"

The fighter grinned playfully beneath his thick red-brown beard. "Ah-ha! That's two!"

Logan flung up his arms as frustration filled his innards and he slowly walked away. He had no idea where he was going; he blindly placed one foot in front of the other and made his way across the barren land toward a small hillock dotted with greenery. All the while his brain played out various rationalizations for his predicament until the number of hypotheses became overwhelming.

Thunderous footsteps shook the ground behind him as the large fighter trailed. "Forgive me," the huge man said. "I am Thromar, the best fighter in all Sparrill and parts of Denzil."

Logan halted and peered at the man in disbelief.

Thromar shrugged his massive shoulders under the gaze. "Well, maybe not in Denzil," he corrected himself.

Shaking his head, Logan resumed his shuffling gait and neared the hilltop. Once again that oddness swarmed in the air about him, the almost physical haze that buzzed silently that Logan did not belong, that he was intruding. The sensation intensified, growing to such proportions that Logan feared something immensely powerful was going to drop out of the sky and crush him beneath it.

Is this what it feels like to go insane?

"Is something wrong?" Thromar queried.

Logan kept walking, his eyes glazed.

Schizophrenic delusions?

"That was quite an impressive display of archery back there," Thromar stated. "You have used a bow before?"

Detached, Logan nodded. Archery, he mused, made sense. He did know about archery, why not have it in this god-awful dream? But his foot . . . and his fist . . . both pulsed with a dull throb. How was that possible?

Cresting the small rise, Logan's feet stopped their mechanical process. Lush greenery spread out before him, and winding, serpentine rivers slid throughout the fertile land. Never in his life had Logan seen so much greenery all in one place, and the air was crisp and clean, with no pollutants fouling the atmosphere . . . only that undeniable twinge of mismatchment.

A large black horse snorted over toward Logan's right, and the young man glanced at it wonderingly. Its eyes flared red, and its mane and tail were the same color. A crude saddle was draped across its muscular back, and weapons and provisions filled the saddlebags.

"That's Smeea," Thromar said proudly. "She's mine."

Logan managed a half-smile as he stared at the magnificent horse. "A black horse with a red mane? Who'd've believed it?"

Chuckling as if Logan had made a joke, Thromar lumbered over to the beast and leapt astride it. Logan watched, slipping further and further into the protectiveness of his rationale. As if the sight of the gigantic expanse of greenery had defeated him, Logan sank in on himself, dumbed and bewildered. He had intended to keep moving, force himself to continue until something happened, but his sudden realization of how large an area he had to traverse reached into the core of his being, and he was suddenly very weary. There is no sense to go on, his mind whispered. Stay where you are. Stay with me. Here you're safe. Nothing can harm you. If you stay here, sooner or later you'll wake up and this whole ordeal will be over. It's only a dream— stay right where you are and inevitably you'll wake up.

Eagerly, Logan gave in to the tempting whisper of his logic, and his strength flowed out of his limbs. Like a marble statue, he stood at the crest of the hill, gazing without seeing at the vast lushness before him.

A tiny portal opened within Logan's subconscious to release a wheezing, disembodied voice that taunted:

Have you no fear of dreams?

Logan blinked.

Know you not that dreams have the power to crush and to rend and to shred?

Frightened by the rasping whisper, strength brought on by fear began to refill Logan's body.

Know you not that dreams have the power to kill?

Logan blinked the glaze away from his eyes and turned his back on the land stretched to the west. The bright rays of the sun splashed the young man's face, forcing him to squint as he realized the danger he was in. It was folly to stay where he was. Whether this was a dream or not, Logan was a survivor. He would not fold up and die as his logic had all but coaxed him into doing. Dreams were dreams—and it would not hurt to keep moving.

Sunspots dancing behind his closed eyelids, Logan spun away from the rising sun and saw Thromar peering down at him from atop his black and red mount. "If I didn't know any better," the fighter commented, "I'd say you were lost."

Logan let out a harsh laugh. "That's an understatement!"

Thromar stroked his reddish brown beard in thought. "If you tell me your name, I might be able to help you," he suggested.

Logan eyed him skeptically. "What could you do?"

"Me?" Thromar responded. "I could do nothing, yet I know of someone who may be able to aid you."

"Who?"

The fighter chuckled. "You first."

Logan sighed. "I'm Matthew Logan from Santa Monica, okay? Now who can help me get out of here?"

"The Smythe," answered Thromar.

Logan waited for Thromar to continue, but when he did not, the young man retorted: "So who's the Smythe?"

Thromar was so taken aback he almost fell from Smeea. "You don't know who the Smythe is? Just where is this Santa Monica place?"

Logan sneered. "Not in this neck of the woods, that's for sure!"

Thromar roared. "Neck? Woods? Since when?"

Another half-smile tried to force its way onto Logan's lips, but he held it back. This Thromar character was an enormous figure of brawn and physical strength, and yet, held an almost childlike quality about him brought about by his innocence. How strange that such a large man could be so simple. Logan wondered how he could dream up such a unique character.

"Do you think this Smythe can get me back?" the young man queried.

"I don't see why he couldn't," replied the fighter.

Logan looked out into the rising sun once more. Survive, a faint voice in the back of his mind advised. Dream or not, live on. Answers are needed—answers to survive. Live on—seek out someone with the answers. *Survive.*

"Which way to this guy?"

Thromar waved a meaty hand westward. "He's off some way—in the Hills of Sadroia. Likes to be left alone. That's

the way these spellcasters are. In fact, I think they do it on
purpose to make it difficult for the person searching for their
help. Nasty batch, then, don't you think?"

Spellcasters? Logan asked himself. Jesus Christ, I must have
been reading too many fantasy books.

Know you not that dreams have the power to kill?

"Do you think you could show me the way?"

Thromar grinned with his yellowed teeth. "Of course; I have
nothing else to do. I'd offer you a ride, but Smeea doesn't take
kindly to strangers."

Strangers. The word made Logan wince. That damnable
feeling of misplacement kept hovering about him, as if the
fertile land detested his presence.

"I'd rather walk," Logan remarked.

Hooves sounded behind the pair, and Thromar stood in
Smeea's saddle. From the eastern side of the hillock, backed
by the rising sun, a small band of Reakthi rode toward the
pair, blood-red light gleaming off their chestplates.

An expectant grin was on Thromar's face as he glanced
down at Logan. "You did pretty good with my arrows," he
stated. "How are you with a flail?"

Logan frowned. "A what?"

"That bad, eh? Well, take my extra sword. You do know
what a sword is, don't you?"

Logan grasped the heavy blade. "Is spinach green?" he
asked back.

Thromar scratched his great tuft of hair. "I don't know. I've
never fought one."

Once again Logan found an odd weapon in his hands. Like
the bow, the sword was larger and heavier than the ones Logan
was used to handling. Nervously, he gripped the hilt, studying
the sword. Double-edged, he mused, and a straight blade. The
hilt was molded so that the wielder could make a sweeping cut
in more than one direction, so the weapon was intended for
both cutting and thrusting. There were a few grooves in the
steel to lighten the weapon, and the point was diamond-shaped
with a concave face for the greatest amount of stiffness without
additional weight.

The four Reakthi drew their horses to a halt near the crest
of the hill. Three of the four were clad in the normal bronze
and golden chestplates; the fourth Reakthi, the obvious leader,

wore a white chestplate. He gripped an odd-looking, jagged-edged sword that Logan thought resembled the barbs of an Igorot spear. Or, he mused with morbid humor, a double-edged saw.

"Thromar!" the lead Reakthi barked. "We have come on request of Spellcaster Groathit not to battle with you but to accompany your companion to Vaugen's castle. We have no wish to quarrel with you. Give us the stranger and you shall be spared."

Thromar spat at the white-chestplated man. "Let that be my answer, Reakmor!"

The quartet of warriors charged, and Smeea snorted in furious response. From the ground, Logan knew how vulnerable he was, but the Reakthi went to encircle Thromar. With a sweat-slickened grasp, Logan swung wildly at one of the soldiers, his weapon catching the Reakthi in the solar plexus. Sword and chestplate clanged as the Reakthi was knocked from his mount. Logan felt as if the muscles in his arms had snapped loose as he tried to shake off the wavering caused by the impact.

The downed Reakthi snatched at his dagger, snarling up at Logan like a ravenous wolf. Still trying to control the quivering of his arms, Logan swept his sword out before him in a massive arc. As easily as wheat mown under the scythe, the Reakthi spilled to the ground, a horrible gash torn across one side of his face.

Heavy hoofbeats jerked Logan's eyes open, and he spied the corpse at his feet. He gagged involuntarily, but suddenly caught sight of the Reakmor rushing toward him. Swallowing the bile that had risen in his throat, Logan tried to lift his sword, yet his entire body was quivering.

Know you not that dreams have the power to kill?

"Friend-Logan!" Thromar yelled. "Beware!"

The dark horse was nearly atop him as the white-chestplated Reakmor reached down to grip Logan's sweat jacket. Half-jumping back, Logan shot up his sword, grazing the arm that groped for him. Crimson fluid leaked from the wound, and the Reakmor jerked back his arm, clutching it tightly to his chest. Red stained the white armor, making a stomach-churning contrast of colors, as more hooves trampled the ground.

Logan turned to see Thromar and Smeea head toward him, the former's eyes ablaze. The remaining Reakthi were slowly staining the soil with their life fluid.

"There were only four of us," the Reakmor shouted from a safe distance. "We only wanted one man. If you had surrendered him peacefully, no harm would have befallen you. Instead, you have cursed yourselves! The Reakthi will hound you until we get what we want, and we want you, man from another world!"

The Reakmor spurred his horse and vanished into the blood-red sun.

Man from another world? Logan repeated to himself.

"You fight well," Thromar complimented, shattering Logan's thoughts.

The young man shrugged diffidently, handing the bloodied sword back up to Thromar. The fighter's beady eyes went wide.

"What is this?" he exclaimed. "Are you giving me back your weapon? By the gods, keep it! You have earned it!" Thromar grinned. "Besides, I don't use that blade—come to think of it, the Reakthi I took it from is in no condition to use it either, if you know what I mean."

Muttering an unfelt thanks, Logan took back the weapon and the leather sheath, strapping it about his waist as they continued onward. The weight of the massive blade became a constant reminder as Logan withdrew into his mind, searching, thinking, pondering, puzzling. More and more things were making it seem less and less a dream. Things were happening far too fast for Logan to make any sense out of them. That Reakmor had called him a man from another world; was that truly the answer? Was Logan really in this strange world of castles and warriors? Or was it just a plausible solution that Logan had incorporated into his dream as an explanation?

Traverse not into folly, the long-haired businessman had suggested. What the devil had he meant? Or did it mean a thing? It was, after all, nothing but another stupid, idiotic dream.

Have you no fear of dreams?

By the time Logan glanced up to actually see where he was going, the sun was being swallowed by a range of mountains in the west. A large valley lay before the young man, and, even in the faint light of dusk, Logan could make out the glittering rivers that wound their way on either side of the valley. Stars began to dot the darkening sky as Thromar brought Smeea to a halt and dismounted. Faint spots of light played between the two rivers, and Thromar jerked a large finger in the direction of the will-o'-the-wisps.

"We'll enter the valley at sunrise," he declared. "For tonight, we'll stay on the east side of the Lathyn."

"What for?" Logan wondered.

"*What for?*" Thromar exclaimed. "That's Eadarus! It's a great town by day, but, at night, it becomes a thieves' quarters! Everyone from Moknay to Roshfre could be there, all just as willing to slit your throat!"

Logan gently fingered his neck. "I take it it's not too safe?"

Thromar responded: "Not once the sun has gone down." He gazed longingly at the flickering torches that marked the town. "Too bad, too. Eadarus has the best women this side of the Roana!"

Stifling a yawn, Logan felt the vitality run from his frame and tiredness take control. His feet hurt as if he had been walking all day, and his stomach growled in hunger. Abruptly, the young man blinked, his hands going to his face.

"Hey!" he cried. "I've got my contacts in!"

Thromar peered at him curiously.

Logan ignored the fighter, glancing about him frantically. Contact lenses! he screamed to himself. I've got my goddamn contact lenses in! Never had a dream been so precise! And how was he supposed to clean them? He had no saline solution, no heating unit, no carrying case.

"Friend-Logan?" questioned Thromar. "Is something the matter?"

Logan did not hear the rumbling voice as he stared wonderingly out at the world through his contact lenses. Neither contact had been bothering him; never once had a speck of dirt gotten into his eye and irritated the lens, nor had they felt uncomfortable at any time during the day. And yet, they were there! Logan could not see without them!

With fearful expectation, Logan reached into his right eye and pulled out the soft lens.

"Your eye!" Thromar bellowed. "You have plucked out your eye!"

Logan glanced at the fighter, holding up the small lens so he could study it in the dimming sunlight. "I haven't plucked out my eye," he replied. "It's a contact lens; it helps me see."

"Of course it helps you see!" Thromar boomed. "The lens of your eye is what emits eye-beams! From these eye-beams we gain our sight, and you have simply pulled yours out!"

"It's not my cornea!" Logan returned. "It's my contact lens!"

And it's so damn precise it all but proves I'm really here!

"*Cornea?*" Thromar repeated. "What tongue is that?"

"It's not your tongue, it's part of your eye."

"Which part?"

"The lens part!"

"The part that you have just torn off! Oh, friend-Logan, you have blinded yourself!"

Logan screwed up his face, replacing the lens and blinking it back into place. Immediately, it slipped over his cornea, and his vision cleared. Contacts, he breathed. Dreams are *not* this exact!

Casting a quick glance at Thromar, Logan saw the fighter was gaping at him. "See?" he retorted. "I'm not blind."

"No, indeed!" Thromar roared. "You must be a spellcaster!"

"I'm no spellcaster!" Logan shouted in frustration. "My God!"

"Your god?" wondered Thromar. "Which one?"

Logan's eyes blazed as he turned on the fighter. "You're the most infuriating dream I've ever had!" he accused.

Thromar released a thunderous laugh. "And you are by far the most interesting, friend-Logan!"

Logan shook his head in submission, sitting heavily upon the grass below him. A thousand words were tumbling over and over in his mind; half-formed explanations swirled within him and died before birth. Contacts! There was no way to comprehend how the lenses had gotten there—dreams were just not that accurate!

Learn to decipher dreams from reality, unreality from false-hood, falsehood from truth, or doom shall fall upon your worlds!

With a frown of puzzlement, Logan flopped back onto the grass and stared up at the star-filled night. The unsettling presence of wrongness rematerialized, almost as if it were taking a substantial form over the young man and circling like an invisible bird of prey overhead.

Surrounded by the unnerving feeling, Logan slept.

A thin mist hung in the air as Logan awoke. For a moment, the young man thought he was back in Santa Monica, but the recurring disharmony rudely reminded him of where he was. Small beads of dew clung to his body like transparent leeches, losing their grip as he moved and splashing to the ground. His breath escaped in a white cloud of haze as he got to his feet and spied Smeea eyeing him with her brilliant, crimson eyes. Her rider was nowhere in sight, and an uncomprehensible fear swelled within Logan's breast as he feared being alone in his madness.

A massive hand clamped down upon Logan's shoulder and he wheeled about, twisting as he grabbed the hand. Thromar let out a holler as he flipped over Logan's back and landed upon his backside, his chainmail tinkling like bells.

"By the gods!" the fighter boomed. "Never have I been bested so easily!"

Logan suppressed a relieved smile as he helped the large man to his feet. Thromar's black eyes were wide as he peered down at the young man, inquisitively stroking his reddish brown beard. "You're quite sure you are not a spellcaster?" he asked.

Logan sneered. "Positive."

"Spellcaster or not, you are probably rather hungry," Thromar declared. He tossed Logan a small roll and popped two into his own mouth. "Eat, friend-Logan, and, when we get to Eadarus, we will set about getting you a horse."

Logan stopped chewing the slightly stale bread. "A horse?" he replied. "You don't have to buy me a horse—I don't want to be a bother."

Thromar flashed him a crooked smile. "Who said anything about buying you a horse? We're going to steal you one."

"Steal me one?" exclaimed Logan. "I don't need a horse that badly! The last thing I need to happen is to get caught! Then I'll never get back!"

"Caught?" Thromar boomed. "Caught by whom?"

"The police—or whatever you'd call them here!"

Thromar took a swig of wine from a leather flask. "The only

ones who would try to stop you are the King's Guards," he said, wiping his mouth with the back of his hand, "and they're too fearful to come within a league of Eadarus!"

"But what about whoever we steal it from?" Logan objected. "What happens to him?"

Thromar sighed heavily. "Friend-Logan, let me tell you something about Eadarus: Everything there does not belong to the person who has possession of it. One owner stole it from another, who, no doubt, took it from someone else, who must have snatched it from the first thief, who had to have stolen it from some store to gain possession of it in the first place. Do you understand?"

Logan chewed as his head bobbed up and down slowly. "Oddly enough," he responded, "I do."

The pair crossed a stone bridge stretched across the river and began their descent into the valley. Like rats fleeing a sinking ship, Logan could see hunched figures clad in black hastily scrambling out of the town and into the foliage surrounding the outside gates. Watching the dark forms, Logan could sense his contacts rolling about on his eyes, as comfortable as if he had just placed them in. He had almost believed this ordeal to be real when he had first discovered his contacts in place, but now, only in a dream could he sleep with his lenses in and feel no discomfort.

Traverse not into folly.

Musing silently, Logan trailed Thromar into the cluttered town and down a cobblestone street. Carts and horses wound their way across the narrow roads, the noises they made drowning out the cries of the merchants along the roadway. Large clusters of people milled about small shops made out of some kind of canvas, and larger groups meandered through the wood and stone structures behind them.

The clothing, Logan noted, was anything but medievalish. The young man had been prepared to see men and women dressed in Elizabethan styles, but an assortment of costumes and materials paraded before Logan's curious eye. And those Reakthi had thought *his* sweat suit was weird!

As the two ventured farther into the town, the small canvas shops gave way to women. Multitudes of scantily clad females lined the cobblestone paths, eyeing prospective clients as they rode or walked by. The men who walked the streets wore darker clothing, and hoods covered much of their features. Obviously not the better portion of town, Logan thought.

A sudden voice rang out from the crowded walk: "Thromar!"

Logan swung his head around to see a girl race toward them.

"Bella!" Thromar roared.

Bella happily charged Smeea, gripping Thromar's leg with long-nailed fingers. Logan saw she was rather short and stocky, but her face could classify her as "fetching." Bobbed black hair reached almost to her shoulders, and the slits in her light blue gown seemed to go up to her arms.

"Thromar," she breathed, "come with me. It has been so long since your last visit."

The huge fighter was about to leap from Smeea when he spied Logan out of the corner of his eye. He cleared his throat loudly until he had Bella's attention and then nodded in the young jogger's direction. Bella gave the fighter's companion a brief smile, her lips painted red.

Logan took an exaggerated step backwards. "Hey!" he exclaimed. "Don't let me stop you! I don't want to be a bother!"

Thromar grinned with his yellowing teeth and sprang from Smeea. "Thank you for your understanding, friend-Logan," he said. "I shall not be long."

Bella jerked on his arm in silent protest.

"Well, not too long. Await my return; I would hate to lose an ally such as you."

Logan waved the two off. "Don't worry about me," he told them. "This is my dream; nothing'll happen. Maybe I'll *shop* around for a horse."

"Just don't purchase anything until I get back," advised Thromar as he was led by an impatient Bella into a nearby building.

Feeling confused and awkward, Logan shoved his hands into his jacket pockets and wandered off through the town. *Is* it my dream? he asked himself. Since when had he ever had complete control over what was going on? Never. That didn't mean it *wasn't* his dream, but it certainly didn't confirm it.

Logan spied a building that looked as if it could be a bar, and, as he neared, he was sure of it. Two men staggered out, bumped into one another, and sprawled flat on the ground.

Another man sauntered out, grabbed hold of a whore, and slung her over his shoulder. Logan started forward but immediately restrained himself. He had no need to get involved with this idiotic land. He only wanted to wake up.

As Logan approached the tavern with the hope of getting some answers, he was forced to sidestep one of the drunken men on the ground. In doing so, he bumped into a trio of men as they stepped through the doorway. The three glared down at Logan, their eyes red with intoxication.

"Get a load of him," one of them slurred. "The little man from Droth thinks he can bump into us."

Logan took an uneasy step backwards. All three, he noticed, wore swords that glittered as fiercely as their bloodshot eyes.

Cold fingers of fear pressed against Logan's neck as he remembered the rasping whisper: *Know you not that dreams have the power to kill?*

Logan did not want to find out.

"Maybe he's a Guardsman?" another snarled. "Is that the new uniform?"

The third man pointed a large finger toward Logan's nose. "Naw, he's just a scrawny little harpy turd. Let's show him what we can do to him."

Logan's hand shot for his sword as the trio advanced. Hands seemed to reach out from all about him and tear at his limbs, forbidding him from freeing his weapon and protecting himself. Unexpectedly, one of the men spilled backwards, his chest smeared with crimson. Another crumpled to the ground immediately afterward, blood fountaining from his neck. The third took an uneasy step back, gaping at the small golden hilt protruding from his stomach. As blood welled up around the dagger and splattered the street, Logan's third assailant crashed to the cobblestones.

Logan wheeled about in astonishment and disgust. He expected to see Thromar behind him, grinning his crooked, yellow grin, but the large fighter's enormous frame did not back the young jogger. A lithe man clad all in grey was stanced in the street, daggers strapped across his chest in a menacing display of weaponry. Two more of the slim blades glistened in either hand.

"Morning to you, my friend," the stranger said with a smirk in greeting. "I hope you don't mind my rude interruption of your discussion, but it seemed your companions were getting a little out of hand. Tell me, whom have I the honor of saving?"

"Matthew Logan," Logan answered cautiously. "Why?"

The black-haired stranger shrugged. "Moknay the Murderer always lets the engraver know the proper name to place upon the gravestone."

Moknay stepped forward and a dagger sailed from his hand, glinting silver as it screamed toward Logan's neck.

·2·

Murderer

Glistening with metallic splendor, the dagger glinted as it spun toward Logan's throat. Immobile due to shock, Logan shut his eyes tight, flinching as a hollow "thwunk" reverberated in his ears. When he risked opening one eye, he could see the golden hilt of the dagger gleaming at him wickedly as it protruded from the Murderer's target: the wooden doorframe of the tavern.

Moknay the Murderer smirked, his trim, black mustache twitching along with his lip. "I didn't have to miss," he advised.

Logan opened his other eye and gulped. "I—I believe you," he stuttered, "but why did you?"

Moknay twisted free the blade and inspected it with eyes as cold as the dagger's own steel. "Because," he answered, "you are different; and I am curious. You're not from Sparrill, and yet, you're not a conquest-greedy Reakthi either. Where *are* you from?"

Logan nervously eyed the strap of daggers crossing the Murderer's chest. "Santa Monica."

"Santa Monica?" Moknay repeated, raising an inquisitive eyebrow. "Never heard of it. Where is it—somewhere south of Magdelon?"

Logan heard a faint splatter of liquid as he shifted his weight and looked down at one of the corpses at his feet. The bread Thromar had given him for breakfast tried to come up as Logan pulled his Nike out of the puddle of blood. "It's south of Los Angeles," he said, choking.

The grey-clad Murderer looked at Logan carefully, peering at the sweat suit and heavy sword at his side. "How is it you wear a Reakthi sword?" he questioned, the smirk returning to his face.

Logan threw the weapon a quick glance. "It was given to me," he explained, hastily, "as a gift."

"By who?" the Murderer queried, fingering a dagger. "A Reakthi? Once they earn their blade, they rarely ever part with it."

"Look," protested Logan, taking a step back and hearing more blood splash, "you said yourself that I wasn't a Reakthi!"

"I'm having second thoughts," Moknay answered. "Now tell me, why do you wear a Reakthi sword?"

Logan swallowed hard as he tried to take another step back. Either a corpse or one of the unconscious drunks blocked his passage, and he was forced to confront the dark-haired Murderer. The sunlight flashed off the many blades hooked across Moknay's chest and his grey cape appeared to conceal many more weapons strapped to his belt.

Know you not that dreams have the power to kill? The hideous whisper snickered from Logan's subconscious.

"Look, this fighter named Thromar gave it to me when I first got here," Logan finally spat out. "We ran into some Reakthi and I didn't have a weapon. Thromar gave it to me and wouldn't take it back once I had used it."

The young jogger glared at the lithe form in front of him. All right, he wanted to shout, do you believe me now? Go ahead! Stick one of your goddamn daggers down my throat! *I* don't believe it—why should you?

There was a flicker of recognition in Moknay's grey eyes. "Thromar?" he murmured. "Here? Back in Eadarus?"

Logan blinked. He believes me?

The Murderer turned on Logan, a wide smile spread across his usually grim mien. "Where?" he wanted to know. "Where is Thromar?"

"Why should I tell you?" Logan retorted, suddenly and unexplainably defiant. "Why do you want him?"

"He and I were war-siblings," Moknay grinned. "Back when I was a young and foolish thief, I attempted to steal some supplies from Thromar while he camped east of the Jenovian. I soon found out the reason he was resting was because a troop of Reakthi had been hounding him for weeks. As I was about to make good my escape, the Reakthi ambushed him. As I said before, I was quite foolish, and, like some damned warfiend, I threw down my ill-gotten gains and helped him. Needless to say, we shed enough Reakthi blood to dye the Jenovian red! Ever since then, Thromar and I have been war-siblings."

Logan was silent a moment. "I don't believe you," he declared.

The Murderer barked a laugh and started for Logan. The young man tensed, however, Moknay continued past him, entering the tavern. "Come with me," he said. "I'll buy you something. Any friend of Thromar's is a friend of mine."

Cautiously, Logan followed the grey figure into the tavern. Moknay strode through the dimly lit bar undauntedly, winding his way through a maze of wooden tables and benches. Torches crackled against the walls, casting shadows upon the floor that leaped and danced like specters.

Moknay leaned up against the bar, smirking as Logan trailed him. "I'll have an ale," he said to the barkeep, "and my friend here . . . ?"

Logan turned away from inspecting the scenery and shrugged helplessly. "Same thing, I guess." Be too much if I asked for a hot cup of coffee, he mused.

Two mugs clunked down before them, overspilling with froth. Moknay's gloved hand snatched up the nearest mug and waved it in Logan's direction. "Drink up," he proclaimed. "A stranger in a new land is always happy to have a few friends!"

Logan raised the mug, wincing. There was that blasted word again! he muttered. *Stranger.* Never before had that word meant so much to the young man. It was that unnerving feeling of disharmony that did it, he surmised. It kept surfacing constantly, reminding him that he did not belong in this place. Which was stupid, because it was—after all—his dream.

Logan almost choked as he took his first swallow of the ale. The beverage tasted slightly like beer, only much stronger. There was something in it that Logan thought tasted like malt, and some tiny seeds of some sort swirled within the dark liquid. Hops! Logan recalled. The little seed-things are called hops. Yeech! Worse than drinking orange juice with too much pulp! Nonetheless, the young man had not had anything to drink in this dream, and his throat was rather dry, so he greedily emptied the large mug. Moknay pounded the bar when he noticed the mug was no longer full, and the barkeep refilled it.

Logan downed his second mug in seconds.

"If you want anything else to drink," Moknay quipped, "the Sea of Hedelva is about twenty-three leagues north of here."

Logan wiped his mouth with the back of his hand as Thromar had earlier that morning. "No, thanks. I didn't know I was that thirsty."

Moknay smirked, turning his back on the bar. Picking at a hop that had gotten stuck between his teeth, Logan pondered how he could have dreamed such a drink. He wasn't one for beer—never had been—but this ale certainly tasted similar. And why was he so thirsty? Dreams didn't usually have the dreamer stop to eat or drink. Sometimes a dream could supposedly last over a number of months and never once would the dreamer stop to have dinner or go to the bathroom.

Logan blanched. Bathroom! *What do I do if I've gotta take a piss? Huh? Since when had he ever thought he'd need to go to the bathroom in a dream? Christ, Matthew! Wake up before you drive yourself insane!*

The smug Murderer beside Logan twisted around, tapping the young jogger upon the shoulder. He waved a gloved hand in the direction of the door, and Logan blinked. There were two figures silhouetted in the doorway, and the dim light was glinting off what could have been a blood-splattered chestplate. An arm with an ugly sword wound running across its flesh lifted in Logan's direction, and a finger extended accusingly.

"Friend," whispered Moknay, "I think you have visitors."

"Aw, shit," Logan cursed.

Moknay grinned, his grey eyes twinkling. "Fear not," he soothed. Suddenly he bounded onto one of the tables, glaring down at one of the men seated there. "What?" he roared. "You think grey is drab? Cur!"

A grey boot lashed out, catching one of the men on the chin and knocking him out of his seat. The man's companion jumped to his feet in astonishment, eyes wide.

"Hey!" he shouted. "You can't do that!"

Another man one table over got to his feet. "Seems to me he just did," he answered, delivering a wild punch at the fellow.

A chair hurled across the tavern and fragmented against the far wall. Like an erupting volcano, shouts and yells echoed throughout the building as more and more drunken patrons joined in on the brawl. Mugs sailed overhead, and benches and tables overturned as bodies thumped to the floor.

Logan let out a frightened cry and leapt behind the bar for protection. A mug crashed above his head, showering ale down upon him, and he almost got clipped by a fist when he stood up to look for Moknay. In the dim lighting, the Murderer had simply disappeared, and Logan felt a twinge of guilt since he had doubted the fellow's sincerity. Still, he could not see the two Reakthi, and that much relieved him.

When Logan attempted to find Moknay again, there was a sudden blur of white before him. Breaking through the cluster of bodies and dim light, the Reakmor leapt forward, drawing his jagged sword. Logan's death gleamed in his eyes as he sprang for the young man, releasing a triumphant war cry as he hurdled the bar.

Logan stumbled back in surprise, his hand jumping to his own sword. Intense fear swelled up inside him as his hand slipped and missed the golden handle which was slippery from spilt ale. Logan could only gape as the Reakmor he had wounded dove over the bar and lunged for him.

Warm fluid sprinkled Logan's cheek as the Reakmor jerked to one side, his war cry becoming garbled as blood filled his throat. A fine stream of crimson trickled from his lips, and the color drained out of his face. His barbed sword clattered to the floor as he crumpled upon the bar, twitching fingers futilely grasping for the dagger that was lodged in his neck.

Feeling his stomach twist in protest, Logan bolted to his right, eager to get out from behind the bar. He had been safe from the brawl Moknay had started as a diversion, but a sitting duck should the other Reakthi corner him back there!

As Logan ran, a gnarled figure in a silver chestplate barred his way. A black robe covered the lean body, and short, blue-grey hair spiked outward from atop his skull. Flaming, sunken eyes glared at Logan from a shriveled and taut face while bony hands clenched and unclenched at his sides.

"Get out of my way!" Logan demanded, this time firmly gripping his sword's hilt.

The silver-chestplated man smiled cruelly. "What will you do if I do not, man from another world?" he queried sarcastically.

That's twice somebody has called me that! Logan noted.

"Man from another world nothing!" he spat back. "This place isn't real! You're all my creations!"

A spiked eyebrow raised in question. "Are we?" the new-comer remarked. He slowly shook his head, the shadows of the tavern playing across the many wrinkles of his face. "I should think not . . . although . . . we may become so later. As for this place being real . . . I can assure you, we are *quite* real."

Logan's mind was screaming. Truth! Holy Mother of God, why do I sense truth in what he's saying? *He's telling the truth!*

"I am Groathit, greatest of the Reakthi spellcasters," the silver-chestplated warrior announced. "You are to come with me."

Logan, shaken, partially withdrew his weapon as his rationale raged in silent turmoil. "I'll go with whoever I damn well feel like going with!" he roared.

Truth! God damn it to hell, how can he be telling the truth? I'm dreaming! Listen to me, goddamn it! You're dreaming! You're not really here! You can't be here!

Another voice entered the fray within Logan's mind: *Learn to decipher dreams from reality, unreality from falsehood, falsehood from truth, or doom shall fall upon your worlds!*

A warning! Logan's mind howled. Falsehood from truth! Maybe he is lying! Maybe the truth I sensed isn't really there at all!

The young man froze both physically and mentally as he realized something: *Worlds.* Not "world" but "world*s*"! It *was* a warning! He *really* was there!

Now more than ever he wanted to get back home!

"The Reakthi can use you in the conquest of this land," Groathit was saying. "With your help we shall crush these barbarians."

Barbarians? the young man repeated in his mind, suddenly filled with a hellish anger. These "barbarians" had helped him! Thromar and Moknay had aided him! He would have been dead—*really dead*—if it hadn't have been for them. All the Reakthi had done had been to rain war and danger upon Logan and his newly acquired friends.

Without Thromar and Moknay, he could have gone mad!

With a roar of defiance, Logan lunged, blade first.

The lean Groathit waved a gnarled hand, and Logan's thrust sent him directly through the wizard. Eyes wide, Logan spun about as the sensation of mismatchment deadened his nerves and caused his head to swim. Through blurry contacts, the young man saw Groathit's form waver and become solid once more.

"It is futile to fight," the spellcaster growled.

Gritting his teeth, Logan ignored the buzz of disharmony and charged. He slashed at Groathit's midriff with all his might behind his weapon, anger feeding an inhuman strength to his muscles. The wizard barked a harsh laugh as the sword passed through his body, throwing Logan off balance. Glancing up from the floor, Logan saw Groathit step toward him, a hideous frown upon his face.

"I am to bring you to Vaugen," he informed Logan, a bench thrown in the brawl passing harmlessly through him. "He has need of you."

The spellcaster smiled, and Logan froze. The wizard's teeth were gradually lengthening, elongating into large, needle-sharp fangs. His sunken eyes flared red, and the tips of his bony fingers erupted, releasing iron claws. There was a sudden blossom of flame, and the concussion threw Logan backwards as he was once again beset upon by the feeling of dissent.

Shaking the numbness from his mind, Logan looked up to find himself outside the tavern. His sword lay on the cobblestones beside him as fearful screams exploded from within the tavern. A tidal wave of people rushed free of the building, blindly fleeing some unseen terror inside. Unexpectedly, two men were batted skyward as the demonic Groathit crashed out of the tavern, flames belching from his fang-rimmed mouth. Malevolent red eyes trained in on Logan, and the transformed mouth drew back in a crocodilian smile. With a strangled shout, Logan scurried to his feet, gripping tightly to his sword. The metamorphosed Groathit disregarded the weapon, lumbering menacingly toward the young man. A grey form suddenly leapt atop the wizard, a dagger plunging deep into his neck. Roaring in anger rather than pain, the demon-wizard pulled free the blade, releasing a geyser of blood. An arm swung about, catching Moknay on the side of his head and flinging him head over heels. Logan watched in horror as the Murderer sailed across the street and landed with a crash in a silversmith's shop. The terror increased as Logan saw Moknay slump against a circle of bricks and lay still.

Waving an iron-clawed hand, Groathit healed the wound on his neck. The rush of blood slowed to a trickle until that too faded to pink scar tissue. The gleam in the spellcaster's eyes intensified as he slowly turned to face Logan.

Staring at the still form of the Murderer across the street, Logan could feel the fear mutate into a raging fire of anger. Moknay! He had befriended him! He had attempted to rescue him from these infernal Reakthi! And now he was injured—dead, maybe! And it was because of Logan's meddling!

Teeth clenched, Logan swung about to face Groathit. Although his vision was blurred by his intense hatred, he could make out the demonic form of the wizard, fanged mouth drawn back in an evil sneer. Overtaken by his rage, Logan's arm thrust outward, jabbing the point of his sword into a flashing red eye. Streams of blood babbled down Groathit's face as he staggered to one side, screaming in agony, his black-clawed hands protectively covering his injured eye.

"I shall return for you, man from another world," the magic-user warned, spitting blood. "Consider yourself fortunate that you are of no use to Vaugen as a corpse!"

Smoke swelled up from the cobblestones, surrounding the wizard with a dense, black curtain of haze. When it dispersed, Groathit was gone.

Drained of his anger and strength, Logan made his way to the silversmith's shop, dragging his sword through the cobblestones behind him. Odd, he told himself, the silversmith's was empty. But where had Moknay gone?

A sudden glint of silver caught Logan's eye, and he hurried over to one corner of the shop. There, embedded in a barrel, was a slim dagger. Beneath it, scrawled in what could have been charcoal, was the message: "Must go. Keep this or I will cut your head off."

Smiling with relief, Logan freed the weapon. It was perfectly balanced, he noticed, so it could be used as a missile, but why had the Murderer left so hastily? You would think Logan would at least be able to see him up one of the streets.

The young man froze as he gazed up one road. A small squad of men hurried toward the tavern in military order, all dressed in uniforms. Guessing them to be the Guardsmen Thromar had mentioned, Logan crouched down behind the barrel and waited. Beads of perspiration dotted his brow as he observed the Guards march into the tavern, inspect the damage, and start off again, splitting into smaller troops. A sigh escaped Logan's lips as he scurried out from behind the barrel and started back toward the building where he had left Thromar and Bella. His unexpected entrance may cause some embarrassment, but he could not stay in Eadarus any longer. If he got caught by these Guardsmen, he'd never get to that spellcaster and go home.

As Logan jogged around a corner, another squad of uniformed men came into view. One of the Guards shouted, pointing in Logan's direction, and the others echoed his shout, jerking their swords free of their sheaths. Numerous feet pounded the cobblestones, and Logan glanced around frantically. He couldn't go back—the other troop had been scouting that area.

Logan sprang to his right, clambering upon the closest horse and jerking back the reins. The yellow stallion reared, twisting around and charging down the street. Hooves clattered noisily upon the cobblestones as the stolen horse and thief thundered westward. He had no idea where he was going, Logan realized, but he didn't need to go too far from Eadarus if the Guardsmen didn't pursue.

They pursued.

Its green mane and tail billowing out behind it, Logan's horse galloped onward. More Guards materialized from around corners, expressing their surprise and trailing after the young man. Gripping the reins protectively, Logan chanced a look behind him and almost fell out of the saddle. Three Guardsmen kept up the pursuit, mounted on darkly colored horses. Muttering an unhappy curse, Logan turned back around and swerved his horse to the right. The town suddenly dropped away behind him, and Logan was back out in the wilderness, following a northwesterly path. The trio of Guardsmen were gradually falling behind, their own mounts tiring much faster than Logan's stolen horse. Still, urged on by the fear of being caught, Logan drove his horse further, directing it off the path and into the forest. Foam began to spot the horse's mouth as Logan spied a large outcropping of rock to his left.

"Not much further," he told the horse. "I don't think they'll look for us by the rocks. The area might be too treacherous for them to consider . . . I hope!"

The yellow-and-green mount raced onward, its head bobbing up and down as if in response to Logan's comment. Clods of dirt the size of silver dollars were kicked up into the air by the thundering hooves, and the many trees and bushes of the forest were green and brown blurs of color.

Logan began to feel the soreness creep into his rump as he continued bouncing up and down in the crude saddle. Abruptly, the stallion broke free of the forest's greenery and Logan drew in the reins. A small, sparkling pond lay before them, positioned just outside the outcropping of rocks. A few large boulders surrounded them, and a cavern gaped in one knoll of stone. A tiny froglike creature sprang into the pool of water and submerged; the water was so clear Logan could still see the amphibian as it descended to the bottom and hid beneath a rock.

Logan dismounted and knelt beside the pond, splashing the clear liquid onto his face. His horse placed its snout into the water, shaking its head back and forth to clear its mouth of its spittle. As some water dribbled down Logan's face, a few droplets splashed into his eyes. An odd tingle filled his sockets, and his contact lenses swirled and blinked themselves clean. Immediately, Logan's vision increased, and he wonderingly touched his face as the sensation in his eyes faded.

The young man was drawn away from the odd feeling when his horse jerked its head up and stiffened. Logan did likewise, turning in the direction of the dark cavern. His ears picked up an almost inaudible crunch, and he hastily led his horse behind a boulder for safety. There, crouched in the shadows, Logan listened, straining to pick out any more noises. Beside him, his newly acquired horse pawed the ground uneasily.

There was a pause of about two minutes until Logan felt that he was just being jumpy. He flashed his mount a grin and began moving around the boulder back toward the pond. The horse, however, balked like a stubborn mule. Logan was almost jerked back as the reins went taut, and he turned to pull the horse out from behind the boulder by force. His clear vision happened to skim the sparkling pond as he turned, and he caught the reflection of the monstrosity behind him.

With a startled exclamation, Logan spun about and faced the creature.

The sunlight reflected off iron scales as the giant, newt-shaped beast lumbered free of its cavern. Two bullish horns grew from its grotesquely lizardlike face, and massive claws extended from its four limbs, each impaling the ground effort-lessly with every shuffling step it took. Its large, oval-shaped eyes flickered as it spotted a prospective meal, and saliva oozed from its mouth.

Swallowing hard, Logan withdrew Moknay's dagger. He was no longer dreaming, he remembered, and the possible death facing him had become much more real.

The creature advanced, its forked tongue flicking between its inch-long fangs.

· 3 ·

Jewel

Logan stanced himself for battle, legs spread slightly apart for balance and Moknay's dagger shimmering in his right hand. His arm shook with fear as the iron-scaled creature shambled forward, an angry hiss sounding from its mouth. As the beast took another step in Logan's direction, the fear became overwhelming, and Logan almost swooned. His head felt light and airy, and his legs turned to quivering pillars of gelatin. His grip on his dagger faltered as he realized the monster before him could be his death coming to greet him warm-heartedly.

A pestering buzz filled Logan's airy skull, swarming through his cranium with its message of disorder. You do not belong here, it accused him. How dare you set foot in this land? You are out of place. Go back to where you belong.

A self-righteous anger rose up within Logan. I didn't ask to be sent here! he yelled back at the buzz. And I *am* going back home, but not because you're bothering me! I hate this place! I hate it! Do you hear me? *I hate this place!*

A gurgling snarl sounded in Logan's ears, and he looked down to see the reptilian creature facing him bolt forward, its enormous body swaying to and fro in its charge. Brewing with anger, Logan turned on the beast. It is of this world! he snarled. I hate it as well! Wildly, he lashed out with his dagger.

The blade skimmed off the creature's forearm, leaving a faint white streak across the grey scales. Gargling, the beast took three quick steps to one side, oval eyes flaring. Hardly two feet separated the combatants; but it was Logan who made the next move. Ablaze with his hatred, the young man swung about, plunging Moknay's gift directly into a nostril. Blood spumed into the air as the monster howled, rearing back its head in pain. With a silver flash, the dagger thrust out again, sinking in between the scales to penetrate the flesh of its throat. Crimson liquid splattered Logan's hand as he ripped the blade through the soft skin and tore it free.

Blood bubbled from the creature's nostrils and mouth as it careened to one side, crashing to the earth with a faint gurgle. A limb twitched spasmodically, and the life in the large eyes dwindled and went out.

Eyes narrowed with an unrelenting anger, Logan stared down at the corpse and then turned his sight inward. The buzz had also left him, as if he had slain it along with the monster, but Logan knew it would be back. As long as he was stuck here, that persistent feeling of wrongness would continue to plague him. But, for now, at least, it was gone, and Logan felt completely justified by what he had just done.

Cleaning off Moknay's dagger and his hand, Logan turned around to see his green-and-yellow mount standing behind the large boulder where he had left it. Surprisingly, it hadn't bolted when the monster had charged, but it was reluctant to approach the grey-scaled corpse. Slowly, Logan replaced his weapon and mounted. He guessed it was about one in the afternoon, and instinctively glanced at his watch. He was surprised to see the digital display was gone; no numbers played across the surface. They had been replaced by a strange red-and-silver glow that faintly radiated from the watch's face. Frowning, Logan tugged his sleeve back over his watch and started his horse ahead at a slow trot.

The young jogger looked about him as his mount made its way through the greenery. Trees, grass, and bushes flanked him, each almost identical with its neighbor. As anxiety began to gnaw its way through Logan's stomach, he realized he was badly—and irrevocably—lost. He had followed the path out of Eadarus, but God knows how far he went when he veered off the road. Now he could hardly tell north from south and east from west . . . and there was foliage all about him.

Aimlessly, Logan let his horse lead until the sky turned a bloody shade of red as the sun began to disappear behind him. Hoping he had not unwittingly passed Eadarus, Logan dismounted and tethered his horse to a nearby tree. As the red sky turned dark blue, the young man noticed the leather saddlebags hanging from the horse's sides. In his desperate flight from Eadarus he had not noticed them, nor had he seen them after his battle with that creature. Curiously, he opened them and withdrew four smaller pouches.

Rifling through the first sack, Logan came across a few pieces of black bread, cheese, some fruit, and an odd-looking roll of what Logan guessed was beef jerky. The supplies did not look all that appetizing, but Logan's stomach growled eagerly, so he broke off a piece of bread. Then, while eating, he opened the second bag. He was going to whistle in awe, but the bread in his mouth forbade it. Instead, the young man held up the sole contents of the second bag: an enormous golden jewel. Even though the sun had vanished, the jewel glimmered with a resplendent sparkle all its own. Its faceted face reflected Logan's image a thousand times over; it seemed to have no definite center.

Replacing the jewel, Logan turned to the third bag. It was a flask much like the one Thromar had had, and Logan was pleased to smell wine within rather than that hop-infested ale. He set the flask beside the pouch of food and untied the fourth bag. Rummaging around inside, Logan withdrew a smaller pouch and unknotted the leather string. He emptied the contents of the bag into his palm, and his eyes went wide as ten gold pieces spilled out into his hand.

"Gold!" he breathed to his horse. "Do you believe it? Honest to God gold!"

Shifting the gold back into its pouch, Logan closed and knotted the sack, placing it in the same bag with the jewel. Also within the fourth bag was a small metal box. Wonderingly, Logan unclasped the lid then tilted it back. The tin was full of a dark blue powder which Logan thought could have been snuff or tobacco or something like that—then it glimmered with a light blue aura, and Logan clamped the lid shut.

Stars began to twinkle above Logan's head as he stripped off his sweat jacket and folded it into a makeshift pillow. Like a mother hen guarding her chicks, Logan pulled the bags under his arm and lay beside them protectively. He had Moknay's dagger at his belt and Thromar's Reakthi sword at his hip; he would be ready if anyone tried to steal his stolen valuables.

Before he knew it, Logan had drifted off to sleep.

A cricket that had been chirping close by suddenly stopped, and the night was still. Awakened by the stopping of a noise rather than the noise itself, Logan awoke with a start. His hand leapt to the dagger in his belt and freed it, wincing as its blade chafed along the belt and made a noise that seemed to echo across the blackness of night. His contact-covered eyes pierced through the darkness easily, and Logan spotted a shadowy form slinking serpentlike from a protective tree trunk to hide behind a bush. The figure was unmistakably human, and that fact frightened Logan all the more.

Moving as quietly as he could, Logan shifted his legs, staying low to the ground in the hopes that he could meld in with the blackness. The stalker in the forest surfaced from behind its shielding of shrubbery and began moving toward Logan at a swift, loping gait. Triggered by fear, Logan jerked rigid, throwing his right arm forward and releasing the dagger. His water-cleansed eyes saw the stalker dodge to the left, a night-cloaked arm lashing upward and snatching the dagger out of mid-air. A stream of perspiration dribbled down the side of Logan's face as he went to withdraw his sword.

"Does this mean you don't want to keep it?" the night asked.

Logan peered through the blackness. "Moknay?"

The almost-invisible Murderer crept closer to Logan, grinning insanely. He held Logan's dagger by the blade, pinched between his thumb and forefinger. "I thought it might be you," he said, " but I wanted to get closer to be sure. Where did you learn to throw a dagger like that?"

"I didn't," Logan responded. "I just chucked the damn thing. Where's Thromar?"

"I thought you might know," the Murderer replied. "I had to leave town in a hurry, and, from the looks of things, so did you. Are you an outlaw in Santa Monica?"

"No way!" Logan cried. "I just might be mistaken for one here!"

"'Mistaken'?" Moknay repeated. "Sparrill's finest are *all* outlaws, and proud of it! Bloody King Mediyan hasn't done a blasted thing about the Reakthi—lets them wander all over Denzil and Sparrill. The only thing that has kept the chestplated bastards out is the people themselves! That's why we keep the Guards out of Eadarus as well. Thromar himself is an outlaw. Branded a vigilante because he cared about Sparrill and had to bend a few of Mediyan's rules when he killed a Reakthi

Imperator! And what does our fat ruler do? Thank him? No, he calls him an outlaw who has dared to take matters into his own hands!" Moknay snorted contemptuously. "What does Mediyan know about taking matters into his own hands? He just sits on that fat ass of his back in Magdelon where the Reakthi menace hasn't spread . . . yet."

Logan was silent as the anger drained out of the Murderer. Gradually, Moknay's grey eyes dimmed and he turned to face Logan, his expression one of extreme hatred. "Are things as bad where you come from?" he queried.

Logan shrugged. "Pretty much so. People fight one another in supposed times of peace, no one can afford anything with the way inflation keeps going up, lots of people need to steal just to eat, and a number of loonies go around butchering people because they have nothing better to do." The young man caught himself, clamping a hand over his mouth while his eyes bugged out of his head. Stupid! He kicked himself mentally. You're talking to one of these loonies!

Moknay grinned as if he could read the young man's thoughts. "I don't kill people for fun," he explained. "I kill only those who deserve to be killed . . . like those thugs out in front of the tavern. Consider what I do a form of . . . pest control."

Only who decides who the pests are? Logan asked himself. Abruptly, he felt the darker portion of his mind swirl into life and taunt him with the fact that he himself had killed . . . more than once.

The Murderer's left eyebrow shot up in question. "What have you got there?" he wondered, eyeing the bags cradled in Logan's arm.

Logan gave the bags a hasty glance. "Oh, uh, nothing much. Just some provisions, that's all."

"You like food that much?" Moknay quipped. "You're holding it like it contains all of Mediyan's treasures."

Logan forced a chuckle, shaking his head and shrugging at the same time.

The Murderer stepped closer, piercing Logan with his steely grey eyes. "You can tell me what you have," he said, handing back Logan's dagger as if in a gesture of peace. "It could be five thousand pieces of silver, and I wouldn't kill you for it. I'm an exterminator, remember? Not a 'looney.' "

Are you? Logan mused.

A pang of guilt jolted the young man out of his thoughts. This was Moknay, he told himself. A friend. He tried to save you from that wizard and almost got himself killed; he gave you that dagger as a gift; and he saved your life from those thugs and the Reakmor. He may have been called Moknay the Murderer in Eadarus, but it was, after all, just a name.

Logan frowned. Yeah, like Jack the Ripper.

Muttering to himself, Logan opened one bag and withdrew the tin of powder. Moknay flipped open the lid and sniffed at the dark blue grains.

"Phew!" he exclaimed, screwing up his face. "That reeks!"

Logan took back the tin. "It also glows," he reported.

Moknay smirked as Logan extracted the money-pouch; however, when he peered inside the small bag, his smirk turned downward. "Huh? Ten? You're hiding ten gold pieces from me? Holy Agellic! That's not even enough to buy a good sword!"

"I don't want a sword!" Logan snapped. "I've got a sword! I need the gold for food and maybe a change of clothes! These things seem to be a dead giveaway!"

Moknay shrugged indifferently and tossed the gold back to Logan. The young man caught the bag in the air, realizing the Murderer had taken the remaining bags to contain nothing but food. He didn't need to know about the jewel . . . but, if he found out about it on his own, he could get awfully mad . . . maybe even go looney.

"One more thing," Logan told the Murderer. He freed the glittering jewel.

Moknay sprang back in fright, his grey cape fluttering about him. "Where did you get that?" he shouted.

"From this bag."

"Whose bag is that? Whose horse is this?" Moknay rapidly questioned.

Nervousness took root at the barrage of questions. "I don't know!" Logan shouted back. "Why should it matter? It's just a jewel."

"That's not *a* jewel, that is *the* Jewel!" Moknay declared. "You've made a terrible mistake! That Jewel should not be in anyone's hands but a wizard's!"

Logan peered at the gem in his hands, expecting it to suddenly blow up in his face. "Huh? What are you talking about?"

"That thing is the Jewel of Equilibrant," Moknay explained, "and it supposedly has something to do with the Wheel itself! You should have never had left your Santa Monica, my friend."

"I didn't *want* to leave!" Logan barked. "Thromar was taking me to find some Smythe spellcaster to get me back."

Moknay nodded in approval. "You *must* find him now; you must bring him the Jewel—if you didn't steal it from him in the first place. The powers in the Jewel must be controlled."

Logan started to replace the Jewel when a fearful thought lodged in his mind like a bullet. "Oh, my God," he breathed. "That Reakthi spellcaster is after me, and, if he catches me, he catches this Jewel as well. If it has as much power as you say . . ."

Moknay was still nodding gravely. "The only thing we can do is go back to Eadarus."

"Go back?" Logan blinked. "And walk into the Guards?"

"We need Thromar," the Murderer stated. "I have no idea where the Smythe hides—Thromar does. And besides, if we're going to be realistic, you and I would not survive long with the Jewel in our possession and Groathit dogging our heels."

The Murderer turned to face the black forest and brought two fingers to his lips. A shrill whistle rent the night, and a grey horse with a black mane and tail thundered free of the gloom. Logan hurriedly untethered his own horse and scrambled into the saddle, glancing down at the saddlebags as he did. *Just what I needed—complications!*

Spewing up dirt, Moknay's grey horse bolted off. Logan jerked on the reins and turned his horse to trail the Murderer. All the while a familiar voice was playing in Logan's head: *Have you no fear of dreams?* Only now, Logan knew, it was no longer a dream.

The sun had been up for a half an hour when Eadarus finally came into sight over the treetops. The morning mist had already dissolved as the two horses galloped down the path, making their way toward the protective wall of the town. Through the early morning hours, a third rumble of hooves sounded, and Logan and Moknay threw one another expectant glances.

"Someone's coming," the Murderer whispered, motioning Logan to pull in behind him.

As the pair readied themselves to confront any Guardsmen, the third rider came into view. With an arrogant snort, Smeea tossed back her head, flinging her red mane behind her. Thromar's reddish brown hair whipped in the wind as he brought his horse to a stop, his black eyes wide beneath his bushy eyebrows. Moknay let out a sharp chuckle as he eyed the fighter, shaking his head in disbelief.

"Well, well, well," he said with a smirk, "look who has seen fit to honor us with his presence."

Thromar opened his mouth in astonishment. "Moknay?" he queried. "What brings you out of Eadarus, Murderer?"

The lithe man continued smirking. "Have you been battling Reakthi so long that their chestplates have blinded you? Look behind me, oaf."

Thromar jerked his head back in surprise. "Friend-Logan!" he roared. "So this is where you ran off to!" The huge fighter gave Moknay a glance. "If I had known you were going to make friends with the lowest, murderous, most treacherous man in all Denzil I would have never have left your side!"

"What?" Moknay replied, indignant. "Have I no good points?"

"Those *are* your good points," Thromar responded, laughing good-naturedly. He gave the road behind him an anxious glance. "I would suggest you turn around and follow me; Eadarus is swarming with Guardsmen. It seems a fight broke out in one of the taverns and two Reakthi were involved. And Mediyan's buffoons actually thought *I* had started it! Indeed!"

"We know what happened," Moknay interrupted. "We were the cause. The Reakthi came looking for Logan, and I attempted to foil their plan by starting a brawl. We made a hasty retreat; still, I don't see why the Guards are suddenly so interested in Eadarus and Reakthi? Hmmm. Oh, well, anyway, during our escape, we've stumbled upon the Jewel of Equilibrant. We were coming back for your help."

"My help?" Thromar boomed. "I'm not a bleeding spell-caster! Maybe friend-Logan can do something. Have you seen him take out his eye yet, Moknay?"

"Logan is the one who found the Jewel," the Murderer retorted, "and, no, I have not seen him take out his eye. But what you don't seem to understand, Thromar the Thick-headed, is that Groathit was one of the Reakthi in Eadarus. He and Vaugen seem to have an interest in our strangely dressed friend, and, now that Logan's stumbled upon the Jewel, if they capture him, they also receive the most powerful item in the entire multiverse as an extra gift!"

"By Brolark!" Thromar blurted. "I see what you mean! Well, no sense in waiting around; Mediyan's dungheads should be catching up with us any moment now. We'll just get off the roadway and travel at a slower pace until our mounts are rested. No sense in tiring ourselves out being chased by Guardsmen!"

The three led their horses into the surrounding foliage and started their trek westward. By noon Logan was positive he would never be able to find Eadarus again. He had been completely enclosed by trees again . . . and that bizarre sensation of mismatchment had returned. In an attempt to ignore the feeling, Logan turned toward his two companions.

"Why are the Reakthi trying to invade your land?" he wondered.

Thromar glanced over at the young man, a perplexed expression drawn across his bearded face. He abruptly remembered Logan knew nothing of the Reakthi and took in a deep breath.

"Well, friend-Logan," he said, "it began long ago, years before I came into being. The Reakthi are a people who lived in a land far to the east, across the Sea of Hedelva. With many ships they set sail for Denzil, their eyes aglow with the prospect of more lands. When they first landed, we knew nothing of these chestplated strangers, and they were able to easily conquer the eastern portion of Denzil. After that, of course, the people started fighting back. Nonetheless, the Reakthi have strong spellcasters and were able to retain their conquered lands.

"I grew up learning to hate the Reakthi since they made constant attacks on my home, which was in the western regions of Denzil. We were forced to flee into Sparrill as the Reakthi steadily advanced westward, but the people, when they realized they would get no help from Mediyan, rallied together and decimated any Reakthi troop. For many years the Reakthi were daunted, held back by a throng of loyal citizens who, unlike their King, cared about what happened to their homelands. Still, four Imperators took charge of the Reakthi Stronghold about ten years ago. They were Vaugen, Ikathar, Agasilaus, and Quarn. Agasilaus, a crafty devil if ever there was one, suggested a slow and almost unnoticeable advance into Denzil. The others agreed, and small bands of Reakthi made their way deeper into our land. By the time they were noticed, Vaugen and Ikathar had already half completed building fortresses on the very western border of Denzil, and the Reakthi Stronghold had moved just north of Lake Xenois. Any city or town the Reakthi had crept past, they now went back to and destroyed.

"One of the first things I did against the Reakthi was seek out Agasilaus and slay him. That seems to have saved Sparrill from the same fate as Denzil. Vaugen is the only Imperator we must be cautious of, although he is not as devious as his friend was. Quarn and Ikathar can be ignored; Ikathar is too brash and impetuous to do anything right, while Quarn does not seem all that interested in conquest any longer. Oh, we still have problems with small bands roaming through Sparrill, but the Reakthi can never close around us like they did in Denzil so long as Eadarus still stands. If the Reakthi gain Sparrill, the thieves and cutthroats there would lose their trade, and there is nothing more furious than a thief who has been replaced by a Reakthi."

Moknay glanced over at Logan, nodding. "As I mentioned before," he stated, "Sparrill's finest are the outlaws."

Logan nodded back to the two men, and the unnerving buzz came back. "What about Droth?" the young man continued. "Everybody thinks I come from Droth. Where's that?"

Thormar tilted back his massive head and laughed. "Droth is a small island north of Dragon's Neck. It has always been known as the setter of many strange customs."

Logan grinned. "Like L.A.," he remarked, chuckling. The young man winced as he spoke the name. Like a swarm of hornets, the disharmony converged on him, demanding he return there. Gritting his teeth in response, Logan asked his companions: "Just why are the Reakthi after your land?"

Thromar and Moknay both blinked. "What?" they both asked.

"Why are they after your land?" Logan repeated. "There has to be a reason. I don't see why they should come all this way just to conquer you unless they wanted to gain something."

Thromar scratched his beard. "You ask puzzling questions, friend-Logan. I had always thought the Reakthi were just lusting after lands, but your inquiry has opened my eyes to the fact that, when Agasilaus was in command, they were somewhat disciplined, as if they were searching for something in particular."

"Any idea what?" Logan persisted, fighting back the mismatchment.

Moknay ran a finger across his mustache. "I have none," he admitted, "and I do not think the Reakthi do either."

Thromar nodded in agreement with the Murderer, looking over at Logan. "You are very good at asking questions, friend-Logan," he complimented. "Is that what you did in Santa Monica?"

"No, I was the focus operator for a film crew."

"Focus operator? Is that why you are able to take out your eye?" Thromar wondered.

"I don't take out my eye!" Logan replied, raising his arms. "Jesus! What would you have done if I had had a glass eye?"

"Glass eye?" Thromar mumbled. "Is that anything like a glass jaw?"

"Or glassware?" Moknay added, grinning in jest.

Thromar looked around. "Glass where?"

With a mischievous smirk, Moknay sprang from his saddle and looked about them carefully. Logan halted his horse, watching the Murderer inspect the forest. When he was about to ask what Moknay was doing, the Murderer turned back to his companions.

"I think we can stop here for a while," he said, glancing up and narrowing his eyes.

Following Thromar's lead, Logan dismounted and tethered his mount. He looked about the trees as Moknay had done and was satisfied when he could see or hear nothing forbidding amongst them. Thromar had plopped down on the ground beside him, hungrily shoving raisins into his mouth. Feeling hungry himself, Logan withdrew his beef jerky and tore off a piece. He stuffed it in his mouth and began to chew, and immediately made a sour face. The stuff tasted like cardboard! he mused. And it had the same texture as well! Blecch! Still, Logan had to eat, so he diligently kept gnawing away.

Thromar spoke up, his mouth full of dried grapes: "Looking for something, Moknay?"

Logan turned to see the Murderer was still staring skyward, his grey eyes flickering. Curious, Logan turned his gaze heavenward and peered into the blue sky. He didn't see anything out of the ordinary . . . in fact, there weren't even any helicopters or jets to fly overhead. There was only a lonesome hawk circling through the clouds.

To Logan's surprise, Moknay withdrew a dagger and silver flashed. The hawk veered to the left, diving sharply toward the trio as it dodged the weapon. Now Thromar was on his feet, his bloodstained sword held tightly in his meaty hand. Confused, Logan turned on the two.

"What are you doing?" he said to Moknay. "Practicing on birds?"

Moknay reached into his belt and withdrew an oddly shaped weapon. It had a golden hilt like all the Murderer's daggers, but it branched into three curved blades, one on the right near the base of the hilt, one on the left closer to the top, and the third slightly off-center and arced like a crescent moon. At first Logan had no idea what the strange, many-bladed thing was; then he recalled reading about throwing knives and recognized Moknay's weapon for what it was.

"That bird," Moknay snarled, holding the knife in his hand, "may just be Groathit's doing. A spy."

"A spy?" Logan exclaimed. "A spying bird?"

"Of course," Thromar put in. "You wouldn't think Moknay would waste daggers on some harmless flock of feathers, now do you? If that bird is working for that Reakthi scumcaster, it will tell him where you are . . ." The fighter lowered his voice. " . . . and the Jewel."

Moknay nodded his head dismally. "And there may be no escape."

The ebony-winged bird banked, swooping to the right and winging its way eastward. It opened its beak and cawed loudly, "No escape! No escape!"

The three watched it diminish into the clouds.

The afternoon slowly gave way to evening, and the blood-red hue began to tint the sky as the sun dropped down behind the mountains. The grey, yellow, and black horses slowly wound their way through the labyrinth of trees, and Logan could see the path out of Eadarus to his right; Moknay and Thromar had promised him that they would return to it by nightfall.

As the moon floated into the sky, the trio did direct their horses back onto the dirt road, and they continued their leisurely pace. Pale trickles of moonbeams sprinkled the path, and the moon itself hung directly before them. Logan was almost sure that if he could ride to the end of the road, he would reach the moon.

A dark spot marred the yellow-green moon before them, as if the moon were issuing forth some black object toward the three. The closer it came, the more detail it attained. Leathery wings flapped in rapid succession on either side of the figure, and skinny, sticklike limbs protruded from its humanoid body. It continued to grow, taking on more features with each beat of its wings. Large, toadlike eyes glared in the moon's light, and a small, rounded mouth opened wide, releasing a soul-wrenching shriek.

Veering sharply, the pale creature swooped.

"By Agellic!" Moknay exclaimed. "Is that a Demon I see?"

Thromar nodded calmly. "That it is," he stated, freeing his sword. "What's wrong? Afraid of a puny thing like that?"

"Demons are not a common sight in Sparrill, Thromar," the Murderer answered, slipping two daggers from his chest strap, "but we know for certain Logan does indeed have the Jewel. The Demon must have sensed its powers and wants it for itself."

"Well, let it come!" bellowed Thromar. "I'll take it to Gangrorz's Tomb with three blows! Hack! Slash! Tear! Then I'll dance on its corpse!"

Moknay turned away from the Demon, smirking. "Would you care to wager on that remark? Say, five gold pieces?"

"Make it ten!"

"So be it! Ten it is!"

Thromar stood up in his crude saddle, his huge sword held before him. "That's more like it," he grunted, slashing downward as the Demon came into range.

The swooping Demon screeched, halting itself in mid-air. Thromar's weapon ripped across a leathery wing, bringing a yellowish white blood to the surface of the pale skin. The fighter, however, spilled out of his saddle, unbalanced by his mighty swing.

Emitting a triumphant scream, the Demon flashed downward.

Yellow blood spurted as the creature impaled itself upon Thromar's upraised sword. Releasing a victorious cry of his own, Thromar tore free his weapon and swept it in a massive arc. The heavy blade met little resistance as it passed through the thin neck and severed the Demon's spinal cord. In a spatter of blood, the decapitated Demon crumpled to the ground, its toadlike eyes still blinking on its separated head.

"Hah!" Thromar boomed happily. "I win!"

"Oh, no, you don't," Moknay grinned.

Thromar made a face, shuffled over to the cadaver, and pounced up and down a few times. "I must look like an utter fool dancing like this!" he grumbled.

"Would you like to hear something just as amusing, Utter Fool?" Moknay snickered. "I left all my money back in Eadarus."

Thromar stared dumbly at the grinning Murderer, angrily wiping the blood off his boots. Logan, impressed by Thromar's display, suddenly screwed up his face, waving a hand in front of his nose.

"Whew!" he proclaimed. "What a stench!"

Moknay nodded. "Demons tend to stink more than most things once you cut them up. That bothersome odor will attract quite a number of beasties on the prowl for food. I suggest we put some distance between ourselves and the corpse before stopping for the night."

"I agree heartily," Thromar put in. "Not only for safety, but also so I may forget how I was tricked into dancing upon a dead Demon!"

"Cheer up, Thromar," Moknay jeered. "Think of it as something you can tell your children—if that creature wasn't one of them."

"You tread a thin line, Murderer," Thromar playfully growled, mounting up.

Logan pulled back his sleeve and stared at his glowing watch; the red and silver light was still there. He guessed he had been on watch for about one hour, so it must have been somewhere around four in the morning, but, without his watch, he could not be positive. He tossed a look behind him at where his horse was tethered and the leather saddlebags were hanging beside its flanks. Muttering unhappily, Logan opened the pouch of food beside him and ate the remaining pieces of jerky. Chewing, he threw a few small twigs into the campfire before him. He stared as the sticks blazed with red, yellow, and orange light and let the image blur. It looked as if Logan was amazed by the fire hungrily consuming the twigs, but, in actuality, he was bored. Wishing he could suddenly reappear in his apartment, Logan continued gazing at the dancing tongues of flame. His eyes sprang open when the fire finished feasting upon the twigs and belched.

Logan brought up his head, his blue eyes wide in astonishment. Beyond the fire, peering out from the shrubbery, was the strangest-looking face Logan had ever seen. Enormous hands pushed aside the obstructing foliage so the face could stare at Logan expectantly. The face and hands seemed to be a light blue, but Logan could not be sure from where he sat. Unexpectedly, a gigantic leer spread across the squarish face, and the thing lumbered free of the brush.

Logan felt a jolt of fear race through his system. The creature coming toward him stood over seven feet tall! And its skin *was* blue! Its human body was made up of tremendous muscles, and its massive chest was as wide as a barrel. Tattered pants dangled about its tree-trunk-thick legs, and enormous bare feet pounded the ground as it advanced.

It smiled crookedly.

"Foooooooood!"

Mouth agape, Logan scuttled backwards, trying to pull his sword from its sheath. "Hey," he stuttered, "I'm not food!"

"Not foooooood?" the creature asked, crestfallen.

It was semi-intelligent, Logan realized. Maybe he could convince it not to hurt him.

"No," he told the thing, shaking his head slowly, "I'm not food; but I do have some. You want to make a deal?"

The light blue ogre nodded eagerly. "Make deeeeeeal!" it boomed, stepping closer to the fire.

The fear remained churning inside Logan, but it was slowly decreasing. The light blue beast was nothing more than a large human—an ogre. Its odd skin color and enormous size made it startling at first, but now Logan almost expected it to jump up and down and clap its massive hands in anticipation.

Logan continued: "Yeah, I'll make you a deal. I'll give you food, and you don't hurt me."

"Foooooood!"

Logan flinched at the resounding bellow, glancing over at Thromar and Moknay, who—oddly enough—were still sleeping. They didn't need to know about the ogre, Logan concluded. They might wake up and hurt the poor guy.

"Shh!" Logan commanded. "Be quiet! You want to wake up my friends?"

"Friennnnnnnnds?" the ogre queried, cocking its head to one side.

"Yeah, those guys," Logan responded, pointing to one side.

The light blue ogre nodded its massive head and clamped a huge hand across its mouth. Unable to restrain a grin, Logan pulled out his food pouch and handed some over to the ogre. The large creature snatched at it greedily, wolfing it down in one swallow.

"Foooooood!" it rumbled cheerfully.

"Jesus!" Logan exclaimed. "Eat it fast, why don't you?"

The ogre grinned. "Faaaast!"

Logan peered back into the pouch; the leather sack was empty. The fear increased as he looked back up. The ogre stood on the opposite side of the fire, a massive hand extended for more food. That hand could fit right around my skull! Logan noted, swallowing hard. And if it squeezed . . .

Fearing the worst, Logan said, "Uh . . . I'm afraid there isn't any more."

The ogre cocked its head to one side again. "No moooooore?"

Cringing, Logan nodded. "Yep, sorry."

The light blue hand closed and slowly retracted as the ogre took a few thunderous steps back. "Sor . . . ry," it repeated, dejectedly vanishing into the surrounding foliage.

A large black hawk glared from atop a tree, its eyes flickering in the firelight below.

·4·

Wheel

Logan glanced over his shoulder at the treetops backed by the cloud-filled sky. The black hawk ignored his gaze, continuing to flap from to tree. The sunlight seemed to sparkle upon a malevolent intent glittering within the bird's eyes as it glared down at the three.

"It's been watching us all day," Logan muttered, turning back around.

Moknay sneered in vexation, one hand going to the throwing knife at his belt. "Damn bird," he snarled. "It just sits there—like it's waiting for something—and it always evades anything we throw at it."

"Let it come closer and I'll mash its beak!" Thromar declared.

"It did; and you missed," Moknay reminded. "At least we've been able to guess that it has to return to wherever Groathit is to give him a report on our progress. I only wish I knew what the damn thing was waiting for." The Murderer glared up at the treetops with his own namesake glinting in his eyes.

The ebony bird spread its wings and fluttered to the next treetop.

Logan gave the saddlebag hiding the Jewel a swift glance and then turned back to the hawk. Groathit's tactics worked better for them than for him, Logan discovered. The spellcaster could have led them on this stupid bird trail all the way to the Hills of Sadroia before doing something himself, and, of course, by then, it would be too late. The Jewel would be in the Smythe's hands, and Logan would be safe at home in his Santa Monica apartment. A wild grin suddenly spread across Logan's face and he directed his horse closer to Moknay's.

"It might be waiting for us to mention where we're going," the young man whispered.

Moknay's eyebrows shot up, and Logan's grin was reflected on the Murderer's mien. "You may have something there, friend," he whispered back. "We're pretty close to Debarnian; perhaps we can lose our feathered foe for a few days."

"How?" Thromar questioned. "It will surely follow us into the town."

Moknay's eyes flickered. "Not if we give it some information to tell Groathit," he said with a smirk. Then, in a loud voice, he proclaimed, "Not much further. We should arrive in Semeth in a few weeks."

"We will?" Thromar asked, startled.

Moknay hushed the fighter with a fierce glare and turned to watch the bird. The hawk flapped its wings triumphantly, flying eastward. "Semeth!" it croaked. "Semeth!"

"Into the town!" Moknay ordered.

The three horses shot forth, leaving an enormous cloud of dust rising in their wake. The wind shrieked past Logan's ears as he urged his mount on at what seemed to be an impossible speed. Before he could adjust his senses to the incredible pace, the horses entered Debarnian and Logan had to fight the reins for control. People scattered, screaming, as the trio of horses charged recklessly through the town, hooves clattering upon the cobblestones.

Logan jerked back on the reins and finally pulled his yellow-and-green mount to a halt. Thromar reined up beside him; dismounting in front of them was Moknay. He walked over to the two, leading his horse and smirking in victory. Thromar also dismounted, gently patting Smeea upon the nose. Logan remained on his horse, watching the two from there as if the spectacular run had left him as winded as the horses.

With a cheerful "Ah-ha!" Thromar began to move forward, taking Smeea along behind him.

Moknay raised a curious eyebrow as the fighter walked past him. "Where in Imogen's name are you going?" he queried.

"In there," Thromar remarked, pointing to a nearby tavern. "If we're going to hide from that bird, we may as well do it in style."

"So," the Murderer grunted, "Thromar the Fat heads for the nearest tavern! I should have guessed as much. Well, Logan and I will be at Agellic's Church; I've a friend there who may be able to help."

Logan jumped from his horse and gave Thromar a last look before the fighter ducked into the bar. An unease began to take residence in Logan's stomach as he followed Moknay down the cobblestone street. The last time he had been separated from Thromar he had almost been killed—three times! And he had been forced to retreat without the fighter's aid. No, Logan did not like the idea of Thromar leaving them, but he could not demand the fighter accompany him. Thromar had his own life to lead . . . Logan was only getting in the way with his being there.

The sensation of incompatibility returned as if on cue.

Moknay halted before Logan and opened a massive ivory door. The feeling of wrongness practically vanished as Logan looked up at the Church. It was built out of massive stones, and battlements lined the roof like a castle tower. Triangular windows made of glass stretched up the walls, and four huge pillars supported the roof above the entrance. The architecture seemed to be a cross between the structures of ancient Greece and of the High Middle Ages.

In awe, Logan entered the Church and was stunned once again. Crystal and gold adorned the tables and walls, and the marble floor sparkled black and white as sunlight streamed in through the windows. Enormous pillars stood sentrylike within the foyer, and Logan realized the black-and-white floor made an odd design under their feet. A small wooden door, carved with intricate designs, stood off to their left, and double doors which led to the main body of the Church lay ahead of them.

His boots clicking upon the marble, Moknay went for the smaller door.

The two stepped into a cluttered room filled with tables and littered by strange objects and devices. Rows of candles lined all the tables but one. This table was covered by a collection of papers and scrolls, and a somewhat plump man dressed in a red tunic and blue pants bent over the parchments, his back to his guests.

Silently, Moknay crept up behind him, poking a dagger at the man's back. "Stand quite still and give me all your money," the Murderer growled menacingly.

The man at the table went rigid. "I give up!" he cried. "Take my money! Take my clothing! Take everything! Just don't hurt me!"

Moknay grinned back at Logan. "Turn around very slowly," he instructed his victim.

The chubby man did as he was commanded, shuffling about with as much grace as a worm caught in a spider's web. When he saw his attacker, he straightened considerably, tugging on his tunic and clearing his throat.

"Fooled you, didn't I?" he snorted. "Knew it was you all along! Just wanted to give your morale a boost!"

"Of course you did, Barthol," Moknay agreed, his voice tinged with sarcasm.

"Oh, I did!" protested Barthol. "If I had not have recognized you, a real thief would have tasted my fury! Stab! Into his bowels! Slash! Off goes an arm! Blood everywhere! Marvelous!"

"You remind me an awful lot of Thromar," Moknay sneered, "but that's not why I'm here."

Barthol turned his back on the Murderer, waving his hands in annoyance. "If it's money you want, you've wasted your time. The collection box has been empty for weeks, so I haven't gotten . . . uh . . . I mean, the Church hasn't gotten anything for a long time."

"I don't want your money," answered Moknay. "I want you to help my friend."

Barthol looked over his shoulder and spotted Logan for the first time. With a startled yelp, he sprang back, knocking into a table and spilling a number of leatherbound volumes. Moknay glared at the priest, tapping the fingers of his right hand upon his left arm.

"Calm yourself, Barthol," he commanded. "He's a friend."

Barthol sneered back. "Well, he can't have any money either." The plump man took a curious step forward and peered at Logan. "And besides, people from Droth aren't allowed in Agellic's Church."

"For Christ's sake!" exclaimed Logan. "I am *not* from Droth!"

Barthol blinked, turning to Moknay. "For whose sake?" he wondered.

Moknay's eyebrows lowered, transforming his face into a grimace of impatience. "Stop aggravating me, Barthol," he said, gritting his teeth. "You know you're very good at it."

"Yes," Barthol replied, "you say that every time you visit me and ask for money."

"I don't want your damn money!" the Murderer fumed.

"Then why did you come here?" Barthol threw back.

Moknay's gloved hands shot out and grasped the front of Barthol's tunic. The stumpy man cringed for a moment as Moknay drew him closer, then threw back his shoulders and met the Murderer's glare. "Don't hit me," he warned, "or I'll turn into a living blast of power and whiz about you until you won't know what hit you."

Moknay continued glaring, his teeth clenched. "You'll find that quite difficult without a head," he snarled slowly.

Barthol's brow furrowed in thought. "You know," he pleasantly responded, "I think you're right."

"Now listen to me and listen carefully," Moknay instructed. "My friend here is not from Droth, nor is he from Sparrill, Denzil, or Magdelon. He says he comes from Santa Monica, which could be another part of the world—Imogen knows I've never heard of it! We've run into a bit of a problem, and I want you to check your charts to see if Logan's . . . arrival has been noted."

Barthol beamed. "Ah! My charts!" he happily cried. "You have come to the right man! I shall answer any questions you may have . . . if you'll let me go."

Moknay released the priest and watched as he walked to an empty wall. Dimpled fingers picked up a pouch and reached into it. Between his thumb and forefinger, Barthol was pinching some glittering dust when he extracted his hand, and Logan thought it looked like glitter he used to buy as a kid at a magic shop. Knowing he had an audience, Barthol himself put on a magic act, adding meaningless gestures and ridiculous jumps as he sprinkled the dust before the blank wall. For a moment, nothing seemed to happen; then the wall shivered, almost rippling like water. Gradually, a dark square formed on the wall, dotted with points of light. Logan blinked a few times at what appeared to be a window, only it did not look outside at the town of Debarnian but stared out into the blackness of space. Strange illuminated symbols accompanied the stars as they went about their celestial dance.

Barthol leaned closer to inspect his chart.

"Hmmm," the little man muttered, "Bergyls has shifted, and Rewyt seems to have dropped Wheelward. Aetwindan is increasing, and Gereord is diminishing. IukIan and Paell have interchanged, and Tolmaessa is veering Gymmward."

Logan scratched his head. "What's all that mean?"

Barthol turned around, shrugging. "I don't know."

"You don't know?" Moknay bellowed. "What do you mean you don't know?"

Barthol waved his hands frantically. "I never did understand all that cosmic claptrap!" he admitted. Unexpectedly, something on the chart caught his eye and he began staring. "What's this, then?" he mumbled. "There's a rift in the Wheel, causing it to tilt slightly to one side."

"Any foreseeable danger?" interrogated Moknay.

"Oh, no," Barthol consoled him. "The Wheel continuously dips from one side to the other—part of the cosmic cycle of events."

"Anything about the Jewel of Equilibrant?" Logan abruptly questioned, shifting the leather pouch he carried in his arms.

Barthol turned away from his chart, his eyes trained on Logan. "Why do you ask that?"

"Can you find it on your chart?" Moknay pressed the question.

Barthol swung around to face his chart. "Of course I can find it on my chart," he retorted. "The Jewel acts as the force that balances out the system of forces within the Wheel and produces equilibrium for the . . ." The priest nosed up to his mystical chart, peering at it. "It's not there," he gasped.

"Do you know who owned it?" Logan inquired, recalling Moknay's comment about stealing it from the Smythe. Wouldn't that just be dandy? the young man thought. The man I was looking for was in one of the first places I was, and I may have not only left without seeing if he could help me, but stealing his horse as well!

In somewhat of a daze, Barthol turned to some scrolls to answer Logan's query. "The Jewel has been in the possession of one of the mightiest spellcasters in all Sparrill, a magician by the name of Zackaron. In his experiments with the Jewel, Zackaron accidently triggered a portion of the energies and bestowed upon himself almost godly powers. This transfer alone has kept him alive for almost two hundred years.

Unfortunately, powers that practically give Zackaron control over nature also drove him quite mad. So, in order to keep the Jewel's powers in check, he gave it to his servant-boy, Pembroke." Barthol swung his gaze from his scrolls back to his chart. "And it seems Pembroke has lost the Jewel!" He went silent for another moment. "Holy Agellic!" he cried in fear. "If the Reakthi should happen to get their slimy hands on the Jewel, I'd hate to think what would happen to Sparrill!"

"No need to worry," Moknay grimly advised. "Logan has the Jewel."

"Moknay, this is no time for your macabre humor," Barthol snapped, still glaring at his shimmering chart. The priest's eyes abruptly widened. "By Harmeer's War Axe, you're right! That's why the Wheel is beginning to tilt! The rift seems to be from your friend's 'arrival,' but the tilting is because the Jewel's powers are not being kept in check. We're doomed! Doomed, I say! Doomed! That Jewel has got to be given to a spellcaster who can hold the powers in. If the Jewel continues to leak its cosmic energies, there will be nothing to stabilize the forces of the Wheel and act as equilibrant! The Wheel will have no means to achieve equilibrium, and it will tilt until it entirely flips over and destroys us all!"

Logan took in a sharp gulp of air as a burning anger chewed its way through his brain. "So it's up to Matthew Logan to save the universe," he snarled venomously.

"Huh?" queried Barthol. "What was that?"

Logan turned on the priest, eyes blazing. "I didn't want to come here!" he thundered. "Blast it! All I want to do is get back to my quiet, apathetic, Earthly home! I don't want to have the outcome of an entire world on my shoulders! It's not fair! It's not my fault I got zapped here! Why is it my fault that this Wheel is tilting?"

"It's no fault of yours, dear boy," Barthol soothed. "Only a spellcaster should have that Jewel; the powers inside it are what keeps the Wheel balanced, and you can imagine the force those powers must have. A magician must constantly keep the Jewel's energies in check. Oh, some leaks out now and again, but the Jewel easily replenishes itself. However, if there's no one around who knows how to keep the Jewel's powers in, they'll start escaping—slowly, mind you—but still escaping."

Moknay was nodding all through the priest's explanation. "How long do we have until all the powers are free?"

Barthol studied his chart. "Not very long," he reported dismally. "You will see signs of the escaping powers: earthquakes, storms, and such, all unnatural, of course, since the natural balance is faltering. Then larger disasters will begin. When this occurs, there will not be much time before the Wheel tilts on its side."

"And, if I remember my schooling correctly," Moknay continued, "once the Wheel goes over on its side, there's no reversing it. it will continue to tilt the rest of the way until this entire place goes up in flames."

Barthol nodded in silence, scanning his chart over and over.

Fists clenched at his sides, Logan stood behind the two, the anger still within him. This was worse than a dream, he grumbled to himself. It was a nightmare slowly going from bad to worse. It was suddenly up to him whether this land lived or died, and that didn't seem fair to Logan at all. He was an accident . . . a quirk! He wasn't supposed to be here! Why did this task fall to him? He didn't mean to steal the Jewel from Pembroke—why should he have to face the consequences? He was having a hard enough time as it was!

The young man's anger started to diminish as a faint sound reached his ears. For a second, he thought that infernal buzz of mismatchment was upon him, but then the noise faded, leaving Logan floundering in a million possibilities.

"Should we give the Jewel back to Zackaron or continue toward the Smythe?" Moknay was asking Barthol.

"The Smythe, by all means!" Barthol replied. "Agellic knows what Zackaron could do with his mind gone and all. It's a wonder he never forgot to keep the Jewel in check himself."

"We could use your help in finding the Smythe," Moknay invited.

The priest shook his head. "I'm afraid I'll have to abstain, not that I envy your task. My duty lies with the Church."

Moknay was nodding when Logan jumped toward him. Wings! the young man's brain was screaming. That noise is the beat of wings!

The Murderer went to the floor wearing a startled expression as something tore the air and splintered against the far wall near Barthol. Cursing, Moknay rolled to his feet, his grey eyes flaring angrily. Standing outside Barthol's open door was Groathit, a ghastly smile drawn across his lean face. Flanking him were six chestplated Reakthi, one leveling a crossbow at the Murderer's chest.

From his vantage point on the floor, Logan saw the spellcaster's left eye was glazed, as if he were blind in that eye.

"Groathit!" Moknay barked. "You worm! How long have you been here?"

The magic-user continued to smile. "My men and I have only just arrived, but I knew of your secret . . . 'cargo' beforehand." His good eye flicked to the crossbowman at his side. "Now hand over your companion and his prize."

In reply, Moknay swerved, and two daggers flashed. The crossbow twanged, and the blatant noise made Logan flinch. Moknay, however, expertly dived to one side, releasing the throwing knife at his belt. With an agonized cry, the crossbowman went down, one of the Murderer's daggers projecting from his cheek. Another Reakthi toppled, the Murderer's dagger and throwing knife embedded in his flesh.

"Get them and bring me the Jewel!" Groathit roared at the remaining warriors.

The quartet of Reakthi advanced, pushing into the cluttered room. Logan yanked free his own blade, swinging at the closest soldier. The warrior let out a shout as the blade tore across the top of his wrist, freeing blood. Moknay sprang atop one of the tables, three daggers screaming from his hand in rapid succession. One Reakthi fell backwards, a dagger lodged in the side of his neck. Another winced as a spinning blade skimmed his left shoulder and thunked into the wall. The third dagger spun for Groathit, who waved once and scattered the weapon's molecules throughout the chamber.

"Logan!" Moknay called. "The Jewel!"

Logan pulled the sack out from under his arm and made ready to toss the pouch to the Murderer. Unexpectedly, the hilt of a sword crashed into the back of his head with terrific force, and Logan pitched forward with a weak groan, the sack falling out of his hands.

Moknay's eyes narrowed as he watched the Reakthi behind Logan bend to grasp the Jewel. Groathit stood in the doorway, a triumphant grin across his skull-like features. A booted foot suddenly smashed into the Reakthi's jaw, knocking the warrior to the floor. Spitting blood, the chestplated soldier readied his sword, glancing up to see Barthol now in possession of the Jewel. Growling like some savage animal, the Reakthi shot forward, his sword thrusting for Barthol's stomach.

Barthol moved with astounding speed, snatching up Logan's fallen sword as he scurried to one side. His wild lunge, however, sent him reeling into a table, and the priest expected the Reakthi's sword to pierce his back at any moment. A scream sounded instead, and Barthol whipped about as his attacker toppled to the ground, one of Moknay's daggers just above his chestplate.

The Reakthi with the wounded wrist started for the priest, who sprinted back, pushing over the table he had bumped. The warrior stumbled, slipping in a puddle of blood made by his companions as he gripped tightly to his wrist. When he regained his balance and glanced up to find the fat priest, shining metal met his eyes and white-hot pain seared into his face. Blood splattered as Logan's blade bit into the Reakthi's eyes and across the bridge of his nose before shattering his skull.

Barthol watched as a hand twitched and went still.

"By all the gods!" a voice boomed throughout the Church.

Groathit wheeled about to see Thromar stride into the chamber, his massive sword ripping free of its sheath and streaking for the Reakthi spellcaster. Frantically gesticulating, Groathit burst into a titanic tongue of fire and vanished. The last Reakthi collapsed to the bloodstained floor as Moknay slit his throat.

Thromar let out a snort, replacing his sword. "Huh! Next time I shall know better! I went looking for some fun in a tavern and it's in a Church instead!"

There was a dim glow generating from somewhere within the room and a persistent throb in his skull as Logan feebly opened one eye. All the muscles in his body ached, and he winced at each heartbeat as if the flowing of his blood strengthened the pounding in his head. With his one eye open, Logan could make out a strange, iron-wrought symbol hanging on the wall above his supine form, and a soft substance lay beneath him, so he guessed he was on a bed of some sort. When he attempted to turn his head, the sharp jab of pain shot through his nerves, and Logan slumped, groaning. Through the ache, the young man heard satin rustle and peeked his eye open again to observe a slim figure leaning over him, a candle sputtering in one hand.

The candle's faint yellow glow illuminated a lovely face ringed by dark brown hair, and eyes filled with concern looked down at Logan. A red satin robe clung to her shapely form, closed by a black satin belt about her slim waist. She smiled when she saw Logan's eye pop open.

"Don't move," she whispered. "I'll fetch Barthol."

Barthol, Logan mused. That's right—he and Moknay had gone to see Barthol and had been attacked. *The Jewel!* he suddenly recalled, attempting to sit up. *What had happened to the Jewel?*

Dizziness and nausea consumed Logan, and he was forced back onto the bed. Helplessly, he stared up at the iron symbol, wishing the pain in his head would go away as he recognized the ornament as the same design that had been in the foyer. Quiet footsteps sounded as the girl returned, trailed by Barthol and Moknay; to Logan each step was a booming cannon.

"How are you feeling?" Barthol inquired softly. "That was a nasty rap you took."

Logan reached a hand behind his head and flinched as he lightly touched the enormous bulge on the back of his skull. "I feel like a bunch of elephants are doing a fandango in my head," he moaned.

Barthol glanced back at Moknay. "Fandango?"

Moknay glanced back. "Elephants?" he queried. Silently, he approached a window and peered out behind the curtains. "If you're wondering," he said over his shoulder, "we still have the Jewel."

Logan attempted to nod, and his head was flooded with pain. Instead, he croaked, "How the hell did Groathit find us? I thought we had tricked his bird."

Moknay shrugged. "He must have been waiting for us to ditch his spy and had a troop of Reakthi trailing us. He probably just teleported in from wherever he was hiding." The Murderer flashed Logan a grin which—to Logan—seemed to glare like a million suns. "Still, he doesn't know if we were lying when we said we were going to Semeth. Any fool could have guessed we had run into Debarnian."

Barthol placed a gentle hand on Logan's shoulder. "You'll be staying here tonight," he told him, "in Mara's room. She's an apprentice priestess of Lelah, so feel free to ask her for anything . . . if you know what I mean. She's never had a visitor before, but she does very well in her studies."

Logan blinked a few times, thinking he had misheard. "Huh?" he sputtered. "You mean when you're a priest you can . . . ?"

Barthol chuckled good-naturedly. "Of course! Lelah's the goddess of love, so all her priestesses are taught the goddess's art. It's different where you come from, eh? That's too bad you can't . . ."

"Who the hell says I can't?" barked Logan. "It's some of the priests where I come from who can't!"

The young man fell back onto the bed, clamping his hands to the sides of his head. His own shouting had hurt, and it felt like someone had activated a triphammer in his forehead.

"Get some rest," Moknay instructed him. "We'll be leaving early tomorrow morning. I can't say I like staying here when Groathit knows where we are."

Logan did not even attempt to nod as Moknay and Barthol left the room. He muttered unhappily to himself and at the rhythmic beat within his brain. Mara sat on the edge of his bed and gently placed a cloth behind Logan's head. For a moment, there was a flash of pain, but then it was gone and Logan realized how near the girl was to him. As she backed away, Logan cracked an awkward grin, recalling what Barthol had said.

"I—I wish I . . ." he stuttered, cursing himself for not being able to talk straight.

What rotten luck! he grumbled. Mara was one of the loveliest girls he had ever seen—in Sparrill or in Santa Monica. The way she arranged her hair was absolutely beautiful, and she had the most alluring green eyes that sparkled as if they were emeralds. Her smile was one of understanding and compassion, and her figure . . . ! Thank God someone put a blanket over me! Logan thought. Without it, his reaction to Mara's beauty—and Barthol's comment—would have been six and a half inches more than obvious!

"What Barthol said . . ." Logan tried again. " . . . I can believe that . . . uh . . . what I mean is . . ."

Mara bent forward, placing a slim finger on Logan's lips. "Shhh," she hushed him. "Rest now. You received quite a bump."

Logan almost flustered as he misunderstood the priestess and feared the blanket did not cover him as much as he thought. The panic slowly drained away, and Logan realized she meant the bump on his skull. Frowning to himself, he noted what headaches could really do to one's sex drive.

"Perhaps you could come back under less strenuous circumstances," Mara suggested. "I'd like to know more about you and your world."

Logan tried to smile and succeeded, although his facial muscles screamed in protest. "I don't think I can come back," he answered. "Once I leave Debarnian, I don't think you'll ever see me again."

Mara brushed one of the spiraling wisps of her long dark hair out of her face. "Why not?"

"Homesick," Logan shrugged, and the pounding intensified. "I'm giving my 'cargo' to some Smythe guy and going home . . . I hope."

Mara nodded, more of her dark brown hair spilling about her. "Then sleep," she told him. "Your journey will be arduous, and you will need your strength."

The young girl rose from the side of the bed and started across the room, her satin robe parting as she walked to give tantalizing glimpses of her bare legs.

Groaning, Logan shut his eyes and tried not to think about the priestess. It was reassuring to know, he noticed, that this god-awful world hadn't confused *all* his feelings. Only why did he have to find out now?

When Logan reopened his eyes, another priestess had entered the room, clad in a satin robe of dark blue. She was as beautiful and as shapely as Mara, but her hair was the color of beaten gold.

"Riva," Mara said, "bring in some more pillows, please."

The golden-haired priestess nodded in silence and fetched the goose-feathered pillows. She placed them on Logan's bed, gently lifting his head as she slipped one behind him. Her light blue eyes glistened, and a seductive wink made Logan panic. His thoughts tripped and staggered over one another as he tried to think of a response. The priestess was gone even before he thought to grin.

Mara stepped quietly over to her bed and untied her satin belt. With the rustle of satin, the red robe spilled away from her luscious frame like crimson water, and Logan clamped his eyes shut. Of all the times to have a knock on the head! he cursed silently.

Logan could hear Mara's breath as she blew out the candle, and more fabric rustled as the priestess climbed into her bed. Even behind the safety of his closed eyes, Logan was not free. The image of Mara slipping out of her robe continued to tease him, and, with nefarious mirth, his imagination took over and she and Logan were together. The pounding in his head lessened as his blood began to flow to other portions of his anatomy, and Logan begged for release.

Taking its cue once again, that infernal sense of wrongness heard Logan's unspoken plea and descended, swirling about his already shaken skull. Images of Mara, flickers of pain, and that mercurial buzz sloshed about in utter chaos, and Logan cursed his luck and the foul world in which he was trapped.

Gradually, his release was granted, and Logan slept.

"What? Blast it! There's got to be a way!"

The voice arose from the eddying tidepools of red and silver light, shattering the stillness with its tone of wonderment and confusion.

"Oh, wait! Yes, wait a minute! I think I'm getting something!"

Matthew Logan blinked his eyes repeatedly, staring at the spiraling vortex of blood and metal that encircled him. A strange sensation of déjà vu assailed the young man, and, puzzled, he tried to remember where he had seen this place before.

"Excuse me. I'll be there in a moment. I'm having a devil of a time trying to get a clear picture. Whatever you do, don't wake up. I may not be able to pick up your alpha waves again."

The asthmatic voice receded into the ocean of red and silver as a shadowy form took shape before Logan's bewildered eyes. Overwhelmed by the feeling of repetition, Logan watched as the figure advanced. It was a robed, monklike form that walked with a purposeful stride toward Logan, its features hidden by a large hood. Questioningly, the monk's hood tilted to one side as the figure halted.

"*You're going to be the one?*" the monk asked in that same, wheezing rasp. "*Hmmmm. Seems it works out. At least you're not dead, yet. My idea must work since you're not denying you're here. Well, that's good to know.*"

Hands pulled the hood away from the face, and Logan blinked in recognition. Before him stood the long-haired businessman, only now his face wasn't so ferocious. But why was he now wearing a robe? In Logan's world he had worn a suit; in Sparrill he wore a robe. Was there any significance?

Snow began to fall about the two, and the long-haired businessman appeared to be just as surprised as Logan. They watched the miniature flakes of white for a moment before the businessman/monk turned his gaze back to Logan.

"*Remember what Lord Byron once wrote,*" he said enigmatically. "*'I had a dream which was not all a dream.'*"

Logan lifted his eyebrows in question as the robed figure melded into the whirlpool of snowflakes and red and silver. Icicles began to sprout from the snow-covered ground like strangely jagged blades of grass, and one touched his throat from somewhere out of his line of vision. It was freezing and cold to the touch . . .

Logan's eyes fluttered open as the dream dissolved. Very dim light hinted to the young man that it was a little before dawn, but his subconscious did not wish to give him up. The icicle was still at his throat and a weight was upon his chest, restraining his arms.

"Hand me the Jewel or die," a throaty voice commanded.

That was not my subconscious! Logan realized, instantly springing awake. Someone was straddling his chest, their legs pinning his arms to the bed. And, if that wasn't bad enough, that icicle was no mere piece of frozen water! It was the cold, cruel blade of a dagger touching the unprotected flesh of his neck.

"What Jewel?" Logan inquired loudly.

"Silence!" the voice rasped in command, and the dagger nipped at his throat as it edged closer.

In that second of movement, Logan thought he heard the faint rustle of fabric.

"I want the Jewel," his attacker growled.

His night-hidden foe did not weigh much, Logan noted. The voice was raspy, but high—obviously disguised. Logan surmised he could probably unseat his assailant by arching his back, but he couldn't stop the dagger before it slit his throat.

"You will give me the Jewel or you shall die," the voice threatened.

"Then you'll never get it," Logan smugly retorted, once again purposely loud.

There was silence for a moment. The cold dagger eased up as Logan's attacker shifted its weight. This time Logan was sure he heard fabric rustle as his foe settled back down. A slim and shapely backside rested upon Logan's abdomen, and he knew his opponent had to be female. He moaned inwardly, praying his assailant was not Mara. Absolute power corrupts absolutely, he grimly reminded himself.

"I shall use you," his foe advised in a harsh whisper. "You for the Jewel."

Logan let out a laugh, and his injured skull throbbed in reply. "My friends know the importance of the Jewel," he snapped, ignoring the pain in his head. "They're not going to make a stupid deal like that!"

"I will not tell you to be silent again," his attacker warned.

The weight upon his chest and the dagger at his throat was suddenly gone, and a loud thump echoed in Logan's ears and affected the pounding in his skull. His vision became blurred as he struggled to look to one side; all the while the throbbing in his head grew worse. Through the pink of the coming dawn, however, he could make out two forms struggling in the shadows.

"Hurry!" Mara cried out, grasping the wrist of Logan's assailant. "Run!"

Logan sat up, and the room twisted inside-out. His stomach leaped and churned, and vertigo seized control. The throbbing in his brain became frantic, beating and pounding at the walls of his skull. Trying to adjust his vision, Logan saw silver flash and watched in fear as Mara forced the dagger away from her bare breast. The robed assailant threw itself back, satin billowing noisily as it freed its arms from Mara's grasp. In response, the priestess lunged, nude and unarmed. She once again caught her opponent by the wrist, desperately trying to force the dagger out of its grasp.

Stumbling in the pink light, Logan fell out of his bed. His head felt twice its size and growing larger with each pulse of pain. Gasping for breath, the young man blindly lunged, and his fingers latched onto fabric. His sense of balance dispersed, but he did not care. Pulling the robed assassin down with him, Logan crashed to the ground, followed by his attacker and Mara. A slim leg cracked into Logan's chest, and the pain in his head reached down into his ribs. All the breath went out of the young man, and he collapsed to the floor, stars and supernovae playing behind his eyelids.

"I can't . . . !" Mara breathed. "Matthew Logan, you must run!"

The voice reached into Logan's mind, and his last remaining ounces of strength stirred themselves into action. Feebly, he crawled to his hands and knees and stood, leaning up against the wall for support. Something whistled beside his ear, and his brain casually registered that the dagger had narrowly missed slashing Logan's throat. *Narrowly missed?* Logan blanched, realizing the importance of the message and momentarily forcing the pain away.

Satin tore in Mara's hand and Logan's attacker viciously backhanded the priestess across the room. The dark-haired girl spun backwards, crashing into a small table and lying very still. From where he was leaning, Logan could tell her full breasts continued to rise and fall, so she was not dead. His attacker, however, snatched up the dagger and started for the priestess. Rage boiled inside Logan and his hands clenched into fists— and he felt cold steel on the wall.

Inhaling, Logan fought back the pulsing in his head and pulled the iron-wrought symbol down from the wall. Its massive weight was too much for him, and the young man succumbed to gravity, clumsily twisting around as the huge design dropped earthward. Logan's attacker crumpled under the iron ornament, its dagger clattering noisily beside it. Logan also fell to the floor, his hands still clutching the enormous symbol. He had no idea how long he lay there before he pushed himself away from his assailant and crawled serpentlike to Mara's side.

His head continued to scream in agony, and the pain dimmed the other sensations in his body as Logan touched numb fingers to Mara's naked leg.

His head swirling, Logan thought an explosion had gone off when light suddenly flooded the room. Mumbling what he hoped was a curse and not some word he had made up, the young man turned to see Barthol hurry into the chamber, a torch crackling above his head. The flames seemed to bore into Logan's skull, and the pain became too much for him. His head dropped, resting upon Mara's thigh as he battled the fury raging in his brain. He suddenly saw Riva nearby, her robe torn open and blood staining her golden hair red. The iron symbol lay atop her skull, and her exposed chest failed to rise.

"Holy Agellic!" shouted Barthol. "What have you done?"

Hurt, Logan's thought whimpered. Voice hurts. Shhh. Mara hurt. Help her.

Moknay glided in behind Barthol, his feet making no sound upon the floorboards. "Calm yourself, Barthol," he advised. "The details of the struggle are quite clear to me."

"Not to me!" the priest retorted.

Unsteadily, Logan pointed a shaking arm at Riva. "She attacked me . . . wanted . . . wanted the Jewel." He collapsed back upon Mara's soft leg. "Mara saved me."

Moknay nodded slowly, clamping a friendly hand upon Logan's shoulder. "Come on, friend," he said. "We've got to be leaving."

Logan shrugged off the Murderer's hand and protectively tightened his grip on Mara's thigh. Handing the torch to Moknay, Barthol leaned down and picked the unconscious Mara up in his arms. Logan's hands slipped away and a terrific wave of loss swept over the young man. Someone who had saved him had been injured, just like Moknay himself had been. Logan longed to help Mara, but he did not know how. Best to leave as Moknay had suggested and get out of the priestess's life before he brought more injury.

Painfully, Logan pulled himself off the ground and walked with Moknay's help out the door.

There was still a small ache in the back of his head, but the broth Barthol had made for him had lessened the pain. Quietly, Logan sat atop his mount, gazing apologetically down at Mara.

The priestess stared back at him, a faint smile on her lips. She did not blame Logan at all for her injuries but thanked him for saving her life, something Logan hardly thought himself worthy of after what he had caused. He had been the one to put her life in jeopardy in the first place!

"Don't worry about it, my boy!" Barthol spoke up, noticing the two staring. "Mara's all right. In a few days she'll hardly remember the incident!"

"I'll remember," Mara whispered in answer, never taking her eyes from Logan.

"You've got the Jewel?" inquired Thromar from atop Smeea.

Logan patted one of the saddlebags in response, casting his eyes down as he was unable to meet the priestess's gaze any longer.

"May Agellic aid you in your search for the Smythe," Barthol told the trio on horseback. "We dare not let such powers fall back into Zackaron's hands or Groathit's."

"We shall try not to," Moknay told his friend. "Very well then, Barthol, perhaps I shall see you once this journey is over . . . or perhaps I shan't."

Barthol grimaced at the Murderer's gloomy humor but waved cheerfully as the colorful horses turned and galloped down the cobblestone streets. Mara kept her emerald green eyes trained upon Logan until the horses turned, and he was out of sight.

"Which direction?" Moknay queried as they rode.

"Straight west," Thromar replied. "We'll be leaving the path, but moving directly for Plestenah. From there it's straight into the Hills."

The Murderer stroked his bare chin with a gloved hand. "But that leaves us Roana, Lephar, and Ohmmarrious to forge without a bridge."

Thromar made a sour face under his beard before answering. "The Roana's gentle enough to cross, and I believe there's a bridge outside of Plestenah that will take us over the Lephar. That leaves us with only the Ohmmarrious to cross on our own."

The three raced out of the town, Thromar and Moknay tossing possible routes back and forth between them. Logan's horse thundered behind them, its rider taunted by visions of a shapely young priestess with eyes as green as fir. There had been something about Mara that had piqued Logan's interest, and it was definitely more than just Barthol's suggestion. And Logan had caused her to be hurt.

"But if we go all the way to the bridge, that takes us too far south!" Thromar was arguing. "We want to go to the Hills, not Gelvanimore!"

"You want to try crossing the Ohmmarrious near the branch of the Lephar?" the Murderer retorted. "We're not riding waterfoals!"

"Quiet!" Logan ordered his companions in a hushed voice.

The pair glanced back at him; he no longer wore his dour expression and alarm sparkled in his eyes. Immediately, Thromar and Moknay obeyed and went silent.

"Keep riding," Logan whispered, "only glance to the left when you get the chance."

The fighter and Murderer did and saw what Logan had glimpsed. Snaking from tree trunk to tree trunk was a thin, lean figure with spiky black hair. A sharp, long nose jutted from the narrow face, and tiny black specks hidden in the crevices of his brow were his eyes. A tattered cloak fluttered behind the figure, and clothes as rumpled as his hair covered the scrawny skulker.

"It's Pembroke," Moknay murmured. "He's found us."

• 5 •

Druid

Pembroke sprinted across a small clearing and disappeared behind a thick tree trunk, his tattered cloak marking his whereabouts for only a second before vanishing. His lean face materialized from beside the bark, ebony eyes riveted to Logan's green-and-yellow mount and the saddlebags at its side.

Weasellike, the black-haired servant scampered to another tree.

"That's Pembroke?" Logan questioned softly, amazed by the rodentlike movements of the gaunt figure.

Moknay nodded gravely.

Thromar snorted in contempt. "Hrrumph! Let him come! I'm not afraid of that little maggot!"

Moknay threw Thromar a glance. "He may be a maggot, but Pembroke is most certainly the swiftest and slyest maggot alive . . . and almost as insane as his master, Zackaron. Barthol told me certain rumors have it that he wields a Triblade. If we were to fight him, one of us is surely to perish."

"Triblade?" repeated Logan.

"A huge, heavy weapon," Thromar answered. "You'd have to be mad to use one! Has something near three blades on a razor-sharp hilt with barbed teeth atop the center blade. The deadliest weapon in existence, if you're strong enough to lift the damn thing let alone swing and thrust with it! I had no idea this Pembroke fellow could." The huge fighter grunted again. "Oh, well, he's still a maggot."

Their horses having slowed, Logan turned to peer through the trees. His blue eyes filled with puzzlement as he was unable to pinpoint the wiry servant amongst the foliage. With

an urgent move of his hand, he pointed out the empty forest
to his companions. Moknay's eyes glittered in thought but he
remained silent; Thromar snorted.

"Hah!" the fighter exclaimed. "He's run off! Must have
recognized me for who I am!"

Moknay grimly shook his head. "I doubt if he's run off,"
he muttered. "It may not have occurred to you, Thromar,
but Pembroke has followed us all this way *on foot.* I don't
think he's going to spot us and then run off without trying
to get his horse back. He'll try something before summoning
Zackaron."

The Murderer's horse suddenly reared up in fright, and
Logan almost spilled to the ground as his horse did the same.
Only Smeea remained on her feet, although she snorted like
her master.

Blocking their path was the gaunt Pembroke, a mindless
smile drawn across his lean and hungry visage. His villain-
ous Triblade flashed in the sunlight, and Logan gaped when
he saw the servant used only one hand to wield the titanic
weapon.

"He has caught you at last," Pembroke grinned wickedly.
"You are very observant to assume Pembroke would try to
regain that which is his. Now give it to him. Return the beast
and Child to Pembroke."

"Child?" Thromar wondered, asking the question for his
companions as well. "We don't have any bleedin' child, maggot!"

The Triblade glinted as it wavered in Pembroke's hand.
"Child," he sighed. "Pembroke's Child. Infant of Pembroke
and the multiverse, she is. Beautiful . . . Most beautiful." The
insane servant turned on them, his eyes radiating hatred. "*Jewel!*" he shrieked. "*Give me my Jewel!*"

The scream seemed to drive into Logan's brain, and his
horse and Moknay's skittered backwards fearfully. There was
something about the madman that triggered reactions of terror
within man and beast. It's no wonder why Logan's horse ran so
swiftly from Eadarus and remained with the young man rather
than return to its rightful master.

"Give you your Jewel?" Moknay retorted in a resentful
tone, and Logan immediately feared for the Murderer's life.
"What do you take me for? A fool? I am Zackaron's new

servant! The old one was done away with! I care for the Jewel now."

Pembroke's dark eyes flared as he stood in thought. An almost comical frown crossed his gaunt features, and his Triblade lowered somewhat as he pondered. Then he spat, "No! You lie! Pembroke is faithful! He would not be done away with! Give him his Child! Give me my Jewel!"

Logan swallowed hard, glancing about in all directions. There did not seem to be any escape from the black-haired lunatic before them. Moknay was closest to the servant and boxed in by Logan and Thromar behind him. If anyone made any move, Pembroke would surely slay the Murderer and then go for the others. Maybe they should give him back the Jewel regardless of what Barthol had advised.

"*Give me my Jewel!*" Pembroke howled, raising his Triblade to strike the Murderer.

"Stop!" Logan cried out, stretching out an arm as if to hold off the blow.

Pembroke's dark eyes flicked like a serpent's tongue to land upon Logan. The unbridled fierceness within those eyes made Logan shudder as he reached down for the leather pouch hiding the Jewel.

"I'll give you your stupid Jewel," Logan told him, sweat breaking out across his brow as the black eyes brightened, "but not if you hurt my friends."

"Friend-Logan!" Thromar protested, his beady eyes going wide.

"No one's going to die for me!" Logan snapped, cutting off any other comments. "He can take the Jewel and his damn horse! I'm not letting Moknay get killed to save me!"

"A noble sentiment, friend," Moknay answered, "but you need that horse to get back home; and Sparrill needs someone more trustworthy than Pembroke to hold that Jewel."

"Silence!" Pembroke roared, saliva spraying. "Pembroke *is* trustworthy!" The servant turned back to Logan, smiling hideously. "You are a smart one," he said. "Give him his Child."

Logan looked down at the magnificent Jewel he now held in his hands. Golden light leapt from the gem as the sunlight streamed into its many facets, and a halo of energy surrounded the Jewel. As if jealous for Logan's attention, the sensation of displacement rose up.

Pembroke's smile widened as he stepped closer to take the Jewel.

There was an unexpected screech from the heavens, and a blur of darkness descended upon the servant. Wings flapping, Groathit's spy swooped again, its beak flashing like a dagger's blade.

"Cannot!" the bird croaked. "Belong to Groathit! Cannot!"

Pembroke let out a startled shout and stumbled back. The ebony hawk dove a third time, forcing the wiry man away from the three on horseback. Losing his balance, the mad servant tumbled down a small slope, a cloud of dust rising into the air behind him.

"Go!" Moknay yelled, digging his heels into his horse's flanks.

The colorful horses charged forward, leaving behind Pembroke and the angry bird. Clutching the sparkling Jewel to his chest, Logan glanced back to see Pembroke leap to his feet, his black eyes blazing. A razor-sharp talon struck him above his eyebrow, and Pembroke stumbled back, blood dribbling down his forehead. Instantly, his Triblade came into play, blazing silver as it severed the air. Feathers and blood flew into the sky as the three-bladed weapon creased the bird's breast. With a furious squawk, Groathit's hawk veered to the right, picking up momentum as it swooped for Pembroke's face. A second flash of the Triblade separated the bird's head from its body.

"I would love to wade through your vile blood, fowl," Pembroke mocked the corpse, "but I must be after my Jewel. It is mine, and mine alone!"

Logan blinked as he saw Pembroke stagger back onto the path, the blood of Groathit's bird sparkling upon the many blades of his weapon. Bloodied feathers had adhered themselves to Pembroke's spiky hair as he sheathed his Triblade and sprinted after the three.

"He's coming after us!" warned Logan.

"That maggot killed the bird!" Thromar boomed. "We couldn't touch it, and that maggot kills it! He *must* be dangerous!"

The trio of horses charged on, relentlessly pursued by the lean Pembroke. The servant's legs blurred as his pace increased, and his tattered cloak whipped out behind him. Logan's eyebrows raised in shock when he glanced back again to see the mad servant was even closer.

"Holy shit!" he cursed. "He's gaining on us!"

"Pembroke has been around the Jewel long enough," Moknay replied, not bothering to turn around. "Keep moving, friend. You did not want to see me dead—I have no desire to see you in a similar state."

Logan urged his yellow-and-green mount to faster speeds, grasping tightly to the Jewel. The feeling of disharmony remained about the young man as he rode onward, his face beaten by the high winds. For the first time, his eyes began to smart as the wind slashed into them and forbade him from blinking soothing tears into his contacts. His vision began to blur as his contact lenses began to dry, and it hurt for Logan to even blink. His eyes were red and sore, and the horses' bits were covered with foam by the time the trio lost Pembroke. Gradually, and somewhat reluctantly, Moknay slowed his mount; the nearly blind Logan and Thromar did the same.

The young man from Santa Monica hardly heard Moknay as he tried again and again to blink some tears onto his dry lenses while replacing the Jewel.

"We appear to be in more trouble than before," the Murderer was saying. "Not only do we now have Pembroke to contend with, but Groathit's out one spy. The next pawn he sends out may be just as fast as that bird but deadlier. The three of us will never get the Jewel to the Smythe if that happens."

"What do you suggest?" Thromar asked. "Find more help? Unless we go out of our way, there's not a town for leagues."

Moknay nodded curtly. "You said we're heading for Plestenah; maybe from there we can head toward Wailvye or Gelvanimore. Better to go out of our way than to never reach our destination."

When his eyes did not bother him quite so much, Logan put in, "But remember what Barthol told us: We don't have that much time before the Wheel tilts."

"Friend-Logan is correct," Thromar agreed. "Still, I might get us some help in Plestenah. Fraviar's a good friend of mine—what help he'd be I can't guess."

"Fraviar?" echoed Moknay. "The tavern owner?"

Thromar nodded with a shrug. "I said I didn't know what help he'd be."

The Murderer sighed grimly. "Some help is better than none."

Logan heard the voices of his companions as he lightly touched a fingertip to an eye, gently moving the lens on that eye. His vision blurred as the lens slid off to one side, then gradually corrected itself as the contact slipped back into place. Because of his blurry vision, and the movement of his horse, Logan almost disregarded the dark object he spied lurking through the trees . . . until it sprang out of the shrubbery and blocked their way.

Logan jumped, staring at the creature he had seen hiding in the bushes. It stood some three feet in height, covered with shaggy brown fur. Tiny eyes peered out from beneath all its hair, and a mouth filled with little sharp teeth also hid below the fuzz. Long arms dangled at its side, and it grasped a dagger in its five-fingered, almost human hand. With a loud, perturbed screech, the fur-covered creature bounded forward, waving its lengthy arms frantically. Its tiny eyes glittered, and a smile drew across its face, exposing two pointed fangs.

Halted by the strange beast, Moknay, Thromar, and Logan peered down at it and at the dagger it held. Sneering, Thromar placed a hand upon his sword hilt.

"Do not hurt him, please," the forest suddenly said.

The three men turned to see a dark-haired young man step free of the greenery, his boots making no noise upon the forest floor. A black robe covered his body, tied at the waist by a silver cord. He held a thick oak staff in one hand, and, with the other, he motioned for the little monkeylike creature to step back.

"You must excuse Munuc," he told them. "He always gets a little excited when strangers enter our forest." The robed young man smiled faintly. "I am Druid Launce."

"Druid?" repeated Moknay. "You live out in the forest?"

The druid nodded. "The land was given to us by Brolark, populated by Agellic, and made beautiful by Lelah; we should all learn to use it well." He pointed into the greenery. "My home is that way. Will you not come with me?"

Moknay gave the druid a skeptical glance and turned to his companions. Thromar, however, was eyeing Munuc, his meaty hand still at his sheath.

"Are you sure it's safe," the fighter queried, "giving him a dagger and all?"

Understanding the question and considering it an insult to his intelligence, Munuc released an angry screech and flailed his long arms at Thromar. The fighter, never having seen such a creature before, leaned back on Smeea and continued to watch the monkeylike beast carefully.

Druid Launce faintly smiled. "Munuc is very touchy," he explained, turning to his anthropoidlike companion. "Munuc, you must stop this misbehaving or I shall take your dagger away."

The little mouth dropped open in shock, and Munuc tried to hide his weapon beneath his fur. Launce watched his hairy friend lope off into the surrounding foliage before turning back to the trio.

"I found him roaming the woods one day," he stated. "I am not sure, but I think he is the only one of his kind—a most lonely kind of life." Starting off through the vegetation, Launce motioned with his staff. "This way."

His eyes better, Logan followed Moknay's example and jumped off his mount, leading it through the heavier foliage by the bridle. Thromar walked behind them, cursing as his massive boots stumbled and tripped through the shrubbery. Logan and Moknay also found the greenery a hindrance, but not as much as Thromar. Druid Launce, however, walked on, unhampered by the forest. It was almost as if the brush drew aside for him like a curtain of green.

Thromar let out a startled bellow as Munuc playfully sprang out of the treetops and onto Smeea. The horse started but did not object to the furry creature. Thromar, on the other hand, peered hard at the beast.

"Munuc has taken a liking to you," Druid Launce noted with a faint smile.

The monkeylike Munuc grinned at the fighter.

"He must have mistaken him for one of his kind," Moknay quipped.

Thromar brushed off the remark as he grinned back at Munuc. "It would appear I have a new friend," he boomed, looking over the little creature with more interest than fear.

The young druid broke through the bushes to a clearing overgrown with strands of ivy. An outcropping of rocks loomed to the right, and a hillock of grass rose ahead of them, partially obscured by a toppled tree. Massive oaks stood sentry about the ivy-strewn clearing, and Logan could hear water trickling in the distance.

Druid Launce pointed with his staff. "Welcome to my home," he declared.

Moknay blinked. "You live here?"

The druid nodded his head of dark brown hair. "I care for the forest, and, in turn, the forest cares for me." He snapped his fingers, and Munuc sprang from Smeea. "Munuc will see to your horses. Come."

Launce walked to one side of the hillock and disappeared. Following behind him, Logan slipped down the first, ivy-hidden step and searched for the second in the shadows of the fallen tree. Gradually, the young man was swallowed by the earth as he continued down the earthen staircase, descending farther and farther into the ground. He could hear Moknay and Thromar trailing him, the latter grumbling as he lost his footing. Unconsciously, Logan had been counting the steps, and, by the thirteenth stair, a torch flickered against the wall. When Logan left the twenty-seventh step, he found himself in Launce's home.

The druid's abode was a wide chamber, its walls neatly covered in clay. Furniture made out of wood filled the room, and a thin window with no glass allowed sunlight and fresh air to stream into the chamber. Logan saw a narrow hall, cloaked by shadows, that wound off to the right.

"Incredible," Moknay breathed.

The druid's chairs were padded with cushions filled with a type of moss, and clay bowls overspilled with odd fruits. Two unlit lanterns hung in the far corner of the room, near the narrow hallway, and a third dangled in the center of the room from a gnarled tree root which stretched across the roof of the chamber.

Moknay glanced out the slim window and peered at the ivy-covered clearing. "Can't somebody see this opening?" he wondered.

Druid Launce's faint smile appeared. "Did you?"

The Murderer barked a laugh.

Munuc energetically bounded into the room and flopped onto a table, snatching up a piece of fruit with his toes. Grinning, the little monkeylike thing tossed the bulb of fruit to Thromar, who was forced to stagger back before the fruit struck him in the beard.

"Go ahead," Druid Launce coaxed, "eat. There is much more. The forest is plentiful."

Thromar bit into the fruit and smacked his lips noisily. In reply, Logan's stomach growled blatantly, and Munuc jerked his almost humanlike head toward him. Still grinning his mischievous grin, the anthropoidlike beast hurled another fruit, this time directing it at Logan. As he caught it, he swung his gaze to Moknay, who was cautiously sniffing at the fruit bowl. Sensing Logan's eyes upon him, the Murderer glanced at him and nodded. At least the food was not poisoned.

Logan turned the red-and-yellow bulb of fruit about in his hand and waved it under his nose experimentally. There wasn't much of a smell, so he chanced a bite. The taste was unique: a kind of sugary sweet, tangy taste accompanied by a juice that soothed Logan's dry throat. Marveling at the fruit—since Logan was not one to enjoy fruit—he turned to the window and almost choked. Prowling outside, ebony eyes aglow with hatred and madness, was the gaunt Pembroke.

"Pembroke!" gagged Logan, trying to swallow and speak at the same instant. "He's outside!"

Moknay wheeled around, grey eyes flashing. "What?"

The Murderer leaped to Logan's side, glaring out the narrow window. His gloved hands instinctively went to the strap of daggers across his chest.

Druid Launce looked over their shoulders at the odd figure in the rumpled clothing. "You know that man?" he questioned.

"He's pursuing us," Logan briefly explained, saying nothing more.

"He is your enemy, then?" the young druid inquired.

Moknay nodded.

"He's a maggot!" added Thromar from the table.

"Look at him," the Murderer breathed in awe. "He's sniffing around like a dog. He'll find this house for certain."

Druid Launce calmly picked up his staff and approached the hall caped in shadows. "Remain here," he ordered, then slid through the corridor and out of sight.

Pembroke jabbed at the vegetation with his fingers, his wild eyes scanning the immediate area. His movements were rodentlike as he jerked and scurried from one bush to another.

"He knows you are here," he called mockingly. "Come out and give Pembroke back his Child." There was no answer, so he kicked at a bush angrily. "Come out, I say!"

An almost inaudible snap whispered behind him, and the wiry man swung around, black eyes blazing. His Triblade slid silently out of its sheath as the servant glared at the young man emerging from the shrubbery, an oak staff held in one hand.

"He's going to get himself killed," Logan moaned, watching the druid from the hidden window.

Munuc let out a frantic bark and leaped to the window, scratching his furry head in bewilderment as he fixed his eyes on the two men outside.

"You are looking for something?" Druid Launce questioned Pembroke.

The servant's mouth drew back in a sneer. "No business of yours, holy man!" he spat.

"Perhaps it is," responded Launce. "I may be able to show you what you seek."

"Bah!" Pembroke scoffed. "You are a holy man! What do you know?"

"I know of many things," Launce answered. "I know of the forest. I know of the elements." He smiled faintly. "I know of you."

Pembroke raised his dark eyebrows and his eyes glittered. "Know you of me?" he repeated, stepping forward in interest.

"You are the one called Pembroke," the druid stated. "Now what do you seek in my forest?"

"I search for three men who have robbed me of what is mine," Pembroke growled, eyeing the young druid cautiously. "A grey man, a fat man, and . . . another. They hold the Jewel of Equilibrant—my Jewel. Pembroke's Child! Have you seen them?"

Druid Launce was silent for a long while.

"No," he finally answered. "I have not seen them."

Pembroke's jet-black eyes flared. "You lie!" he accused. "You have seen them! Where are they?"

The mad servant dived, his Triblade severing the air. Casually, Launce stepped to one side, easily evading the deadly weapon. Releasing an angered shriek, Pembroke lashed about, whiplike, swinging the three blades viciously.

"Where are they, holy man?" he screamed. "Where do they hide? Tell Pembroke or he shall kill you!"

Launce shook his head sadly. "I am sorry, but you may not do that."

The lean Pembroke halted, amused. "Oh, no? Then Pembroke shall prove you wrong."

The Triblade howled, and Logan turned away from the window, guilt seeping into the pores of his body. Moknay, however, chuckled, and Thromar roared with delight as they peered out the opening. Dredging up his courage, Logan glanced out the window to see Druid Launce finish knocking aside the Triblade with his staff. Pembroke was forced to back up or else lose his hold on his heavy weapon.

"You are quick for a holy man," the servant said between clenched teeth, "but not quick enough!"

The Triblade split the air, and Druid Launce flipped backwards, a booted foot rushing up and slamming into the servant's wrist. The many-bladed weapon spun into the sky, the sunlight glistening off its murderous points. With a metallic clatter, it struck the ground beside the outcropping of rocks, some distance from Pembroke.

As the mad servant went to retrieve his blade, Druid Launce placed two fingers to his lips and blew. Pembroke jerked about as a shrill whistle rent the forest, but then, scowling, he bent to grasp his Triblade.

A sudden, throaty growl caused him to stumble back in shock.

"By my Jewel!" he cursed.

Snarling from atop the outcropping of rocks was a large wolf, slavering as it watched over the massive Triblade. Growling like the wolf itself, Pembroke turned on Launce and blinked as two more grey forms padded silently beside the druid. For a moment, the insane servant was confused, flicking his night-filled eyes from wolf to wolf. Then, with reflexes impossible for a normal human, Pembroke sprang, snatching up his weapon and scampering off into the forest. The wolf atop the rocks slowly brought up its head to glare at Launce, its black lips drawn back in what could have been a canine grin.

"Thank you, my friends," the druid said, gratefully patting the wolf nearest him. "You may go. Remember to call for me should you ever need my help."

The three wolves stalked back into the foliage as Launce began descending the hidden stairwell of his home.

"That was remarkable!" Moknay laughed as Launce entered.

The druid shrugged off the compliment. "A few friends I called to aid me," he replied simply. All at once, his eyes grew harsh as they riveted upon Logan. "Why did you not tell me you carried the Jewel of Equilibrant?"

Logan swallowed hard, casting a pitiful gaze to his companions. What could he say to the druid? So far a Demon and a priestess had gone out of their way to steal the Jewel—and Launce's appearance had been all too unexpected. The druid had just frightened off Pembroke, but, at this point, Logan was no longer trusting anyone he met. It was too dangerous—and costly.

"We are trying to get the Jewel to the Smythe," Moknay told the druid when Logan said nothing, "and cannot be greatly delayed since the powers are escaping. We were trying to be cautious with our secret cargo."

"And you thought I may prove to be a danger?" Launce said, and his faint smile reappeared. "You honor me with abilities I do not have. But, to prove myself a friend, we shall remain here tonight. Then, at dawn's first light, I shall escort you to Plestenah. And you have my word as a friend that I shall not rest until you—and the Jewel—are there safely."

His oaken staff before him, Druid Launce sat upon his horse as it made its way through the forest. The greenery politely peeled back for the four horses, closing behind them once the mounts had passed. The saddlebags had been filled with fresh supplies, and the three had bathed before starting off. Both Moknay and Logan had shaved with daggers, the latter bearing the wounds to prove it.

"We are approaching the Roana, my friends," reported Druid Launce from the lead. "I can hear the sprite's song."

Logan blinked. "The what?"

Druid Launce's faint smile spread across his face. "The land of Sparrill—and some believe Denzil—was guarded by three sprites, Roana, Salena, and Glorana. With the aid of a magical Bloodstone, the very Heart of Sparrill's beauty and magic, the sprites kept our land pure and bountiful. One day a vile *Deil* was sent by the Voices of the Dark. So horrid and evil was this creature that all the Demons alive today could not match its wickedness. It had been sent by its masters to wound and destroy the Heart of the land, and, for many years, plague, famine, war, and strife reigned throughout Sparrill.

"Seeing the pain that Sparrill suffered, Roana became determined to cast the foul *Deil* out and called upon the magics of the Bloodstone to aid her. The creature, called Gangrorz by its masters, learned of her intent, and a vicious battle followed. In the course of the battle, the powers intensified and *Deil,* sprite, and Bloodstone were all lost.

"It is believed Gangrorz was struck full in the face by the Bloodstone's blow and was sent reeling into the heavens. When he landed, ablaze with the cosmic fire of the Air, he struck with a thousand thunderclaps. A large crater was gorged into our beloved land, and the Sea of Hedelva rushed in and drowned the hideous *Deil,* filling the wound he had created with horrid, putrid waters. This became known as the Demonry River and stagnant Lake Atricrix. Roana, meanwhile, was similarly lost, and, with her, the Heart of Sparrill. Following the belief that Roana herself became part of the river, it was so named after the sprite. I know she does indeed live on in the river, for I have heard the sprite singing."

A cloud of silence hovered over the quartet for a moment as the druid completed his tale. Interesting, Logan mused. Guardian sprites and a Heart for the land itself . . . and the ability to blame all mishap on the "Voices of the Dark." Then again, what were myths and religions but ways to explain things that would otherwise be unexplainable? Such as the formation of a lake?

"What about the other sprites?" Logan asked out of curiosity.

"Glorana and Salena deeply mourned their sister's departure

and melded with the remaining two rivers in Sparrill to be with Roana. That is why all rivers intersect."

Munuc, sitting with Thromar on Smeea, abruptly screeched. Pulled forcibly out of his thoughts, Logan jerked his head up as Druid Launce reined in his horse. Thromar extracted his massive sword, peering about the foliage with a distasteful glare. Moknay also withdrew his weapon, straining his ears to pick out any unnatural sounds. Only Logan was unready for what happened next.

Two dark horses emerged from the forest.

"This is as far as you shall ever get," a familiar voice croaked.

Logan swung his head to the left and snarled to himself. The jagged, blue-grey hair and silver chestplate seemed to shimmer mockingly back at him, and the glazed left eye singled out Logan and voicelessly accused him of its blindness. The second rider was examining the quartet as curiously as they were examining him. Folded across a pitch-black chestplate, his thick arms were riddled, as was his face, with white lines of scar tissue. Grey-black hair was neatly groomed atop his head, and dull grey eyes scrutinized the four.

For no apparent reason, a smirk drew across his face.

"So this is Matthew Logan."

The silver chestplated Reakthi nodded.

"So, Groathit," growled Moknay, "who's your friend?"

The black-chestplated man smiled. "Allow me to introduce myself: I am Vaugen."

· 6 ·

Imperator

The foliage rustled and four horsemen emerged beside Vaugen and Groathit, their chestplates blazing in the morning light. Logan heard more hooves to his left and pivoted about to see eight more men flank them. Another eight sprouted like weeds on their right, and five more horses blocked the rear, their riders certain they had boxed in their quarry.

Moknay's grey eyes leapt from Reakthi to Reakthi, his fingers twitching around the daggers he held. "I fear we are in trouble," he noticed, his grim expression growing even fouler.

Twenty-five Reakthi, Logan counted, plus Groathit *and* Vaugen! What could be so important about Logan that the Reakthi Imperator would leave the safety of his castle and come after him himself? That just didn't make sense to the young man as he sat and gaped at the warriors surrounding him.

Descending upon invisible wings at the most inappropriate of times, the feeling of disunion hovered about Logan's head.

Vaugen leaned forward on his dark horse, his grey eyes boring into Logan's blue ones. "I must congratulate you, Matthew Logan, for being the only man to anger Groathit and still be alive." He paused a moment to give the half-blinded spellcaster a snide glance. "It was so unfortunate that you took up sides; you and I are so very much alike—we would have gotten along so well. And besides, we had need of you." The Imperator stroked his chin. "Still, you do have something that may be of value to us."

Cocky little bastard, isn't he? Logan asked himself, clenching his teeth as Vaugen held out a scarred hand.

"The Jewel, Matthew Logan," he said softly. "Give me the Jewel."

"Blow it out your ear," the young man retorted, searching desperately for any breach in the Reakthi ring.

Vaugen turned to Groathit as if expecting a translation of Logan's statement. Gradually, he turned back to face the young man and his companions.

Pure, undiluted fear ran through Logan's veins as he looked to his friends for aid. A ferocious frown was drawn upon Thromar's brow as he glared at the twenty-five soldiers, his sword eager to spill their blood and longing to taste Vaugen's flesh. Moknay still held his daggers, and his grey eyes blazed an unspoken command when Logan glanced at him. Ignoring the sensation of misplacement, Logan swung around to see Vaugen gazing at him expectantly, but Groathit's eye was fueled by impatience.

"Well?" the spellcaster snapped. "Where is it? Hand it over, whelp!"

"Kiss my ass!" Logan hollered, brutally jerking back on his horse's reins as he withdrew his Reakthi sword.

Two daggers flashed from Moknay's hands, and the men on either side of Vaugen went down. Emitting a lustful war cry, Thromar charged Smeea directly into a band of warriors, his massive sword catching the light as it sliced through flesh, veins, and internal organs.

"This way!" the huge fighter roared. "Head back!"

"Stop them!" demanded Vaugen.

Several moments of chaos followed. Horses screamed and reared, swords slid free of their Reakthi sheaths, and blood released its coppery smell into the air. Two Reakthi crashed to the ground, knocked from their horses by Thromar's insane charge. Munuc let out a fearful shriek and vanished into the trees. Logan, his horse turned, lashed out blindly with his blade, drawing a bloody gash across a soldier's face.

"They are converging on us!" he heard Druid Launce cry. "We shall surely be cut down!"

Silver glared in the sunlight, and Logan threw up his sword to ward the blow aside. Metal clanged, and hooves rent the air behind him as Logan frantically turned about in his crude saddle. He was just barely able to dodge the flail that whistled above his head, and his own weapon shot out, catching the Reakthi under the chin and skewering his jaw. Droplets of crimson spattered the young man's hands as he whipped around again, trying to spot his companions in the swelling tide of chestplates and weapons.

"Moknay!" Logan heard Thromar warn. "Watch your back!"

There was a gurgling scream somewhere from within the hubbub, and Logan hoped it was not Moknay. White hot pain blazed upon his left arm, and Logan jerked about, stunned by the sight of his own blood bubbling up from between torn flesh. Instantly, the pain transformed to anger, and Logan grasped his sword in both hands. With a furious sweep of his blade, Logan dismembered the Reakthi to his left, sneering in satisfaction as the sword arm dropped to the dirt in a shower of blood.

"An opening!" Druid Launce exclaimed, smacking his heavy staff against a Reakthi's skull.

Cursing under his breath, Logan attempted to bring his horse around as he saw the young druid bolt free of the swarming Reakthi. The pain in his arm and the feeling of wrongness in his ears gave Logan the strength necessary to cut a gruesome path toward the druid. Shouting joyfully, Thromar and Smeea rammed through the chestplated warriors, also finding the safety of the forest. Logan was close enough to take advantage of the hole made by the fighter and dashed through the clustering soldiers. Out of the corner of his eye, he saw Moknay beside him, his grey clothing spotted with Reakthi blood.

"Stop them!" Groathit screeched, the veins on his neck popping out. "Stop them or I shall have your heads to decorate my walls!"

Vaugen gave the wizard a malicious glare. "*I* am the Imperator, not you. Why aren't *you* earning your rank, spellcaster?"

The magician snarled furiously to himself, kicking at his horse's flanks as he followed the fleeing quartet. Reakthi rode on either side and before the wizard, their weapons flailing and curses flying at their prey. Gesticulating wildly, Groathit could hear Vaugen's horse thundering behind him, the Imperator yelling orders at his men.

Ebony sparks crackled at the spellcaster's fingertips, and a ghastly smile drew across his face as he spied Logan and Moknay through the trees. Death-black rays screamed from his hands, sizzling the air as they howled for the two.

Nausea gripped Logan and bile rose in his throat as the feeling of displacement became overwhelming. The buzz increased a thousandfold, and the young man clamped his hands to either side of his head. This could not be the normal buzz of wrongness, he decided. The only other time he had felt this badly was back when Groathit had attacked him in the tavern.

Uncommonly disturbed, Logan risked a quick glance over his shoulder and spied the twin rays of death. For a second he entertained the thought of leaping from his horse, but then there was no time. Something sliced the air beside him, and the coal-black beams struck.

The immensely powerful sensation remained with Logan as the Reakthi directly beside him dropped his weapon and screamed. His golden chestplate sagged, and the skin of his face and hands went taut before vanishing entirely. Muscles and internal organs erupted in explosive bursts of ebony energy, and only then did the screaming stop.

The chestplated skeleton crashed to the ground and splintered beneath the many horses' hooves.

"Groathit, you bungler!" barked Vaugen. "Them! Not my men!"

Groathit's eye flared malevolently, but he said nothing.

"Friend-Logan?" Thromar inquired without looking back. "Are you all right?"

Logan wiped his forehead and winced as perspiration trickled into his wound. "Sort of," he gasped. "Felt sick for a minute there."

" . . . thirteen . . . fourteen!" Moknay murmured; he laughed. "We downed or disabled eleven of them and got out of that skirmish alive!"

An arrow whined beside Thromar's ear. "Had to open your mouth, eh, Murderer?"

A second arrow thunked into a tree as Logan passed by.

"Munuc," Launce was moaning, "where have you gone? Why have you forsaken your friends?"

"Much good he'd be," Moknay replied, instinctively ducking as an arrow shrieked by his shoulder. "He would have been slain immediately."

"He did the right thing by fleeing," agreed Thromar.

Logan dodged a low-hanging branch as an arrow struck the bark and ricocheted off. Smeea almost toppled as another wooden shaft whizzed free of the forest and skinned her rump.

Pursuing hooves reached Logan's ears, and he glimpsed over his shoulder to see four Reakthi, bows in their hands. "They're gaining on us!" he cried.

"Best Reakthi archers I've ever run into," Thromar muttered, affectionately patting Smeea on the neck as he rode.

Another rain of arrows drizzled down upon them, and Druid Launce cried out, a shaft tearing into the side of his robe. Wincing in empathetic pain, Logan remembered the Jewel in the saddlebags and decided it best to personally guard it. He sheathed his sword and reached carefully behind him for the bags, attempting to flip open the lid as his mount continued its frenzied pace. After a few tries, Logan succeeded and reached a hand in to withdraw the Jewel's pouch. As he pulled it free, an arrow burrowed into the saddlebag, startling Logan so that he lost his precarious grip upon the Jewel. The leather sack slipped and fell from Logan's hand, and the young man cried out as he grasped frantically at the air. By an amazing stroke of luck, one of the leather strings knotting the bag closed became caught between the young man's first and middle fingers, and he retained his grip on the Jewel, pulling it close to his chest and finally remembering to breathe once again.

"Launce!" Thromar boomed. "Are you badly hurt?"

The druid clenched his teeth. "Continue on," he ground out. "We must get the Jewel to safety."

Moknay swiveled his head about, squinting as if unfamiliar with the terrain. "Thromar," he shouted, "just where in Imogen's name are we heading? I've lost all sense of direction!"

Thromar smiled his crooked, yellowing grin. "We've pulled a sneaky turn on the Reakthi scum," he boasted. "They forced us a bit north, but now we're heading west again."

"Damn!" spat the Murderer. "I was afraid of that!"

Logan tightened his hold upon the Jewel. "Huh?" he wondered. "I thought we wanted to go west."

"We're heading directly for the Roana," Moknay explained, his grey eyes lit with dread. "We can't possibly ford the river with the Reakthi on our heels. They'll shoot us down before we're halfway across!"

"What can we do?" Logan queried, still able to see the quartet of archers pursuing them.

"Stand and fight!" roared Thromar boldly. "We can crush the Reakthi slime! Just give me one swing at that harpy turd Vaugen! Wham! Off goes his head!"

"That may be our only alternative," the Murderer grumbled, "but Druid Launce is wounded, and someone would have to carry the Jewel to safety."

"Why don't we give Launce the Jewel?" Thromar suggested.

Logan meant to protest but decided against it. He still did not trust the druid—not after the harsh lesson he had learned at Agellic's Church. Mara had been injured protecting Logan from Riva's greed, and Logan had not given the blonde priestess a second thought when he had first seen her. He did not want to make the same mistake twice.

"I stand with you!" Launce proclaimed, drowning out Logan's musings. "I will not leave!"

"But you've got an arrow . . ." Moknay began.

A determined expression contorted the druid's usually calm mien as he brought his horse about and charged back the way they had come. His blood-spattered staff was raised high above his head.

"Hey!" Thromar bellowed. "What are you doing?"

"Proving my friendship!" the druid snapped back.

Thromar, Moknay, and Logan all slowed their mounts to a stop as they stared in astonishment at the suicidal druid. The buzz in his head began to intensify as Logan gawked at the forest which had come alive. Launce's staff flickered with magical energies as strings of ivy rose up like serpents of green, wavering and coiling. Branches shuddered fitfully, and bushes rustled as if defiled by a strong, nonexistent wind.

The four Reakthi cried out, the leading soldier jerked from his mount by writhing ivy. Two others crashed to the earth, dismounted by a branch that had not been there seconds before. The fourth warrior reined in his horse, keeping himself out of reach of the animated vegetation.

"How in all of Sparrill did you manage that?" Thromar blurted.

Druid Launce rejoined his companions, urging his mount forward. "If we survive, remind me to tell you," he said, smiling faintly.

"Plants won't stop them," Moknay surmised, "but it will slow them up. Perhaps you've given us enough time to get across the Roana."

"Then again, perhaps not," Logan mumbled to himself, exceedingly pessimistic.

The four colorful horses raced onward, outdistancing Groathit's curses and Vaugen's orders. Sparkling light struck Logan full in the face as his green-and-yellow mount burst free of the foliage, galloping for the clear, clean Roana. The water was crystal blue, gurgling softly as it wound its way downstream. Its banks were lined with smooth rocks clad in mossy coats, and bright waterplants dotted the river.

Screaming, an arrow ripped through Moknay's cape and splashed into the Roana.

"Dung!" the Murderer cursed. "That was damn close!" He swung his horse about to face the forest.

Thromar brandished his bloody blade. "Friend-Logan, you can still make it across safely! We'll see to the Reakthi vermin!"

Logan turned his horse sideways, glancing at the opposite bank of the river that seemed so very far away. Maybe he could make it across safely, but what of his friends? He couldn't leave Moknay and Thromar to be slain by the Reakthi—not after all they had done for him! But he didn't want to die. Maybe they did have a fighting chance if they banded together, but against fourteen armored soldiers—many with long-range weapons—it was not very much of a chance.

The first Reakthi archer thundered free of the forest, an arrow twanging from his bow. Moknay let out a strangled curse and threw himself from his horse to escape the shaft. As the Murderer rolled through his dive, the Reakthi drew in his mount and reached back for another arrow. His back arched unexpectedly, and a garbled cry rose in his throat. He flopped to the ground, dead, a dagger lodged in his neck.

Moknay leapt to his feet, eyes narrowed angrily. He caught a glimpse of the Reakthi archer spilling from his mount, and his grey eyes went wide in surprise. Quizzically, he looked down at the two daggers he still held in his hands.

"Good throw, Moknay!" cheered Thromar.

"I didn't throw that," the Murderer admitted.

The second Reakthi to bolt out of the greenery was suddenly snatched back by a pair of hairy arms. Uttering a cry of shock, the warrior was jerked upward like a marionette and sucked into the treetops.

"It is Munuc!" Launce exclaimed. "He did not desert us!"

A furry creature sailed out of a tree, colliding with another Reakthi. Sharp fangs drove into the soldier's neck, and beast, warrior, and horse crashed to the forest floor. Then, its fur matted with blood, the monkeylike beast launched itself at a fourth Reakthi, a black blur amongst the green foliage.

"That's not Munuc!" said Logan. "That one's black!"

Open-mouthed, the four men started as the real Munuc bounded onto Launce's horse. Other furry creatures swarmed out of the trees, descending upon the Reakthi with daggers and fangs. Horses and men screamed their surprise as the forest came alive with the small beasts.

"They are not stopping!" Launce cried out in anguish. "Munuc, your kind cannot possibly hold back the Reakthi! I fear you have doomed your people!"

Munuc grinned beneath his fur and pointed his gangly limbs farther down the river. Obeying the unspoken command, Druid Launce guided his horse southward, Logan and the others following him in puzzlement. As the horses neared the riverbank, a moss-covered stone pushed aside, and a grey-haired Munuc peeked out at the men. Two more hairy creatures sprang out of the opening, leading the horses away as the riders dismounted. Hastily, the real Munuc indicated the portal.

"Quickly!" Launce ordered. "Follow Munuc in!"

Thromar stepped back, fear on his face. "I'm not going in there!" he protested. "I'll never fit!"

"I'll make you fit!" Moknay threatened, gesturing wildly with his daggers.

The bearded fighter grunted and grumbled, finally forcing back his fear and pushing his way into the small opening. With a nasty curse about tight places, Thromar vanished into the ground. In a grey blur, Moknay was after him.

Clear water splashed upon the rock as an arrow plunked into the river. Druid Launce twirled about on his heel, his calm eyes flashing with fury. A Reakthi was running toward them, flailing his bow above his head; a dagger wound marred his forehead.

"He has seen the portal to Munuc's world!" the druid howled. "He must be silenced!"

The black-robed druid flung himself at the warrior, his oak staff smacking into the soldier's temple. With a groan, the man in the golden chestplate staggered back, his empty bow dropping to the ground. Wielding his staff like a sword, the druid brought it forward, plunging its pointed end into the soft, yielding flesh of the Reakthi's leg. Releasing an agonized scream, the soldier crumpled to the dirt.

The oaken staff shattered the Reakthi's skull.

"Enough!" Logan yelled beside the portal. "He's dead! Come on, before someone else sees you!"

Launce drew back the blood-smeared staff, slowly. "Yes," he breathed as if suddenly drained, "he is dead."

The druid turned to face Logan when another Reakthi rode out of the brush. With a triumphant twang, an arrow rocketed from the bowstring and drove into Druid Launce's back.

"*Launce!*" Logan screamed, blindly charging forward.

Smiling, the Reakthi nocked a second arrow into his bow and looked up to aim for Logan. Rage boiling inside the young man, Logan reached the druid's side and snatched up the oak staff. It flew from Logan's hands and rammed into the Reakthi's breastbone. Arrows spilled from his quiver as the Reakthi fell off his horse, stars flashing behind his eyelids.

Blood! Logan's mind demanded fiercely. Retribution! Deal pain to those who usually deal it!

Spurred on by his anger, Logan foolishly converged on the fallen Reakthi, once again picking up Launce's staff. As if he was grotesquely staking a claim, Logan drove the staff into the man's throat, and warm fluid drenched his Nikes.

An abrupt tug on his sweat pants fragmented Logan's intense fury.

The grey-haired Munuc was solemnly pointing at the portal—where Launce was slowly crawling in. Shaking his head in an effort to beat back his rage, Logan followed the creature and ducked into the opening. At the end of a short tunnel was a large chamber, and the bloodthirsty anger within Logan returned. Druid Launce lay near the center of the room, blood pooling beneath him. Munuc stood beside him, his tiny eyes glittering.

Logan made his way to Launce's side, tightly gripping the staff with whitened knuckles. "I kept it for you," he said, handing the staff to the druid. "I thought you might want it back."

Launce brought up his head, smiling faintly. "Thank you, my friend, but it is ruined—stained with the blood of an enemy. It should never have been used for such a purpose."

"But you had to do it," argued Logan. "He'd seen where Munuc and his kind lived. You had to."

Launce nodded gravely and pushed the staff back into Logan's hands. "Do me a favor," he asked.

Logan nodded, kneeling beside the wounded druid.

Launce closed Logan's fingers about the staff. "Take it."

Logan shook his head. "I can't take it. It belongs to you. I have no right."

"I saw you use it," the druid stated with his faint smile. "Keep it, and it will be there to help support you. I no longer need it."

Druid Launce closed his eyes with a sigh and his hands fell away from the oak staff. Abruptly, Munuc let out a wail, and Logan bowed his head, his stormy anger overcome by sorrow.

Somewhere, a pack of wolves howled.

Druid Launce was dead.

· 7 ·

Flood

Logan strangled the reins in his hands as he followed Moknay and Thromar through the forest toward the town of Plestenah. Almost two days had passed since their run-in with Vaugen, and the fury remained within Logan. His anger was similar to that unnerving feeling that continually plagued the young man. It would suddenly descend upon him—without reason and without warning—and Logan would grit his teeth fiercely as he thought of the young druid who had died helping his friends.

The guilt, however, stayed within the young man at all times, slowly tearing away at him from inside. Druid Launce had died helping Logan, while Logan had refused to trust the man—had refused to believe in his friendship. Now there was no way Logan could accept him as a friend—and the guilt drove deeper. It had been, after all, Logan's fault that the druid was dead. If Logan had not stolen the Jewel, and if Munuc had not sent his people against Vaugen, Druid Launce might still be alive.

Vaugen. Logan seethed. How he hated that name. Some mysterious force drove the Reakthi Imperator to trail Logan from Denzil to Sparrill, and, because of him and his chestplated minions, Druid Launce had been slain. His guilt blamed Logan for causing many of the calamities that arose, but his unrelenting anger blamed Vaugen for Launce's murder.

Cursing under his breath, Logan swore vengeance.

The greenery of the forest receded, and the town of Plestenah was revealed. Just south of them, Logan could see denser forest, and his mind turned to the ease in which Druid Launce would have been able to have passed through the vegetation—if Logan had only trusted him.

Plestenah was quite a small town, the young man noticed, made up mostly of shops and markets. A few homes lined the interior, and their pleasant, outward appearance sparked a little hope in Logan's depression; perhaps they would find the extra help they sought.

Moknay suddenly reined his horse in, his grey eyes locked on something down the street. "Logan," he said, still looking away, "see to the horses, will you? Then get us some lodgings in a hostel."

The Murderer tossed Logan a small pouch of gold and dismounted. Logan turned away from his guilt and wrath and caught the bag, peering at it curiously.

"Get lodgings?" he repeated. "How the devil do I do that?"

Thromar interrupted him with a thunderous burst of laughter. "Hah! Moknay's seen a wench that fits his tastes!"

Pulling his eyes away from the pouch of gold, Logan glanced up to see Moknay talking to a young girl who stood along the cobblestone street, her eyes roving up and down the Murderer appreciatively. In reply, Moknay patted the money pouch which he had told Thromar he had left in Eadarus, and the couple started off.

Startled, Logan swung about to ask Thromar what Moknay thought he was doing, but the fighter was gone as well.

The intense ire lurking within Logan reared its head. "Leave it to the man from another world to get the rooms," he snarled, the anger practically becoming one with the young man. Abruptly, he glared at the pouch of gold, weighing it in his palm. "Huh!" he snorted. "They give me money, I'm going to use it for what they're using it for."

With a determined grin, Logan leapt from his mount and peered down the street. He saw a tavern—where he guessed Thromar had ducked into—but decided he did not want to go there. Brawls and hop-infested ale did not entice Logan— what he wouldn't do for a few video games to play to get out his aggression! Still, there were the whores lining the street, and Logan's anger was swift to rationalize his choice of recreation.

The young man dismounted and tied his horse and his companions' to a tethering post. He then turned his interests to the street. A number of girls stretched out before his eyes, but none of them interested Logan. His bitterness would not settle for just any whore—it demanded the best if Logan dared try to force it down.

Abruptly, Logan's blue eyes caught hold and stuck fast. Standing out in front of a store was beautiful young girl, dark blonde hair spilling about her slim shoulders. A white bodice and skirt covered her curvy frame, and her dark blue eyes roved up and down the cobblestones expectantly. Instantly, Logan's anger prodded him forward, demanding the young man do as his comrades and enjoy himself. Gradually, Logan approached, intent on appeasing his never-ending temper.

"How much?" he inquired, stepping up to the blonde.

The girl gave him a casual glance. "How much what?" she asked back.

"Money," Logan's anger explained.

The girl's eyes went wide. "What do you take me for? One of the sluts walking the street?"

At precisely the wrong moment, Logan's anger faded. Caught off guard, Logan backed off, awkward and defenseless. "Uh . . . well . . . yeah," he stuttered.

"*What?*" the girl shrieked, frail fists clenched. "How dare you! Do you know who I am, you chomprat?"

Abandoned by what had given him courage, the young man took another backward step. "No, I—I don't."

"I am Cyrene, daughter of Sire Marchaon!"

Logan flustered. "I'm sorry—I don't recognize the name."

"You don't recognize the name?" the girl fumed. She took a step as if to beat Logan over the head with her fist and then bowed her head. She was silent for a long time. "Not many do, anymore," she finally murmured sadly.

Logan shoved the pouch of gold into his sweat pants and started away. "I better be going," he excused himself.

Cyrene jerked her head up. "No . . . please, stay," she begged. "I need someone to talk to."

"But I just mistook you for a . . ."

Cyrene nodded with a laugh. "You're not the only one. I really shouldn't be standing around like I'm waiting for someone. Father will never come back, but I swear I'll see his murderer slain!"

Logan noted the girl's tightly clenched fists and hoped Moknay had not visited Plestenah often. Fearing that perhaps the Murderer was the cause, Logan queried, "Who killed him?"

Cyrene's deep blue eyes flared. "Vaugen," she spat.

Logan was engulfed by his rage once more and growled involuntarily.

Cyrene's eyes locked on his. "What's wrong?" she asked. "Have you also lost someone to Vaugen?"

The anger churned and boiled within him, and Logan wanted to pound a fist against the nearest wall in frustration. "Yes." He gnashed his teeth. "He killed a friend of mine . . . someone who was trying to help me. We were lucky to escape and make it here without him catching up. I wouldn't be surprised if he found me here with my friends off dicking around!"

"Catch up?" wondered Cyrene. "Are you saying Vaugen's following you?" She took a curious step up to Logan. "Why?"

A battle instantly went off inside Logan. Anger, guilt, and paranoia all clashed head-on in a full-scale war within his mind. His anger wanted to tell the girl of his own personal battle with Vaugen, his guilt wanted to tell her everything about his mission so he would not make the same mistake he had with Druid Launce, and his paranoia brought back the image of Mara, nude and unconscious, Riva's blood-spattered corpse nearby.

"I don't really know why," Logan finally answered. "He wanted me for something—said I could be useful. I don't think he wants me alive anymore, though." Battered by the three conflicting forces within him, Logan uneasily backed away.

"Wait!" Cyrene cried, soft hands grasping hold of Logan's arm. "You said he killed your friend—does that mean you've personally confronted him? You've faced Vaugen himself?"

Puzzlement draped over Logan as he saw the excitement in Cyrene's face. "Why should you care?"

Cyrene shrugged curtly, her blonde hair bouncing upon her shoulders. "I don't know. I was hoping maybe I could join you in wherever you're going."

"Join me?" Logan exclaimed, and the three emotions faded as confusion overpowered them all. "And possibly run into Vaugen himself?"

Cyrene nodded.

Suspicion replaced the confusion. "Oh, no," Logan told her, "I don't want you coming along just to get yourself killed. If you're that desperate to die, save me the guilt and kill yourself when I'm not around." He turned away and started for the nearest hostel.

"You don't understand," Cyrene objected, hurrying after him. "I don't want to kill myself, I want to kill Vaugen."

Swift hoofbeats sounded far off in the distance as Logan went silent. He shook his head, entering the hostel. "I get it," he quipped. "You're not suicidal, you're insane."

"I am *not* insane!" Cyrene snapped, right behind him. "I want to see that murderous whoreson dead!"

"You and about ten thousand other people," the young man retorted, banging a fist upon the desk of the hostel owner.

Blue eyes flaming, Cyrene twirled Logan around, her frail hands gripping him by the front of his jacket. "Listen, you," she snarled. "I'll do anything to see Vaugen dead, and you're the first person I've ever met who's survived a run-in. And you say Vaugen may be following you." Her lips drew back in a horrible frown. "I want a shot at the man who killed my father. You *have* to take me with you!"

Logan glared back at the beautiful girl. "I don't *have* to take you anywhere," he said, sneering back at her. "My mission is dangerous, and you could get in the way."

The fierceness died down in Cyrene's eyes, and it was her turn to eye him suspiciously.

The hoofbeats grew louder, then stopped.

"What mission?" Cyrene queried, jabbing a long-nailed finger at Logan's chest. "Since when did you have a mission?"

"Since he stole a certain horse and found the magical item hidden within a saddlebag," informed a scratchy voice.

Logan and Cyrene whirled to see a white-chestplated Reakmor stride into the hostel. The owner of the building let out a frightened yelp and ran out a back door. Three more men sauntered in behind their leader; only the Reakmor wore a chestplate.

"I am Reakmor Farkarrez," the man in the white chestplate announced, "and unlike those before me, I do not play petty games. Give me the Jewel or my men shall tear you limb from limb."

Logan glared at the Reakmor. "Men? You call those things men?" he scoffed. "They don't even have chestplates!"

Farkarrez grinned, his front teeth chipped. "They wear no

chestplates so these Sparrillian fools will not hinder us as we traverse their land."

Logan's hand shot for his Reakthi sword, but the three soldiers were faster, no longer weighed down by their armor. The young man's anger churned inside as he struggled in their grasp, futilely trying to break the grip of six hands. "Why the hell do I always get into trouble when Thromar and Moknay aren't around?" he muttered.

"You are not alone!" Cyrene proclaimed, withdrawing a dagger from a sheath strapped about her thigh.

Her white skirt flapping, the beautiful blonde dove for one of the Reakthi. The soldier attempted to dodge while still retaining his hold upon Logan, and a scrape suddenly appeared across his forearm.

"By all that is unholy!" he cursed. "The bitch cut me!"

The Reakthi released Logan and grabbed at Cyrene. He caught her around the waist, pinning her arms at her side. Furiously, she tried to ram her dagger into the warrior, but he simply held her off to his right.

"Let go of me, you viper!" the girl yelled.

Logan strained against the four hands keeping him prisoner. "Let her go," he fumed.

Reakmor Farkarrez grinned wickedly, glaring at Logan as he approached the girl. "The bitch means something to you, does she?" He roughly grabbed Cyrene beneath her chin. "I can see why."

Cyrene brought up a slim leg, catching the Reakmor in the groin. Farkarrez grunted, stumbling back in pain, tears streaming from his eyes.

"Touch me again and I shall make it permanent!" Cyrene threatened.

The Reakmor glanced up, agony scrawled across his face. "No one ever harms Farkarrez," he growled, "especially some female! I was going to let you live, but I shall enjoy you better dead!"

Farkarrez withdrew a dagger from his boot and pointed it at Cyrene. The blade rested directly between the girl's full breasts, but Cyrene did not flinch. Defiantly, she glared at the Reakmor, all but ignoring the dagger at her bosom.

"Have you ever had someone dig a blade into your chest?" Farkarrez questioned, his face contorted with fury. "Feel the cold steel as it tears through your flesh? Watch as red blood streams down your pretty, white skin?"

Cyrene did not answer, and Farkarrez struck her across the face. Her head jerked to one side, blonde hair tumbling into her face, but she remained silent. Logan watched the red handprint that developed on Cyrene's cheek, and that familiar fury began to boil and steam, demanding release.

"I should ravage you right here!" the Reakmor growled.

"I'd rather die first!" Cyrene spat back.

Farkarrez slapped her again.

The anger exploded; Logan sprang.

The Reakthi holding the young man stumbled back into one another, unbalanced by the explosive jump. Farkarrez let out a startled shout as Logan sailed into him, hurling the Reakmor into the wooden staircase. Cyrene dug an elbow into the soldier behind her and broke free. Her dagger lashed out and the warrior crashed to the floor, his dying thought concerning the safety that chestplates offered.

Logan's fist smashed into Farkarrez's mouth, guided by his intense wrath. The Reakmor staggered under the onslaught, scrambling for the door. Logan roughly jerked the man back, picking him off the ground and heaving him bodily across the hostel. Adrenaline and rage intermingled, and Logan's sword thrust out, skewering the Reakthi that charged him.

Cyrene, having disposed of the other soldier, rushed the stunned Reakmor.

"Cyrene!" warned Logan. "Stay back! He still has his dagger!"

The girl ignored the warning, her eyebrows knitted above her dark blue eyes. With a sneer of pleasure, Farkarrez hurled his blade. Expertly, Cyrene ducked to one side, batting away the dagger with her own. Farkarrez's weapon whizzed past Logan's ear and lodged into the wall.

The Reakmor's jaw dropped open in shock. "What?" he shrieked. "No one can do that! Not at such close . . ."

Silver and crimson sparkled as Cyrene swept her dagger across Farkarrez's throat. Red liquid bubbled from the Reakmor's lips as he slumped forward, his hands clutching his neck. Gagging, Farkarrez could only watch as his own blood spilled across the floor. Then his vision blurred, and he died.

Logan brushed at his black hair, his fury watching Cyrene

with admiration. The girl turned from cleaning her dagger and focused on the young man.

"He mentioned a jewel," she noted. "What jewel?"

Logan attempted to smile and failed. "You know," he replied uneasily, "a funny thing happened to me on the way to steal a horse."

His frivolity dissipated and he realized how very much Cyrene's hair color resembled Riva's . . .

"Thromar should be back soon," Moknay guessed, stroking his chin as he peered out a window of their hostel room. "We'll be leaving early in the morning and heading southwest. We should reach Prifrane in a week's time; then into the mountains. Hopefully, someone in Prifrane will agree to act as scout through the Hills."

Logan rubbed his hands together nervously. "What is taking Thromar so long?" he said. "I hope he didn't run into any more Reakthi."

The Murderer shrugged diffidently. "He said something about going to see his friend Fraviar, the one who makes the ale." He sneered at no one in particular. "Still don't see what help he'd be."

Cyrene gazed up at the two men, replacing the Jewel in its leather pouch. Her deep blue eyes were filled with awe and trepidation, and Logan prayed that was all. "Shouldn't you keep the Jewel in a safer place?" she wondered. "I mean, a bag doesn't serve as much protection, does it?"

"Hasn't been taken yet," Moknay smirked, and Logan hated the word "yet."

The door flew open and Thromar entered, a silly grin drawn across his face.

"What are you grinning about, O mighty fat one?" quipped the Murderer.

Thromar belched loudly in Moknay's general direction. "Been to my friend Fraviar," he stated.

"Did he give us anything that could help, or just the secret ways of making ale?" the Murderer wondered sarcastically.

Thromar held up three flasks of fluid. "He did give us some of his darkest ale, and a little talisman of magical powers. Says it detects magic." The fighter thrust a huge arm at Logan. "I think you should be the one to wear it, friend-Logan."

Logan took the bulb of stone and inspected it. "It detects magic? How?"

His massive shoulders heaved as Thromar shrugged. "Fraviar says it tingles or something like that. He never used it—his sister did. She's a wizardess."

Logan slipped the talisman over his neck and tucked it into his shirt, turning to the window where Moknay continued his vigil. Beyond the glass, the sky was black, and stars twinkled far off in the darkness.

Wood groaned and creaked as Thromar threw himself onto a bed, yawning.

Moknay turned away from the window and scanned the three before him. "Early in the morning, remember that," he repeated for Thromar's sake. "Cyrene, you have a horse?"

The attractive girl nodded, her eyes narrowing as she studied the Murderer.

Moknay ignored her suspicious stare. "Fine." He faced Thromar. "And if you refuse to get up tomorrow morning, Thromar, I'll personally stick you in the rump with a dagger."

The fighter grinned with yellowing teeth. "What, and break one of your daggers, Murderer?"

Thin, serpentine wisps of color rose into the air, twisting and spiraling like corkscrews. Infinite starlike points of light glittered in the red-and-silver sky, winking playfully as Matthew Logan surveyed the immediate area. A tiny comet sailed overhead, its tail snaking along behind it. Like a mischievous butterfly, the comet swerved, forcing Logan to duck as it crackled over him and sped off into the red-and-silver universe.

It is beautiful, Logan thought. He was standing in midair within the very center of Being. Pleasant tingles coursed through him as the writhing tongues of color touched him and seeped through him as if he himself were a smokelike strand of hues. And the winking of the stars became seductive, like a million gorgeous females all flirting with the young man at once.

A vile sensation of disharmony disrupted the pleasantness, and Logan cast a fearful glance behind him.

A titanic gyroscope was looming down upon him, its wheel

flashing with the hundreds of galaxies revolving within it. Planets and stars began to spin free of the whirling disk, exploding as they tore away from their natural order. A hideous revelation blazed into Logan's mind, and he could tell the tilting gyroscope was going to falter—tip—and everything in it would be destroyed.

Everything.

The young man suddenly saw Moknay, Thromar, Mara, Cyrene, Barthol, and Launce all orbiting inside the Wheel. They, in turn, were peering out at him, hands extended as if pleading. Helpless, Logan wished there was some way he could help his friends, but his mind told him there was none.

A million million screams speared through Logan's brain as the Wheel tilted and everything was torn asunder.

Everything.

That was when Logan realized he held the Jewel in his hands. His stomach twisted in disgust as a horrible gash split across the gem, and blood gushed forth, drenching Logan in a crimson fountain of life fluid. As the Jewel's heartbeat weakened, the blood flow slowed.

The pulsing heart of the Jewel skipped, and the red-and-silver sky dimmed . . . and went out.

Sleepily, Logan tore free of his dream and realized his bed was shuddering to the rhythmic beat of a heart. At first the young man thought it was his own heart, but then he noticed the entire cot was shaking fitfully, and knew the beating was not his own. Another thought struck him and he grasped the stone talisman. No, that wasn't it either, so what . . . ?

A golden flare filled the room.

"Shit!" Logan gasped, watching as the Jewel's bag pulsed with energy.

The leather pouch swelled with an aurora of colors, and light stabbed free and knifed into Logan's face. Blinking, Logan tried to rid his eyes of the afterimage as a high-pitched shriek shattered the night. Thunder roared instantly after. The earth trembled in terror as a blue-white line of electricity forked down from the sky and blazed into the soil. The wailing scream of electrified air devoured the stillness, and a powerful blue-white flash illuminated the room. The rumble of thunder gripped the sides of the hostel and shook.

"Everybody!" cried Logan, jumping out of bed. "Get up! We've got problems!"

The shrill screech of another bolt resonated throughout the night, bringing with it clamorous thunder. The building quaked again as Logan's companions opened their eyes and immediately reacted.

The Jewel's golden glow flooded the room.

"Matthew!" Cyrene cried out. "What's happening?"

"Damned if I know!" Logan admitted as another bolt slashed the sky.

Moknay leapt from his bed, quickly clipping on his cape and strap of daggers. "The Wheel!" he exclaimed. "This is the first disaster Barthol warned us about! Come on! Let's get out of here!"

Screaming, a blue-white saber of radiance struck the hostel. Logan let out a startled shout as he crashed against the wall, striking the almost healed lump on the back of his skull. Lights more brilliant than the Jewel itself played behind his eyelids, and he could barely hear his friends yelling at him to get up.

A pitiful groan resounded in the quartet's ears, and Moknay's grey eyes flickered upward. The wooden support beams of the hostel were creaking and moaning, and the Murderer traced an almost invisible crack across one hovering above Logan.

"Logan!" he shouted, hurrying toward the young man. "Grab the Jewel and let's go!"

Dazed, the young man got to his knees, staring dumbly at the pulsating bag. Splinters of wood sprinkled down upon him as the support beam cracked, a portion of timber breaking free and screaming downward.

Cyrene, attempting to lace up her bodice, glimpsed the falling timber and leaped, catching Logan as she jumped. The young man felt himself suddenly jerked to one side, and there was a tremendous crash as something heavy fell to the hostel floor.

"Bring Logan!" Moknay commanded Cyrene from the darkness. "And don't forget the damn Jewel!"

Logan's vision began to clear as he and Cyrene staggered from the room, the Jewel glaring under his arm. Shouts and curses sprouted from the many rooms they passed, and lightning screeched outside. The fierce glare of the Jewel lit the stairs as the four stumbled down the steps and hurried into the street. A chilling, unnatural gale howled about them, and the quartet made their way to the stables.

"West!" Thromar bellowed over the lightning's din. "We have to go west!"

Grabbing Druid Launce's staff that leaned nearby, Logan mounted his yellow-and-green horse. Cyrene straddled a silver horse beside him, its blue mane and tail whipping in the stormy winds.

The four horses bolted free of the stables, the tempest shrieking around them. A flaring quarrel of blue light split the ground close by, showering the group with clods of dirt.

The Jewel continued to pulse with sorcerous brilliance.

"The hostel owner won't be too happy about us skipping out like that," Logan said, yelling to be heard over the noise.

Moknay frowned. "First you killed four Reakthi in his building, then you tried to fry it with the Jewel. I think he'd rather have us leave than do anything worse!"

"It's not my fault!" Logan roared in retaliation, the anger returning all at once.

Thromar jabbed a massive finger ahead. "By Brolark!" he boomed. "The river's swelling!"

Logan, Cyrene, and Moknay peered through the blackness to see a large, dark object rise and quiver. When a blast of lightning severed the darkness, they could see the water heaving, rising skyward like some behemoth from a long sleep.

Moknay pulled tight on his horse's reins. "We're cut off! We'll have to go back! That blob's engulfed the bridge!"

Logan halted his stallion and glared through the gloom at the throbbing wall of water. A faint feeling of misplacement ran through him as something tickled his left side. Questioningly, he glanced at the Jewel in his right hand, but that had not caused the tingle. His left hand hung at his side, grasping tightly to Druid Launce's staff.

"Moknay!" the young man shouted. "Take the Jewel!"

The Murderer turned in time to catch the Jewel as it spiraled through the crackling lightning. Logan, meanwhile, was glancing down, awaiting the odd tingle. It came again as Thromar decided to turn the horses around and head eastward.

The feathery touch started at Logan's left hand and crept up his arm to his shoulder. As it tickled his chest, Logan clutched at it. It had felt like a big, hairy spider had clambered up his arm, but whatever he had pinned beneath his right hand was not a spider. It was a stone talisman.

Thromar glanced over his shoulder as his horse began back. "Come on, friend-Logan! That blob won't let us get across the river!"

Silent, Logan looked at the fighter, the talisman, the staff, and suddenly a determined expression clouded his features. Teeth clenched, Logan spurred his horse forward, thundering directly toward the quivering mass of water.

Moknay jerked about. "Logan!"

Cyrene and Thromar swung their mounts about as well, staring dumbfounded as Logan rushed the unnatural flood. The young man cast a swift glance behind him and smiled when he saw his companions racing after him. When he turned back, the rising river was closer, towering over him. With a dark grin, Logan noted the river reminded him of Jell-O.

"He's as mad as Pembroke and Zackaron combined," growled Moknay.

A whining lightning bolt splintered a tree, showering Logan with blue sparks. He ignored the rainfall of light, sitting tall in his saddle as he held out Launce's staff. He kept his horse on the path, rushing directly for the bridge that was obscured by the growing tumor of water. As if intent on jousting, Logan charged, leveling the oaken staff in his hand.

"Friend-Logan!" Thromar bellowed. "Stop! For the love of Lelah, stop!"

The sensation of disunity strengthened as magical energy flickered at the tip of Druid Launce's staff. Lightning shrieked about the horse and rider, bathing Logan in a blue-white glare. Moknay, Cyrene, and Thromar trailed behind him, the Jewel flaring in the Murderer's grasp.

"Part," Logan commanded under his breath. "Part, damn you!"

The towering mass of liquid shuddered as the staff brightened. Convulsions ripped through the Jell-O, and the unnatural bulge caved inward. The trio following Logan watched in stupefaction as the depression within the swelling river grew, leaving a gaping wound in the liquid. The wooden bridge reappeared, the waters boiling down around it. Logan's green-and-yellow mount thundered across, the druid's staff still ablaze with magical powers.

"By the bubbling brew of Fraviar!" exclaimed Thromar. "Did you see that?"

"Of course I saw it, you bearded buffoon!" Moknay retorted. "I'm right beside you, aren't I?"

The three horses galloped over the river, their hooves echoing upon the wood. Gradually, the agitated waters subsided.

The feeling of wrongness faded and was replaced by weakness. Sweat dotted Logan's brow, and he took in great gulps of night air to refill his lungs. Unexpectedly, Moknay's voice called out for Logan to take the Jewel, and the young man slowly turned to inquire why.

The pouch, however, was already flying toward him, and Logan's eyes popped open. Frantically he caught the Jewel, embracing it to his chest with his right arm. All at once, the Jewel's glare ceased, blinking out like a candle's flame. The bubbling river reverted to normal, and a lightning bolt vanished as it traced across the sky. A low grumble of displeasure sounded as the winds died with a reluctant moan.

Logan reined in his horse. "Jesus," he sighed, "I don't believe this." He peered at Moknay. "And that was only the first movement of the Wheel?"

The Murderer nodded grimly. "I wonder if Barthol figured out how much time we actually have left."

Logan nodded back and saw the fear in Moknay's eyes. He suddenly realized how much the Murderer dreaded the Jewel and understood he should not have tossed it to him while it was glowing. Next time he'll give it to Thromar.

The young man gulped. Next time?

Slower than before, the four horses trotted onward, leaving the path and allowing the quartet to make camp in a small clearing. Politely, Logan gave his jacket to Cyrene, who was still too frightened to speak. Thromar munched on some food as Logan lay down on the soft carpet of green. The mismatchment suddenly rose up from the very blades of grass, and Logan grumbled as he tossed onto his back. All he needed was to have that stupid feeling keep him awake for the rest of the night!

Fortunately, sleep subdued Logan from behind.

Stars twinkled happily as Logan replaced Moknay as guard. The Murderer had since fallen asleep, his grey form cloaked by the night. Thromar snored beside him, his bearded face not so fierce in sleep, and Cyrene lay nearby. Her skirt had ridden a bit up her leg, and Logan pulled his eyes away from the girl's thigh, mumbling. Since he had come to this land he had been forced to relieve himself in the forest; what about sexually, though? Would he have to see to his own desires? *In the forest?*

Keeping his eyes away from Cyrene, Logan stared up into the night sky. Maybe he could spot a familiar constellation— Orion was an easy one. The sky, however, would not comply, and Logan recognized no pattern in the stars above him. He truly was on another world in another universe or dimension.

Something thudded in the foliage.

Logan's hand pulled free Moknay's dagger, while he glared into the surrounding shrubbery. There was silence all about him, and a chilling unease began to settle in Logan's stomach.

A bush crashed and rustled as if destroyed.

"Foooooooood!" a friendly voice bellowed.

Letting out a sigh of relief, Logan sank back to the ground. The large, light blue ogre smashed through the brush, a huge grin drawn across its squarish face.

"How in the world did you find us?" Logan questioned the ogre.

Its grin widened. "Find yoooooooou!"

"No, *how* did you find us? It's obvious you found us. Are we that easy to trail?"

The huge creature cocked its head to one side in confusion. "Foooooooood?" it queried hopefully.

Logan reached into a pouch and withdrew some of the fruit Launce had given them. He extended a hand toward the ogre, but, as it started forward, the beast halted, eyes wide.

"What's the matter?" Logan asked it. "Don't you like fruit?"

"Maaaaaagic," the blue-skinned creature whispered in awe.

The young man pivoted, expecting to see Groathit emerge from the bushes behind him. "Magic? Where?" he cried.

The ogre pointed an enormous finger at Logan's neck. "There."

Logan bowed his head to inspect himself and felt the talisman bump his chin. He slipped off the magical stone and held it up. "You don't like this?"

The ogre shied away.

"Hmmmm, I guess not." Logan set the talisman aside. "Here, here's some food."

The light blue beast lumbered forward and snatched the food from Logan's hand. Greedily, it gulped the fruit down.

"Now," Logan said, trying again, "how did you find us?"

The ogre grinned foolishly. "Give fooooood! Meeeee find!"

Obviously, the creature felt its answer satisfactory and went silent, leaving Logan in an awkward position. Scratching the tip of his nose, Logan attempted another question:

"Is anyone else following us?"

The creature scratched its stringy black hair. "Skinny huuuuumaaaan!" it remembered. "Maaaaaaad!"

Logan nodded understandingly. "Pembroke," he muttered. Then, he queried, "How far is he?"

The ogre did not hesitate. "Faaaaaar!"

As a reward, Logan gave the beast another handful of food. The ogre happily grabbed the provisions and wolfed them down. It then released a belch Logan was sure could topple a tree.

"Quiet," he hushed it. "Did you see anyone else?"

The ogre was silent for quite some time until booming out: "Whiiite huuuumaaaan!"

"White human?" Logan mused. "As to my knowledge, you're the only person I've seen who isn't white."

The ogre grinned. "Maaaaaagic."

"No, no magic," corrected Logan, pointing at the taliman. "I took it off."

The light blue ogre screwed up its face but its grin soon returned. "Foooooooood?" it hoped.

Logan gave the ogre another handful and it nodded its thanks, clumsily lumbering off into the forest.

Logan was left to his thoughts.

·8·

Warnings

"If we left the road about midday, I'd say Prifrane would be directly west." Thromar's voice shattered the silence.

Logan lifted his head, blinking the sleep from his eyes.

"Groathit knows for certain we're not going to Semeth," Moknay said. "If we stay on the road that long, we're bound to be attacked."

"By what?" Thromar boomed back. "The farther west we go, the harder it is for the Reakthi to trail us! Their stronghold's in the east!"

"Spellcasters have no need for strongholds," Cyrene remarked.

Logan sat up, eyeing his three companions as the early morning mist dispersed. Thromar threw him a pitiful glance.

"Help me, friend-Logan," he pleaded. "They're ganging up on me!"

"That's because you want to take a dangerous route," Moknay retorted.

"But the longer we stay on the road, the faster we get there," the huge fighter said. He looked over at Logan. "Isn't that right?"

The young man shrugged, opening his mouth to say something about not knowing the area.

"We also have Pembroke after us," the Murderer interrupted. "Don't forget about him."

"There's no need to worry about him," Logan stated. "He's far behind us."

Moknay and Thromar both eyed the young man wonderingly. "How do you know that, friend?" queried Moknay.

"Friend-Logan is a spellcaster, Murderer," Thromar roared

happily. "I do wish he'd take his eye out for you! It's the most amazing thing I've ever seen!"

"I'm no spellcaster," Logan answered, grinning to himself. "I just happen to have my own sources of information."

A frown caused Moknay's mustache to droop. "That's another thing," he muttered to everyone but directed it at Thromar. "Groathit is still out one pawn. Whatever he has trailing us now might catch up with us on the road."

"Not if I'm on Smeea!" Thromar declared. "Nothing can catch Smeea and me if we're on the path! We'll ride like the very winds themselves! If we're in the bloody forest, even Smeea can't maneuver through all those damn branches and brambles!"

Druid Launce could, the guilt inside Logan whispered; and the young man flinched in quiet pain at the thought.

"Didn't you say Vaugen may still be riding after you?" Cyrene questioned, brushing at her long, dark blonde hair.

Moknay nodded, looking out toward the Hills.

"Then wouldn't it be better to take the forest route?" continued Cyrene. "Confuse him even more?"

Logan caught an odd flicker passing through Cyrene's blue eyes. The girl was up to something, his paranoia advised him. She sounded so determined to run headlong into the Imperator himself; why was she suggesting a route that would cause Vaugen to lose them?

"I don't think Vaugen will stay on the path," Moknay said, and Logan noticed the brief frown that crossed Cyrene's full lips. "The roads do offer the safety of not running into him!" The grey eyes flashed to Logan. "And if Logan thinks Pembroke is far behind us, maybe the path is our best bet. I'm still a little uneasy about Groathit's new pawn—if he's got one."

Thromar threw up his brawny arms in victory. "We did it, friend-Logan!" he cheered. "We stay on the road!"

Logan, however, was not listening to the bearded fighter. The young man's eyes were trained on Cyrene as she stalked away from the group, mumbling under her breath. She deliberately wanted to take the forest route so that it would slow them down, Logan realized. That way Vaugen would have a better chance of catching up to them. Stupid female!

Cyrene felt Logan's gaze and turned about. The anger that was ablaze in her eyes died abruptly and a strange, oddly friendly emotion took its place. A beautiful smile came to her lips before she swung away and continued for her horse.

Was she flirting with me? Logan wondered, and a little chill of excitement made its way into his sweat pants.

The sensation of mismatchment pounced like a lion, devouring the ideas that formed in Logan's mind. As he reacted, the anger that churned inside him also sprang forth, grasping the opposing feeling in a deathlock. The tingle of disharmony slipped the grip and formulated an attack of its own, and Logan was haplessly caught in the middle.

"Friend-Logan!" Thromar shouted in awe. "Your arm! What's happening to your arm?"

Forcing himself free of the battling sensations, Logan gave his arms a curious glance. His blue eyes enlarged when he saw the bloody glare sprouting from his left forearm near his sword wound. Instant panic consumed him as he feared Groathit was magically draining him of his blood, but then he noticed the tiny silver flecks swirling amongst the crimson, and he pulled back his sleeve.

The blank face of his digital watch was blazing like a miniature bonfire. Red-and-silver light fairly burst from his wrist, slicing into the young man's eyes like the glare of the Jewel the night before. Shaking his head free of the light, the anger and displacement retreated, and his watch dimmed.

The others were staring at Logan dumbly.

"By Brolark," breathed Thromar, "what an array of tricks you have."

The rage Logan thought was gone returned. "I am *not* a spellcaster!" he roared. "If I was a goddamn spellcaster, I wouldn't be here! I wouldn't have this goddamn Jewel leaking energy! I'd have left the very morning I arrived here!"

"We have our problems, friend," Moknay replied, "but Sparrill's not all that bad. Since when was your world a paradise of some sort?"

"It isn't!" thundered Logan. "It's a rat-hole! But at least it's *my* world! Here there's nothing but confusion for me, and people dying every time they lend a hand! Even my world wasn't like that!"

The grimness and pessimism went out of the Murderer's eyes. "Friend, every world has its problems, but every world has its people. I told you before the *people* have kept the

Reakthi out, not the Guards. That's the way we are here. We will gladly help anyone who opposes the invaders . . . even if it means laying down our lives. But we're not fools. We will try every conceivable way to escape with everyone's life intact. And we almost did that when Vaugen and his bastards attacked."

"*Almost?*" Logan moaned. "*Almost* isn't good enough! *Almost* cost Druid Launce his life!"

"Something that happened because he wanted to save us, the Jewel, and Munuc's people from the Reakthi," Thromar put in. "Friend-Logan, you must not blame yourself. Are the people in your world so heroic that no one dies in combat?"

A disgusting realization came to the young man. "No," he sighed, "no one comes to your aid when you're in 'combat.' We all just stand around and wait for someone else to do the helping."

Logan's three companions were still until Moknay clamped a gloved hand upon the young man's shoulder. "I would never have guessed you came from such a world," he said. "Since I have known you, never once have you let someone else act for you. It's unfortunate you want to return so badly, because Moknay the Murderer is proud to call you friend."

A faint smile formed on Logan's lips as he glanced from Thromar to Moknay to Cyrene. Both fighter and Murderer were beaming like proud fathers, and Cyrene was also watching Logan with respect in her eyes. And Logan could tell that—unlike in his world—these people said and meant what their hearts felt.

And Logan's desire to return home lessened just slightly.

There was an opaque gleam in the eye like the glitter of a pearl as Spellcaster Groathit stalked out of the small town of Plestenah and pushed his way through the forest. Horses snorted nervously as the sorcerer rejoined the throng of Reakthi that awaited him in the brush.

Grey eyes as cold as ice trained upon the spellcaster.

"Well?" sneered Vaugen.

"Reakmor Farkarrez did indeed catch up with them in town, and not one Sparrillian even suspected his men as being Reakthi," the wizard reported. "They engaged and battled the one called Logan and some blonde and all four men were slain. Unfortunately, if Farkarrez had used his mind, he could have easily taken the Jewel since the fools had left it in the horse's saddlebag when they entered the hostel where they were confronted."

"Farkarrez was a good man," Vaugen replied calmly. "I am surprised he did not think to search, or, perhaps, even slay their mounts. But we now know that—without chestplates—perhaps we can once again attempt Agasilaus's ploy and conquer Sparrill as we conquered Denzil."

"We have not conquered Denzil," Groathit mentioned, mounting his horse.

The Imperator flashed him a vile gaze. "One town does not make the whole of a land!" he snapped.

"No, but it is almost humorous to think that Vaugen has been unable to conquer one lone city," the wizard mocked.

Rage steamed within the armored chest of the Imperator, and blood rushed to his face, making his scars almost brighten. "You toy dangerously with my anger, spellcaster," he warned. "True, we have been unable to conquer Eadarus, but we have now learned that we can encircle these idiots if we dispose of our armor and keep our movements unseen. Then even Eadarus will be unable to hold off the Reakthi from all sides!" The grey eyes blazed angrily. "It is odd you are so quick to criticize me when the means of our ultimate conquest is wandering around out there with the Jewel of Equilibrant in his saddlebags! Why aren't you doing something about detaining them? I even risked and lost one of my best Reakmors to hinder them."

Groathit snorted contemptuously as the horses skirted the town. " 'Best Reakmor'!" he spat. "Farkarrez is a sadist!"

The Imperator sneered in vexation and something resembling mockery. "Was," he corrected. "Farkarrez *was* a sadist."

The wizard's bad eye seemed to twinkle with foul thoughts. "No," he answered with a skull-like smile. "I mean *is*."

The spellcaster's cackling laughter tore through the forest and sent a chill wafting across the winds.

Logan stared at the ground as the four horses made their way through the trees, lost in his musings. Up until that morning, he realized, he had only tolerated this world. He had been zapped here and had no say in the matter, so he had come to the conclusion that he'd travel across the land, get the Smythe's help, and leave. He had not even noticed the land's good points, especially, as Moknay had pointed out, the people. Still, Logan longed to return to his world, his way of life, his occupation, his apartment with running water and toilets.

Sparrill, he came to the conclusion, was a nice place to visit, but he didn't want to live there.

Peering at the dirt beneath his horse's hooves, Logan did not even see the Jewel in his saddlebag flare yellow and then dim.

Cyrene drew her horse up alongside Logan, and a soft hand touched his shoulder. "Is something the matter?" she asked.

Logan blinked. "No, no, just wrestling with my thoughts," he answered, and could not help noticing the lovely smile Cyrene watched him with. It was odd, but the blonde was almost glad they had reached the forest. Wouldn't she ever stop hoping to run into Vaugen?

Every nerve in Logan's body exploded, and the young man was seized by a paroxysm of agony as the sensation of disharmony brutally ambushed him. Sweat splashed across his brow, and his throat constricted, denying his lungs air. Gasping, he nearly pitched off his horse, but Cyrene's soft hand steadied him. Moknay and Thromar whipped about, instantly alarmed when they saw the young man's pale face and convulsive actions.

A soft hum began to split the air, and Moknay could feel the hairs on his arm prick up as if at attention. Quizzically, the Murderer swung his head in the direction of the buzz, and his grey eyes widened. A swift glove tapped Thromar upon one arm and the fighter also spotted what Moknay had. Wonderingly looking from Logan to his friends, Cyrene caught their startled gaze and also faced northwest.

A flare of man-shaped blackness was steadily making its way toward them.

Sickness flowed throughout Logan as the overpowering feeling started to recede. He thought his eyes were playing tricks on him when he spotted the humanoid figure of blackness stride toward them, a bizarre hum surrounding the form.

"What . . . What is that?" the young man forced out, drenched by perspiration.

Moknay's grim mien was grimmer than usual. "A Blackbody," the Murderer explained, grasping his strap of daggers tightly.

Blackbody? Logan asked himself. Damn, that sounded familiar. Back on Earth a black body was something used in physics, right? Had something to do about being the perfect absorber and emitter of radiation, didn't it? Blast! Logan was no physics major . . . he still had trouble deciphering fractions! But he did recall something about black-body radiation and that its applications were pretty much limited. Now how in the world did a creature such as a Blackbody exist here? Was there a connection between the worlds somewhere?

The Blackbody advanced, flickering with an eerie aura of ebony light. As it neared, the hum accompanying it grew louder, and they all could feel the power vibrating through the air.

Cyrene's deep blue eyes were overspilling with horror. "But I thought Blackbodies were cosmic," she protested. "What in the name of Agellic is one doing here?"

Like an empathetic leech, Logan sensed the girl's terror and felt his own fears bubbling into existence.

"Blackbodies *are* cosmic," Moknay informed the blonde, "but remember what Logan has in that saddlebag. We're carrying something that's threatening the very balance of order, and this Blackbody has probably come to find out about last night's excitement. They *are* responsible for the very fundamental nature of matter and would be a little concerned if matter started to fall apart."

Like on Earth! Logan noted, ignoring the Murderer's sarcasm. Black-body radiation was used by physicists to study the fundamental nature of matter and quantitative . . . ? No, quantum mechanics.

The Blackbody came closer and then stopped, tilting its flaring black head in their direction. Vaguely, Logan could see two white orbs of light where its eyes should have been.

"*You hold sway to the entire multiverse,*" the Blackbody accused, pointing a blazing ebony finger at Logan; it shook its head. "*You should not be here.*"

The young man looked at Moknay. This thing wasn't referring to the Jewel—it was talking about Logan himself!

The fury instantly flared into life inside him. "I don't want to be here!" Logan barked at the astonishing black form. "I *am* going back!"

The Blackbody took two more steps toward them. "*But already you have uncovered a portion of the Macrocosm,*" it stated. "*You must not be allowed to do so again if you ever wish to return to your world. You must give me That Which Balances the Wheel.*"

"Get out of our way, Blackbody," Thromar warned. "We are taking the Jewel to the Smythe, and we're not about to hand it over to some creature that can't control it any better than friend-Logan here!"

"*Silence, inferior organism,*" the Blackbody ordered. "*I am a Being of the Megacosmos and have come to warn you. Know you not that no power was released during the previous revolution of your sphere? There was an upheaval in the natural Balance of things, yet the Equilibrant was quenched before discharging its energies. This has caused much of the Balance to fragment.*" The white orbs flamed. "*There must also be some Order to Chaos. I have come to drink the release that was staunched.*"

At that, Moknay freed a large dagger from his belt and jerked on the handle. A second blade slid free from the first and proceeded to unfold into three separate blades on one hilt. Moknay now held four shafts of steel, and Logan saw the resemblance to the Indian knife, the katar. What the Murderer held was a combination sliding and forking katar, and it looked exceptionally dangerous in his grey-gloved hands.

The Blackbody ignored the knives and continued forward.

There was a moment of quiet as Logan scanned his companions. Moknay and Thromar both were edgy, weapons out and ready. Cyrene had drawn back, her face pale from the fear that billowed up inside her. Turning his attention to himself, Logan disregarded the wrongness that still lurked within him and pulled free his own blade. This ebony thingamajig wanted to bleed the Jewel of more energy—and they couldn't allow it to do so.

"We will not hesitate to slay you," Moknay told the crackling form.

The Blackbody paid him no heed, its white eyes wavering as it closed in on Logan.

Roaring, Thromar rushed the creature, swinging his blood-caked sword in a powerful downward sweep. The Blackbody walked on as the fighter spilled from his mount, his weapon passing harmlessly through the flaring blackness. Logan caught the stifled gasp from Cyrene as the Blackbody approached, its eyes lusting after the Jewel at Logan's side.

"Logan," Moknay said over his shoulder, "perhaps you should take the Jewel and flee. I don't think our weapons will stop it."

Perplexed, the young man looked once more at the oncoming Blackbody. At least it didn't emit radiation ... he hoped.

"I think your friend is right, Matthew," agreed Cyrene. "There's no way to defeat a Blackbody."

"Only because no one has ever confronted one before," Moknay put in, grey eyes locked on the blazing beast.

Angered by his initial attempt, Thromar heaved himself off the forest floor and hacked at the glowing form. Numerous times his sword slashed through the black energy, but the creature's eyes remained riveted to Logan.

Logic beat back the anxiety and Logan felt it better to flee. So far the Blackbody did not appear to be a threat to their lives, nor did they appear to threaten its life. It was probably better to get away from the beast rather than let it walk through the trees to suck the Jewel dry.

As Logan pulled on his horse's reins, the Blackbody shrieked, sensing what the young man had decided. The energy-being lunged, stretching out fingers made up of pitch-black power. Moknay yelled a challenge, positioning himself between the creature and Logan, his katar jabbing out. Thromar let out a frightened curse as the Murderer's hand and knife passed through the beast and almost speared the fighter on the opposite side.

"Harmeer's War Axe!" he cursed. "Call your shots, Murderer!"

Energy crackled and spat as the Blackbody passed through both Moknay and his horse. Agony coursed through the Murderer as his flesh fused with the creature, and his horse reared in pain. Black sparks flared throughout the foliage as Moknay threw himself from his mount, his black hair erect as if charged with static electricity.

The Blackbody continued its lunge.

"Friend-Logan!" Thromar boomed. "Jump! Don't let it touch you!"

Cyrene let out a scream as the Blackbody finished phasing through Moknay's horse and reached out for Logan. It seemed the girl didn't like to battle anything but Reakthi, Logan mused.

Black tendrils of energy stabbed out and seeped into Logan's saddlebag. The young man's green-and-yellow mount reared, terrified by the crackling figure of ebony. Logan's mind, meanwhile, kicked him: Stupid! it barked. Stop thinking about the girl when this thingamajig is after the Jewel!

Setting aside the feeling of misplacement, Logan lashed out with his Reakthi blade. Golden light began to leak from his saddlebag as the Blackbody fed off the Jewel, unfeeling of the steel that passed through its form. Unseated as Thromar was, Logan felt himself fall . . . directly into the Blackbody.

Both Blackbody and Logan screamed as one ripped through the other. Something fiery red was flaming around the young man's throat as he tumbled through the ebony figure, and pain and the sensation of disagreement seemed to short-circuit his brain cells.

Moknay, Thromar, and Cyrene watched as the young man hit the ground, the stone talisman about his neck emitting a blinding red glare. The Blackbody arched its back, energy-formed fingers clutching at the air. Its dying wail resounded in their ears as it shattered into strands of black power and faded.

The agony and wrongness still lingered as soft, gentle fingers lifted Logan's head from the carpet of grass. Thinking his contacts were blurred, he blinked a few times, clearing his vision until he could make out Cyrene kneeling over him. The heavily bearded face of Thromar peered over her slim shoulder, yellowed teeth grinning.

"You're the first person to ever defeat a Blackbody, friend-Logan," he boasted. "Oh, the bards shall sing of this battle!"

"Seems that talisman doesn't detect magic," came Moknay's voice from out of Logan's line of vision. It sounded pain-filled and weary. "Seems to be able to dispel at times."

Logan shook his head and could tell the same weariness the Murderer felt was leaking into his own muscles. "But it *does* detect," he argued. "That was how I knew Druid Launce's staff still worked."

But why, his mind wondered, was the ogre afraid of it? The detecting and dispelling of magic should not have harmed the beast, so why did it shy away? Unless . . . the talisman did more . . .

Pondering, Logan felt himself lifted off the ground by Thromar and Cyrene. He leaned momentarily against the girl until he had his balance, and then took quick steps to his horse. Sliding into the saddle, Logan thought he saw something skulking through the bushes. Wishing his recovery from the Blackbody's attack would quicken, he fixed his eyes on the forest. He frowned when he saw nothing out of the usual. Either the weariness setting in was playing tricks on him, or something dark had briefly flashed by amongst the trees. For a moment the young man feared Pembroke was there, but his mind soon cast that aside. Pembroke—according to the ogre—was far behind them, and he wouldn't have sat idly by while a Blackbody attacked his "Child."

Rubbing his eyes, Logan started his horse after the others, perplexed as to whether or not he had really seen something . . . And the door to his subconscious reopened, and an asthmatic rasp Logan thought he had been freed from responded:

Learn to decipher dreams from reality, unreality from false-hood, falsehood from truth, or doom shall fall upon your worlds!

There was a slightly cooler breeze blowing in from the north as the sun slowly tinted the sky a bloody red. Cool water soaked through Logan's sneakers as his green-and-yellow stallion cautiously waded across the waters of the Ohmmarrious. The young man was having a difficult time holding the reins and all the contents of his saddlebags as well so the water would not ruin them. Thromar was also having a troublesome journey with all his extra weaponry dangling from Smeea's sides. Cyrene, having gotten over the scare of the night before and the Blackbody, had riverted to her usual cold self, even ignoring the rushing liquid when it splashed across sections of her skirt and turned the material all but transparent. And it wasn't helping Logan any as he fumbled across the river with leather pouches bundled in his arms.

"Centaur chips!" cursed Thromar, almost losing his flail, struggling to keep it in his grasp, and almost causing his arrows to spill out of their quiver. "Whose stupid idea was it to cross this stretch of vomit without a bridge?"

"Yours," Moknay answered with a grin, keeping his cape far above the flowing river. "And it's not vomit. If you want vomit, go cross the Demonry."

The enormous fighter screwed up his face and stuck out his tongue. "Imogen, no! I'd sooner wade in Demon-dung than set foot in that cesspool!"

Juggling his provisions, Logan caught their conversation. The Demonry, he recalled, was the river that that *Deil* thing had created when it had crashed back down from above. Odd, but when Launce had told that story, he had mentioned the *Deil* being "ablaze with the cosmic fire of the Air" because it had gone so high. Could that have been a mythological rendition of something reentering the atmosphere? It would be ablaze . . . not that any human could survive it . . . but, then again, Logan had no idea just what a *Deil* was.

The young man flinched as cold water drenched the cuffs of his sweat pants and seeped through to the flesh beneath. Although the current was strong, the waters were sparklingly beautiful. He could almost believe there *was* a sprite in this river—since it was as gorgeous as the Roana—although, at the time, Logan really didn't have the privilege to drink in that river's beauty . . . nor could he at the Lephar either. Only here, at the Ohmmarrious, could the young man stop and admire the beauty of the water and the greenery. Yes, it wasn't hard at all to believe there was a sprite in the river.

A snickering portion of Logan's mind kicked in; and that meant Logan—being in the river—was in the sprite!

Cruelty! The young man moaned silently, wincing and accidentally glancing at Cyrene.

The clinging skirt spattered with crystal-clear water was even more torturous than Logan's imagination, and he forced himself to look away. His sudden movement was enough to unseat him from his horse and send him splashing into the river.

Uncertain of what had happened, Logan pried his eyes open to find himself in another world. Light blue surrounded him, and silver and white stones lined the river's bottom at his feet.

He could see the horses' hooves as they proceeded across the river, and he had luckily thrown his arms up and had kept his supplies out of the liquid. The clear waters of the Ohmmarrious flowed into his eye sockets, and, only for a second, the young man was afraid of losing his contacts to the river. However, as the clear waters of Sparrill had done before, the Ohmmarrious delicately washed and cleansed his lenses far better than any enzymatic cleaner had ever done back on Earth!

As Logan started to lift his head from the clear waters, a faint giggling reached his ears. Quizzically, the young man glanced through the liquid as his head broke the surface. Another giggle came to him, and he swiveled toward Cyrene who was smiling down at him from atop her horse. Like the waters of the Ohmmarrious, confusion washed over the young man as he realized Cyrene's giggle was lower in pitch than the one he had heard below the surface. Had the waters somehow heightened her pitch in some way? Or had he heard two separate giggles?

"I wish Thromar were as apt to bathe as you, friend," Moknay jested. "Agellic knows he reeks like a stable!"

"I am a man of strength, Murderer!" replied the fighter. "Strong of muscle, strong of mind, and strong of odor!" He grinned with yellowing teeth.

As Moknay's horse leapt out onto the western bank, Cyrene slid off her mount and splashed back into deeper waters, offering a hand to Logan. "Here," she said, "give me your stuff before you catch your death."

Without thinking, the young man handed over the pouches he held and began to drag himself from the river. Abruptly his paranoia erupted, yowling at the stupidity of the young man. He had just handed the Jewel of Equilibrant over to someone he had not fully come to trust! How could he be so foolish?

Staring apprehensively, Logan watched as Cyrene waded to the shore and set down the leather bags. Then she turned back to him, once more extending her slim arm to aid him. Relief swamped the young man, and he took her outstretched hand, freeing his body from the cool waters. He turned his blue eyes to the west and grimaced as the sun's final rays were swallowed by the mountains.

"I'm gonna freeze my ass off," he mumbled, wringing out a sleeve of his jacket.

Thromar jerked about on Smeea. "By Brolark! What a sight
that will be!" he boomed. "Will you take your eye out afterward for Moknay and Cyrene to see?"

Warm. Warm, gentle breezes teasingly ruffled Logan's black
hair as they wafted through the night, passing out over the
Ohmmarrious and swirling into the lush foliage beyond. The
young man's clothes did not stick to his body at all as he
lay there on his side, peering at the crystal-clear river. The
waters reflected the red night sky, silver stars glinting in its
vastness. Another warm wind blew over him, and a childlike
giggle sounded from somewhere indistinguishable.

Curiously, Logan propped himself up on an elbow as the
stars gleamed silver in the red sky.

The rushing Ohmmarrious slowed, the constant gurgle of its
waters fading as the sparkling liquid stilled. Pillars of clear
water began to shoot skyward, heralding the approach of someone, Logan guessed. Gradually, through the fountaining shafts
of crystal, a diminutive figure took shape. Logan watched in
wonderment as a woman some five feet in height stepped out
across the river, not wet although she had just walked through
the cascading river.

The petite female was amazingly well proportioned and
gazed at Logan with beautiful, dark green eyes as bright and as
pure as the forest foliage itself. She was absolutely naked, and
long, dark green hair spilled past her bare shoulders and curled
just above her shoulder blades. Her perfect, well-sculptured
breasts were highlighted by the silver stars, and the nipples
were a delicate shade of green. The curve of her waist and hips
made familiar urges flare up within Logan as she came closer,
and he could not help noticing the triangle of hair between her
thighs was also a dark green hue.

Before Logan could remark on the beauty of the dainty
creature before him, another girl stepped free of the fountains.
She was the exact height and build of the first, only her eyes,
nipples, and hair were a light blue. While she slinked across
the water's surface, a third female broke through the jets of
liquid and into the silvery starlight.

Like her sisters, the third was about five feet in height
and had a perfect build, yet there was a hint of experience
and knowledge within her violet eyes. Her violet nipples and

hair were extraordinary, creating an almost alien attraction for Logan. Green and blue were also odd shades, but the third's eyes were stern, more mature than her siblings.

The green-haired one giggled and Logan recognized the pitch. It was the same one he had heard earlier that evening under the water!

"Welcome, Matthew Logan," the three beauties greeted, nearing him with a childlike boldness.

"I hope you did not catch a chill," the green-haired one said.

Stunned by their radiance and sudden appearance, Logan sat up. "No, no, I think I'm all right."

"We're so glad you stopped here," the violet-haired one remarked. "It has been a very long time since we have talked to someone."

"I would like to touch someone as well," the blue-haired one put in.

"You're just jealous that he fell in my river and not yours, Glorana," the green-haired one mocked.

"Oh, I am not!" Glorana retorted. "He would've fallen in mine if that rotten Jewel had acted up!"

"No, he wouldn't've," the green-haired one answered. "He waded through mine but took a bridge over yours. That means you're ugly!"

"It does not!" Glorana whined.

Logan turned a questioning eye toward the violet-haired nymph. "I—I seem to know you," he stuttered.

The pair arguing shut up; the violet eyes of the third flickered in reply.

"You're the sprites," Logan went on, shakily, "aren't you? The three sprites Druid Launce told me about?"

Glorana clapped her hands together in glee. "He knows of us!" she exclaimed. She raced to where Logan sat, her fragile hands clutching his jacket. "I am Glorana," she announced, blue eyes aglow with excitement. "I love you."

The green-haired sprite wheeled about, hair billowing as she dashed to kneel beside Logan. "I am Salena," she told him. She turned on Glorana. "And I loved him first!"

Logan's blue eyes drew away from the green and blue sprites and transfixed on the violet enchantress still at the river's edge. "You must be Roana," he said.

Roana nodded silently, stepping closer.

There was quiet only broken by the continual trickle of the fountains.

"How come I can see you?" Logan finally inquired.

"You're camping by my river," Salena explained.

"And you're special," added Roana.

" 'Special'?" repeated Logan.

Glorana ran an eager hand over Logan's chest. "You're a man," she sighed lustfully.

Salena frowned at her sister. "That's not what she meant," she snapped.

"I don't care," Glorana responded. "I'm enjoying myself."

Logan tried to ignore the soft hands caressing his shoulders. "Would my friends see you if they woke up?" he said.

Roana smiled. "At this time," she replied, "you would not see us if you woke up."

The young man blinked, crossing his legs Indian-style. "Huh?" he exclaimed. "What are you . . . ?"

"You're dreaming, silly!" Salena told him, giggling.

Of course! Logan understood. Red sky and silver stars! Why hadn't he noticed it before? Because nothing out of the ordinary—like businessmen/monks or tilting gyroscopes—had popped up to spoil his dream. Even that infernal feeling of misplacement wasn't harassing him that night. But, now that he glanced behind him, he saw that, in his dream, he was quite alone. Neither his friends nor their mounts were behind him.

Logan turned back to the sprites. "And if I woke up, you'd just go away?" he queried.

"No, Matthew," Roana answered, sitting with him and her sisters, "we would always be here. Remember the story the druid told you."

What a wacko dream! the young man concluded. He had been thinking about that tale too much! He was dreaming about it now! Maybe he had had too much wine before he had gone to sleep!

"I don't think he believes us," Salena noted, a frown crossing her glorious lips.

"I'll make him believe us!" Glorana volunteered, eagerly grabbing Logan and bonding her lips to his.

Logan let out a muffled grunt of surprise as the soft lips met his and almost knocked him backwards. The feelings deep inside him raged and growled like wild animals, pacing up and down the length of their cages, demanding release. When the sprite finally pulled away with a wet smack, Logan knew it was not the warm breeze that was stirring in his sweat pants.

"Believe in us now?" Glorana smirked.

"Probably think you're some sexual nightmare come to torment him," Salena snorted.

"Whether he believes or not," Roana said, silencing her sisters, "we at least have someone to talk to. It's been almost forty years since someone like him has slept beside one of our rivers." Her violet eyes twinkled.

The tingling warmth was racing all throughout Logan's body as he eyed the voluptuous, violet-haired sprite.

"Matthew likes Roana! Matthew likes Roana!" Glorana started teasing, and Logan flustered when he realized her light blue eyes were glued to his crotch.

Salena abruptly stiffened, her exquisite frame outlined by the silver stars. "Matthew!" she cried urgently. "You must wake up! Something is happening! Something terrible!" Her deep green eyes blazed at him. "You must wake up!"

Groaning, Logan lifted his head from his grassy pillow. His sweat suit was still damp, and the clothes underneath were no dryer. He saw the Ohmmarrious through a half-closed eye, its waters rushing and gurgling normally; there were no fountains there. Oh, well, it had been a nice dream while it had lasted.

As the young man went to place his head back down, a faint female voice echoed in his ears: *Matthew! Your horse! See to your horse!* Salena warned.

Shocked into wakefulness, Logan jerked himself up. There was a sudden snort behind him, and the young man whipped around. Hooves thundered as a dark figure snapped Logan's green-and-yellow stallion about and galloped into the dark forest.

"Hey!" Logan yelled angrily. "That's my horse!" He kicked at Moknay and Thromar. "Get up!" he ordered. "Some bastard just stole my horse!"

His voice died down as he realized with mounting terror that, before he had gone to sleep, he had replaced all his provisions within the leather saddlebags. All his provisions . . . including the Jewel itself!

·9·

Quake

Glittering like daggers in the moonlight, Moknay's eyes swung away from the forest and trained on Logan. "There's something I forgot to tell you about the people of this world, friend," the Murderer stated. "They may be loyal to their land—but they're thieving little buggers!"

Frantically, Logan jerked his head about. "What are we going to do?" he shouted. "He took the Jewel!"

"Follow him," Thromar explained and leaped astride Smeea.

"You'll have to ride with Cyrene," Moknay told him, mounting up. "My horse is still a little shaky from that Blackbody attack."

The young man hardly heard the excuse, impatiently waiting for Cyrene to climb onto her horse. Somebody had just made off with Logan's transportation and his problem. A small part of him wanted to say, "Let him go; let him deal with the Jewel," but Logan knew that wasn't right. It was his fault, no matter which way he looked at it, that he had taken the Jewel from Pembroke, and he couldn't let this world be destroyed because of it. If not for the people who had befriended him, then for himself. Who was to say he'd make it to the Smythe before the thief allowed the Jewel to blow? No, Logan had to get that blasted gem back and do his best to make up for the wrong he had caused. Then if it blew while he still had it, he couldn't blame himself for at least not trying.

The horses didn't seem to move fast enough for Logan as they thundered through the foliage. Futilely, he tried to pick up the sounds of his stolen horse's hooves, but only the echoing beats of his friends' mounts resounded in his ears. Dark branches and bushes raced past him, and the half-moon peered down at him like some mocking grin at their attempts to overtake the bandit.

Moknay held up an arm and the three horses stopped. In silence, the Murderer tried to pick up the hoofbeats ahead of them, but it was useless. Somehow, the robber had outdistanced them already.

"He couldn't be that far," Moknay grumbled to himself.

Failure fluttered about in Logan's stomach. "Yes, he could," he replied. "That horse is fast."

"As is Smeea," Thromar answered, "but fast horses leave large prints. Unless he had the time to sweep his tracks away, we should be able to see them come morning."

"Come morning he could be in Frelars," Moknay frowned.

Cyrene sneered. "What makes you so sure it's a he?" she wondered.

Moknay sneered back. "He better hope he's a he because what I'm going to do to him shouldn't be done to a woman! Wouldn't it just be our luck if that idiot bumps the horse right into Pembroke?"

"Could it have been Pembroke?" queried Thromar.

"It isn't Pembroke," Logan stated. "I saw someone hiding in the bushes—or at least I thought I did—after we killed the Blackbody. He must have followed us on foot and stolen my horse when he found our camp and all of us asleep."

"Besides," added Moknay, "Pembroke has a certain . . . aura that frightened the animals. I'm sure the horses would have kicked up quite a fuss if he had been lurking nearby anywhere."

"What about Reakthi?" Cyrene put in.

"Out of the question," Thromar declared. "They want friend-Logan as much as they want the Jewel—wouldn't take one without the other."

Gritting his teeth in frustration, Logan saw the odd stare Cyrene gave him over her shoulder. He ignored the look, turning to Moknay. "Now what?"

The Murderer stroked his mustache thoughtfully. "Can't see any tracks until the sun comes up, but we can't let him get that far ahead. All I can suggest is that we split up and search. You said he was heading southwest, so he was either heading for Gelvanimore or Prifrane. Thromar and I will go south, you and Cyrene go west. The Jewel will probably be the first thing he'll try to sell—after all, it does look like it's worth the most. It shouldn't be difficult asking people if they've seen a man with a large, golden gem that keeps the Wheel balanced. Whatever happens, Thromar and I will meet you in Prifrane in a week's time."

"A week?" Logan echoed. "Do we have that much time?"

"Who's to say?" said the Murderer with a shrug. "If we don't, we'll find out. According to Barthol, much more energy has to be released before the Wheel tips on its side; we don't have to worry about that. Finding the Smythe after we recover the Jewel is something to worry about."

The apprehension and fear of the missing Jewel blinded Logan to the usual unease he felt when splitting up with Moknay and Thromar. Contradicting messages ran from his brain to his eyes: to watch for the thief, and, at the same time, to stare at the diminishing forms of his companions. Abruptly, Cyrene spurred her horse forward, and both commands were lost.

The dark forest blurred past the young man as he clung tightly to Cyrene's waist and her horse.

All sense of time fled, and Logan hardly noticed the sun rise behind him and set directly before him. Two more days of searching passed, frequented by more rests which stimulated Logan's fear even more. Nervously, he paced back and forth, kicking at pebbles and weeds.

Cyrene watched him from where she sat upon a log, sipping some wine. "Calm down," she told him. "Even *he* has to rest. Sooner or later we'll catch up to him—if he's gone west. If not, your friends will get him."

Logan ran a hand through his black hair. "You know," he snapped at her, "you're taking this too calmly. That Jewel means the destruction of your world . . . not mine. Don't you care that someone who doesn't know what he's got is running around not doing anything about it?"

Cyrene shrugged.

Logan's blue eyes narrowed. "Let's put it this way," he said. "Without that Jewel, Vaugen won't be after us with such flair now."

The girl's eyes blazed at the mention of the Imperator, and she focused on Logan. "At the pace we've been traveling, he'll never find us anyway," she retorted. "If I was really that single-minded, I would never have gone so far or so fast. I practically rode my horse to death carrying you and all." She stood up and jabbed a finger in Logan's direction. "I'm here because I want to gain something, just like your other friends— just like you. I want to see Vaugen dead, and you're the best chance I've got of running into him. That's why I'm helping you—so you can help me."

Logan turned away from the blonde, glaring up angrily at the Hills of Sadroia which loomed above him. In three days time he and Cyrene had reached the southeastern base of the Hills, and, if they had the Jewel, they could have already begun the search for the Smythe. Logan saw there were a lot of mountains, but the southern portion was a region of foothills, easily scaled by someone as healthy and as young as Logan. He used to have fun climbing mountains like those back on Earth—backpacking in national parks or just scuttling up reefs at the beach.

Melancholy set in as Logan reminisced about his previous world. It was, at most times, a rat-hole, but it did have its good points. The recreational devices of California were better suited to Logan's tastes than the Sparrillian equivalent. He'd rather ride a roller coaster than brawl in a tavern or slay a dragon. Slay a dragon? He had hardly seen any really bizarre monsters here—only that grey thing that he had killed outside of Eadarus. The other beasts had been explained to him—like the Blackbody and the Demon.

Softened by his emotions, Logan turned back to Cyrene, momentarily forgetting about the thief. "What's a chomprat?" he wondered.

The girl let out a short laugh, remembering she had called Logan that. "A chomprat is a furry beast about the size of a small pony with large ears and a pink nose. It usually eats through anything; hence the name."

A big rat, Logan nodded to himself. A big fat rat that chomps. And a waterfoal, he guessed, would probably be a horse of the water . . . a sea horse! A sea horse? But Moknay had quipped that they weren't riding them! Were the sea horses here big enough to ride?

A familiar buzz suddenly flapped into Logan's brain, and the young man frowned as the sensation of discord returned. For the past three days he hadn't been bothered much by the feeling—oh, every so often it kicked him in the butt to remind him that it was there, but it had not returned with any strength. This time, Logan knew, it was growing stronger.

Cyrene noticed the young man clamp his hands to his head. "Matthew? What's wrong?" she asked, concerned.

Logan snarled, "Just this stupid feeling I get—like when the Blackbody attacked."

Terror welled up within him and Cyrene as they scanned the forest to their backs for another flaring black form. Thankfully, Logan realized the infernal disharmony was not going to get much worse, although it continued to rattle about in his skull.

As the sun hung directly above them, Logan caught a brilliant flare to the northeast, slightly obscured by the Hills.

Some of the mountains gleamed with a golden light as the sensation increased.

"He's behind us!" Logan cried, pointing into the Hills. "He must have entered the Hills and we passed him!"

The golden glow reflected in Cyrene's deep blue eyes and illuminated the fear that surged inside her. She, although not to Moknay's degree, Logan saw, feared the Jewel.

The young man motioned toward her horse. "We've got to get him," he said.

"How?" Cyrene questioned. "He'll keep moving further into the Hills."

The young man gave her an odd smile. "That Jewel is acting like a beacon, and, besides"—he tapped his skull—"I seem to have this built-in radar. Even if he leaves the Jewel someplace, we can find it."

Hope sprang to life within Logan as the two mounted the horse and charged eastward. Cyrene directed her silver-and-blue horse through a small, level pass through the foothills. The Jewel's glare continued to throb to their right, and the buzz in Logan's head amplified. Enormous boulders surrounded them as they thundered onward, pebbles and dirt kicked up under the hooves of Cyrene's mount. There was an abrupt culmination of yellow light in the east, and the horse halted, skidding to a stop in the loose dirt. Logan lost his balance and spilled to the hard-packed soil, the sensation of mismatchment echoing the eruption of yellow.

Shaking the fuzziness out of his head, Logan gave Cyrene a weak glance. A low rumble reverberated through his ears while he grumbled about falling out of the saddle. You'd think he'd have gotten better at riding horses by now!

A deluge of horror burst in the young man's breast as the low rumble magnified, and a shower of dirt drizzled down from the mountains above him. The earth beneath him shuddered violently, quivering back and forth as if wracked by convulsions. Thunder boomed as a boulder broke away from its lofty perch and tumbled down near the two. Cyrene's horse panicked, skittering backwards. Rocks began to cascade from the hillsides, and the golden glow in the east continued pulsating.

"Matthew!" Cyrene was able to choke, as fearful as her mount.

The world seemed to come apart as the ground heaved, a jagged crack gaping wide like a cavernous mouth along the rocky floor. Nearing a frenzy, Cyrene's horse wheeled about, thundering back toward the south. Logan watched in a stunned daze as the girl and horse charged back the way they had come.

A tremendous bellow seemed to blow open Logan's mind, and the quaking below him trembled in expectation. "Cyrene!" he cried out. "Jump! For Christ's sake, jump!"

There was a blur of white fabric as the blonde dived blindly from her mount, and Logan winced at the brutal jarring she took. He crawled desperately toward her and the taste of dust filled his mouth. A hideous, high-pitched shriek momentarily drowned out the rumbling as a titanic ledge of stone gave way and crushed Cyrene's silver-and-blue horse. Clouds of dirt mushroomed into the air, and tears streamed down Logan's dirtied face as he searched for Cyrene. Fortunately, her white clothing stood out within the swirling yellow-brown fog, and Logan grabbed her hand, struggling to get to his feet.

"What is it?" the girl screamed.

"The Jewel!" Logan responded. "The second catastrophe!"

In reply, the entire portion of hill they stood upon crumbled and a violent tidal wave of rock crashed down the mountainside. Cyrene let out a curt shriek as she and Logan fell with the stones, clinging frantically to one another, gasping for breath in the dust-filled air. Pain tore through Logan's left arm as his sword wound reopened, and warm fluid began to trickle down his forearm. A savage shock snapped the young man's head back as he struck bottom, and all the wind was knocked from his lungs as Cyrene fell on top of him. The sensation of disunity heightened, aroused by the chaos about it, and the golden sun continued flaring in the east.

Run, Logan's mind advised, but his legs would not respond. Dazed, he lay there, stones and mountaintops shattering around him. The foliage of the foothills shivered fitfully and a tree careened to one side, a massive stone tumbling into it. Leaves wafted about Logan as he fought his muscles and the trembling earth and clambered to his feet. Unseen bruises ached all over his body, and the sharp, recurring pain in his arm kept reminding him of his vulnerability. Sore, he pulled Cyrene to her feet, and, together, they stumbled across the sloping hillsides. The entire world was bathed in an eerie golden light as the earth shifted and moved under their feet, unscrupulously trying to trip them up and send them to their deaths.

Cyrene stumbled, and, in trying to regain her balance, staggered up against a tree. The earth bucked, and tons of rocky soil broke free as the tree pitched forward. The blonde let out a shout, her slim arms flailing about as she started to fall. Logan's grip on her tightened as he heaved himself backwards, succeeding in pulling the girl away from the treacherous drop that had suddenly appeared before her.

Dust crept into Logan's throat, and he gagged, jumping as a boulder fell somewhere nearby. Yellow-brown dirt covered Cyrene's clothing, and her flowing skirt was torn and shredded. Both their fingers were scraped and bruised, and dust had accumulated in their hair. Their eyes became red and sore from the invading dirt, and particles of dust crawled under Logan's contact lenses, causing flashes of pain to accompany each blink of his eyes.

Half-stumbling, half-sliding, the couple forged their way down a hill and suddenly found themselves in the middle of the sun. Yellow-gold flames surrounded them, yet there was no heat. The buzz in Logan's head and a strange tingling around his neck informed the young man that they had found the Jewel.

An enraged god seemed to cry out, and the Jewel lashed out in a brilliant explosion of gold. Cyrene and Logan were flung backwards, batted away by a massive hand. Grimly, the young man waited for impact . . . the moment when he and Cyrene would smack into an unyielding mountainside and splatter like tomatoes. To his surprise, the pair struck the ground and it was the earth that gave way below them. Stars and flaring Jewels erupted behind Logan's eyelids as the ground collapsed. Cyrene fell beside him, spiraling down into what seemed to be a bottomless pit, and Logan reached out his left arm for her.

Soft fingers curled around his limb, and agony seared through the young man. Damn! he thought. His head was swirling so that he had forgotten the blood-leaking cut on his arm. Nonetheless, Cyrene grabbed hold, dangling from Logan's limp, numb limb. His right hand had luckily grasped the lip of their pit.

"Hold on," he said through clenched teeth.

As if you're going to hold on? Logan asked himself sarcastically. The ground was unmercifully heaving back and forth, pulling away from his hand and then ramming back. Sharp stones ground into the palm of his hand, and sweat and blood made his grip falter. Assaulted by pain, Logan tried to pull himself from the gaping wound in the ground, his blood also causing Cyrene's fingers to slip. She frantically sought out new handholds on his arm as Logan pulled one foot over his shoulder and out onto level ground. At any moment the young man thought he would fall back into the crevasse, precariously perched as he was—half-in, half-out. The insistent buzz and tingle were not helping his concentration either.

Golden light warmly greeted his bloodshot eyes as he raised his head from out of the chasm, bloody fingers scrabbling madly for a hold. His left arm still dangled within the abyss, Cyrene clasping the injured limb with blackness grinning up at her. With a final heave, Logan rolled himself out of the crater, gradually reeling Cyrene up as the earth bucked under him.

The golden fire began to diminish, and the rumble of turbulence died; the clouds of dust began to settle.

"Agellic," Cyrene whimpered.

Logan twisted over until he was facing the direction of the Jewel. Dirt still swirled in the air, but he could see the golden Jewel lying in a deep crater below an outcropping of rock. A form silhouetted by the dust lay next to it.

Logan turned his tear-streaked face to Cyrene and queried, "Are you okay?"

Cyrene nodded, dirt shaking free of her dark blonde hair. "I think so."

The displacement around Logan faded, and, somehow, he found the strength to sit up. He could now see the thief sprawled out near the Jewel's cavity, golden flames lapping at his bare bones.

"Jesus Christ," he cursed, "the Blackbody was right. The combined discharge of the two disasters killed him."

The young man turned away from the skeletal thief and saw Cyrene peering at him. Self-consciously, he wiped the sweat and dirt away from his face. From the way she was staring at him, he thought something might have been hanging out of his nose!

"Is something wrong?" he questioned.

An admiring glitter sparked in Cyrene's eyes. "You saved my life," she breathed. "Three times."

Logan could feel his face flush in embarrassment as he got to his feet, waiting for the shakiness to leave his muscles. His sweat suit, he noticed, was completely dusted, and clouds of dirt spumed into the air as he beat at his clothing. A number of times he hit sore spots and winced as pain nipped at his nerves. Cyrene also got to her feet, frowning as she inspected the rips in her skirt and bodice. Her eyes twinkled, however, every time she glanced at Logan.

Logan offered his hand. "Let's go see if we can salvage anything from your horse," he suggested.

The blonde took his hand, nodding. Before clambering back up, Logan slid into the deep depression and picked up the Jewel, not looking at the fleshless thief. Even the leather pouch had been burned away by the double discharge, he realized, and, uneasily, tucked the Jewel under his left arm. He had no idea where his stolen horse had run off to.

He rejoined Cyrene, who was busily struggling back up, and the two fought their way to the crushed horse. Logan winced at all the blood, but Cyrene tiptoed daintily about the rocks and puddles, tugging out the saddlebags of her mount. Fortunately, most of her rations were intact, and she was able to pull free a heavy cloak. Everything else was lost beneath the rubble.

Logan shifted the Jewel to his right arm as Cyrene approached him. Dejectedly, the blonde sat down at the edge of the slope, staring out over the mountain range and the settling dust.

"Now what?"

Logan wiped the blood off his left arm. "Don't know," he answered, flinching as he touched his wound.

Cyrene looked up at him, her hands going to his injured forearm. "We're going to have to find some way to clean ourselves up," she said. "That cut looks like it got a lot of dirt in it."

Logan blanched. An infected cut? Just what he needed—and no modern medicine! No Band-Aids! No hydrogen peroxide! If they couldn't find water . . . what? Would they have to chop off his arm?

When Logan was able to force his worries away, Cyrene was already sliding down the hillside, trying to keep her balance as she skated over the rocky surface. Puzzled, Logan trailed.

"Cyrene," he called, "where are you going?"

The blonde did not look back. "Saw something," was all she said.

Logan continued to follow, almost losing the Jewel when he reached level ground. Stumbling to keep the gem and his balance, he noticed the gnarled limb of an oak tree half-protruding from the stones. Smiling when he saw it was unbroken, the young man freed Druid Launce's staff and leaned against it as he tagged behind Cyrene. He finally caught up with her near the thief's skeleton and burned-out ditch. He blinked when he saw the small geyser of water spouting from a crack in the mountainside.

Cyrene turned back to him, smiling. "That quake upset an underground spring," she surmised, stepping up to the bubbling water.

While crystal-clear water formed a pool in the crater below the fountaining spring, the pair washed the dirt and blood from their bodies. They were even able to wash the grime from their hair by leaning over the geyser. It was like an upside-down showerhead, Logan thought. And the water was warm, not boiling hot.

The young man was a bit taken aback when Cyrene told him to strip, until she explained she would wash his clothing. Awkwardly, Logan pulled off his sweat suit and handed it to the blonde. His clothing below wasn't in much better condition, and he knew Cyrene was waiting for those as well. Feeling like a complete goon, he shed his shirt, shoes, and socks, but hesitated after that.

Cyrene had a mischievous smile on her face as she watched him. "I don't bite," she quipped, and Logan knew he didn't have to be Freud to figure *that* one out!

His cheeks grew warm and he wondered what brilliant shade of red he had become.

"There's a little grassy knoll to our left," Cyrene told him. "If you want, you can go over there . . . behind some rocks." The glitter in her deep blue eyes grew. "But I want everything," she warned.

Goon! Goon! Goon! Goon! Goon! Logan muttered to himself as he left. You got something against your body? Afraid to show it to someone who's only washing your clothes?

But she's a female! another portion of his mind declared, shocked.

Brilliant observation! Logan mocked himself. Jesus, I made myself look even dumber by standing around not wanting to give her my pants than just ripping them off and giving 'em to her!

But then you'd be naked! his mind cried out in horror.

Oh, great! Logan retorted. It's wonderful to know that I'm so knowledgeable when it comes to the human body!

Still arguing with himself, Logan rounded some boulders and walked across the grass. A few large stones lay strewn about the knoll, probably dislodged from the quake but looking rather decorative in the grassy area. He gave the area a quick scan and convinced himself he was well hidden from anyone in the mountain range. Hurriedly, he stripped off his remaining clothes and threw them over the rocks to Cyrene. In a feeble attempt to get his mind off his state, the young man unsheathed his sword and practiced swinging the blade. After a while, he became relaxed, and the cool, fresh air of the Hills stimulated every portion of his body. A gentle breeze tickled the hairs on his legs, and an oddly natural feeling crept upon Logan, quite the opposite of that disturbing buzz of disagreement.

Logan slipped the talisman over his head and sat down, sighing as the aches eased in his muscles.

"Matthew," Cyrene called to him.

Logan perked up. "What?"

"The water's collecting into a perfect pond," the blonde told him. "If you want to wash yourself, you can just jump in." Then she added, "I won't look."

Logan set his dagger, staff, sword, and the Jewel down beside the talisman. A vital, refreshing feeling flowed through his muscles, and he stood up proudly. "No, that's all right." Then he added, "You can look."

Logan was only slightly surprised when he rounded the rocks and found Cyrene already in the stone-shaped pond. The spring, he saw, was flowing into the crater formed by the Jewel's double discharge, and, like Cyrene had told him, it created the perfect pond. Eagerly, he joined her in the warm liquid while she watched him advance, blue eyes twinkling.

With a whoop, Logan splashed into the water, submerging and shaking his head free of any remaining dirt in his hair. He surfaced directly in front of Cyrene, and the crystal-clear waters were like a shimmering gown on her beautiful frame.

She was eyeing him in a like fashion.

Cyrene kicked through the pond, nosing up to the young man. Her blue eyes were locked on his as she halted an inch away from his face. "How much?" she asked.

Logan wiped water from his face. "Huh?" he exclaimed. "How much what?"

Deep blue eyes trailed up Logan's body. "Money," said the blonde with a smirk. "How much money?"

Logan couldn't stop the grin that spread across his face. She was using his exact lines herself! "What do you take me for?" Logan questioned, softly. "A chomprat?"

Cyrene blinked, striking Logan with a face full of water. "Oh, you!" she scolded.

Logan failed to duck the liquid and sent a wave of his own at Cyrene. The girl's blonde hair darkened as the clear water flooded over her. She jumped backwards, half-out of the water.

Logan's eyes locked on her upper torso as it crested the surface, droplets of water running down her bare chest.

The pond seemed to get warmer, and Logan wished the water wasn't so clear.

Cyrene swam around him, and soft, wet arms draped around his neck. Her cheek pressed up against his own, and the feel of flesh on flesh made every nerve in Logan's body spark to life.

"I can never thank you enough," she whispered into his ear. "You saved my life."

Logan lost the use of his tongue as Cyrene pressed up against him, her firm breasts flattening against his back. A long fingernail traced down Logan's neck to his shoulder, applying just enough pressure to leave a faint red line. Then she was gone, and Logan spun around as she stepped out of the water, brushing back her wet hair. The lowering sun gleamed off the liquid that trickled down her slim curves, and she extended a hand. Together, the two went to the grassy knoll, their wet clothes drying upon the rocks around them. Logan's eyes were transfixed on Cyrene's shapely backside as she led him to the hillock, grasping tightly to his hand. When she turned, her lips met his and her hands roamed across his wet body eagerly. Motions as fluid as water brought them down onto the grass, and the raging beasts of Logan's desires broke out of their cages.

An almost godly amount of restraint halted him.

Cyrene looked at him. "What is it?"

"I—I don't . . ." Logan stuttered. "What if you get pregnant?"

The blonde threw back her head and laughed. "Matthew," she giggled, "we're not wed in Agellic's eyes—we can't bear any children."

The young man raised his eyebrows in question.

"At the ceremony, the priest weaves the spell of bonding between the man and the woman," Cyrene explained. "It is that spell that makes the woman fertile. Before that spell is cast, women can't bear children. It's physically impossible." Her deep blue eyes were aglow with amusement. "Your world isn't like that?"

Logan shook his head in dumbed fascination. "No, it isn't— but I wish it was." Then he asked, "And you can't get pregnant until after you're married?"

"It's that way for every woman on this world," the blonde declared. "And this is one unwed woman who is extremely grateful to you for saving her life."

Their lips fused once more, and all the soreness was gone from Logan's muscles. His questing hands moved down Cyrene's body, traveling across her sleek hips and firm thighs. Desire overpowered him and his actions became faster, his fingers wanting to be everywhere at once on the gorgeous creature below him. Cyrene's own fingers ran through his black hair, her shapely hips undulating beneath him in her own hunger. Invisible tongues of fire remained everywhere Cyrene touched him, and the girl gasped as Logan's hands explored her beauty. Her shapely legs parted invitingly, and Logan paused a moment, drinking in every detail about the voluptuous blonde sprawled beneath him. Yearningly, Cyrene's fingers closed in about his manhood and directed him toward her moist orifice. Slowly, teasingly, his loins aflame, Logan slid into her, gasping for breath.

The fire built as the two gave in to their desires, arms entwined about one another as the rhythm of their hips quickened. Passion Logan thought he was incapable of experiencing burned within his body, and the ecstasy increased as he glided back and then pushed deeper. Cyrene's fingernails raked across his back, her breathing the heavy panting of a wild animal. The fervor heightened until the two shared an explosive release, and their grips slowly eased. Logan withdrew reluctantly from Cyrene's tightness, an arm about her waist. The blonde kissed him once, silently, and sighed as she lay back onto the blanket of grass.

Logan's passion gradually diminished and weariness set in. The harsh days of riding, the narrow escapes from the upheaval, all descended upon the young man until even his sexual drive was quenched.

Holding the slender blonde to him, Logan felt sleep challenge him, and he succumbed.

A gargling rasp pulled Logan out of his deep sleep, and he raised his head with a weary groan. Cyrene still lay beside him, beautiful in sleep, her bare breasts rising and falling as she breathed. The urges of the night before refilled his mind as he stared at the blonde's luscious frame highlighted by the midmorning rays of the sun. Suddenly, the hideous death rattle sounded again, and Logan snapped up and around.

Immediately, the young man looked to find any red and silver, thinking what he saw was a dream, and yet, nothing even glinted with the familiar colors. Pulling himself into a sitting position, Logan stared at the line of figures blocking the knoll. Cyrene stirred beside him and also saw the row of forms confronting them.

Reakmor Farkarrez took a step toward them, his severed flesh rasping as air passed through his windpipe. "How quaint," he mocked, his voice distorted by his slit throat. "Matthew Logan has found a slut."

Instant fury boiled away the fear and wonderment, and Logan made a threatening move. He realized, then, that he was naked and unarmed, his sword, staff, and dagger lying off to one side beside the talisman and Jewel.

"You . . . !" Cyrene gasped, sitting rigid. "You're dead!"

Farkarrez grinned, and the effect was hideous: His mouth and slit throat gave his lean features two smiles. "Oh, yes, I am," he answered, "and so are all my men." He marched arrogantly toward the couple, glaring down at them with eyes unable to reflect emotion. "And soon, so shall you."

· 10 ·

Capture

Logan made a frantic dive for his weapons. His fingers were inches away from his sword when a cold hand clamped around his wrist and held him back. He glanced up to see the skeletal thief smiling down at him, its bony hand locked around his in a grotesque embrace. Although he strained against the skeleton's grasp, the young man could not break free. The creature had no muscles, and yet was denying him his blade.

Farkarrez took another confident step forward. "It is hopeless," he gargled. "You now belong to us."

Cyrene rose into a crouch, her blue eyes flaming angrily. "You bastard," she seethed. "I killed you once—I'll kill you again."

The dead Reakmor smiled down at her with his chipped teeth. "You'll find that quite difficult to do, my dear," he stated, "since you yourself realized I am already dead." His pale, yellowish hand stroked Cyrene's blonde hair. "But it is good to know you are as fiery as ever."

In rage and revulsion, Cyrene went to jerk her head away when dead fingers suddenly snared her hair. She let out a startled gasp as Farkarrez pulled her to him, holding her by her yellow mane. "I suggest you give in," the Reakmor advised Logan, "or I shall do to her what she did to me."

The sight of Farkarrez's living corpse holding Cyrene prisoner sapped the rebellion from Logan. The girl appeared so helpless, so beautiful, so fragile; Logan could not imagine bringing harm to her.

Drained of his defiance, Logan pulled away from his weapons.

Farkarrez grinned, stroking Cyrene's bare shoulder with his free hand. "Good," he rasped. He turned his deadened eyes on the blonde, and Logan thought he saw lust flare in those emotionless pupils. "It is a pity," the Reakmor sighed with his hideous death rattle. "You are as attractive as I suspected." His green-yellow hand cupped a naked breast. "How unfortunate that, in this state, I may not enjoy you properly. But I shall find a way."

The cold, bloodless fingers on her chest sent a million icicles of terror and disgust through the blonde as she tried to rip her hair out of the dead Reakmor's grip. Roughly, he snapped her head back, bringing tears to her deep blue eyes.

"Do not struggle," he growled, and his severed flesh flapped obscenely, "or I may become very upset with you."

Logan yanked his wrist away from the skeleton grinning over him and pointed an angry finger at Farkarrez. "You leave her alone, goddamn it!" he commanded.

The eyebrows above the dead eyes arched upward. "Is that a nice thing to say?" the Reakmor mocked. "*You* certainly haven't been leaving her alone."

Cyrene furiously rammed her slim elbow into Farkarrez's groin. The Reakmor was slightly unsteadied by the blow, but his grip on her remained firm.

He smiled down at her with his double mouths. "You weren't paying attention," he smirked. "Things like that don't affect me any longer."

Turning away from Cyrene's ineffectual attack, Logan scanned the animated cadavers surrounding them. There were over fifteen enclosing them in a half-circle, a cliff at Logan's back. Many of the corpses looked like soldiers Logan and his companions had run into. Yes, he even recognized the crossbowman Moknay had killed in Barthol's chamber. The dagger wound in his face was marred with green, black, and yellow flesh.

The skeletal thief gathered together Logan's and Cyrene's supplies and clothing and carried them away. With a violent shove, Farkarrez threw Cyrene toward Logan and stalked back to his men. He ordered his soldiers to guard the hillock, and the half-circle of cadavers moved closer. Then the sadist leader faced his captives.

"We're going to wait now," he told them, mockingly. "Very soon my scout will reach Vaugen, and the Imperator himself will soon be on his way here. Until he gets here, I suppose we'll just have to find some way to amuse ourselves."

There was a twisting in his stomach as Logan watched the Reakmor's grin widen.

Like a living piece of shadow, Moknay glided out of the darkness and into the midmorning sky, his grey eyes as grim as death. He kept his cape wrapped about him, concealing his strap of daggers as he skated through the cobblestone streets of Gelvanimore. Cautiously, he scanned the area about him before ducking into a building. His steel-grey eyes glistened in the torchlight and locked on the massive form flirting with a barmaid.

Moknay's boot connected with Thromar's rump and got his attention.

Thromar blinked. "Oh, it's you," he said. "What is it? Have you found the thief?"

"Have *I* found the thief?" the Murderer repeated. "What about you? 'Taverns are excellent places to learn information' and 'I'll just talk to wanderers stopping in for a drink. Maybe they'll know something.' Have *you* found the thief?"

The huge fighter stroked his reddish brown beard. "After extensive prying and espying, I can rightfully say—no." His beady eyes flickered. "What about you?"

The Murderer's dark figure seemed to flow into a chair. "Yes," he replied, "in a sense. I ran into someone coming from Frelars and he saw a horrible glare in the Hills yesterday. Ran like a Demon to get here before the sky crashed down upon him. It sounds like our thief."

Thromar scratched his head. "The thief we're chasing glares?" he wondered.

Moknay threw up his arms. "No, but the Jewel does, you thistlebrain! That must have been the Jewel flaring up again."

The fighter nodded. "So the thief was hiding in the Hills, but that's the way friend-Logan went. Do you think he'll see it?"

"I would think so," responded Moknay. "The man I talked to was at least a league from the Hills and he still saw the flare-up."

"So I suppose I'll have to leave this wonderful little information center?" queried Thromar.

"We told Logan we'd meet him in Prifrane in a week, and

that gives us less than two days to get there. I just hope he's recovered the Jewel."

"I think that should be the least of your worries, Murderer," Thromar suddenly declared, spearing the air as he pointed to the tavern doorway.

Moknay pivoted to see the squad of uniformed men entering the bar. There were well over ten of the Guards now inside, and Agellic knew how many outside!

The lead Guardsman stepped forward, his eyes aglow with triumph. "Moknay the Murderer and Thromar the Rebel, you are hereby under arrest by order of His Ultimate Paramount, King Mediyan, for assisting an Outsider dangerous to Sparrill and her Ruler. If you resist, you shall be slain."

A quartet of archers flanked the lead Guard; Moknay and Thromar moved.

The arrows flew.

A shambling corpse pulled the unclothed couple apart and dragged Cyrene over to one side. The smell of the animated dead was unbearable, and the one that had just taken the blonde looked like someone had crushed its skull with a heavy wooden club. Logan swiftly turned to Druid Launce's staff guarded by the undead Reakthi and knew how some of them had been slain.

"We're going to play a little game," Farkarrez rasped, his emotionless eyes roving up and down Cyrene's naked body, "just to pass the time along."

"You whoreson," Cyrene snarled, squirming in the corpse's grasp. "I swear I'll see you dead."

The Reakmor sighed, and Logan's stomach churned as the release of air came from his slit throat. "I grow tired of explaining," he gargled. "I am . . ."

Cyrene's struggles increased. "You have to breathe, don't you?" she shouted. "I'll rip your lungs from your maggot-filled chest!"

Farkarrez leaned back on the grass, smirking. "Oh, that may cause problems, but I'm sure I'll manage. The only reason air passes through me at all is so that I may think and speak for myself." He waved a hand. "Only spellcasters know the secrets of our bodies, and breathing is necessary for the nurturing component of the air to reach my mind and to also activate a special portion of my throat so that I may make sounds recognizable to you. That is the only reason I breathe. My men, on the other hand, can neither speak nor think for themselves. That is because Groathit did not feel it necessary for them to do so."

Hideous! Logan's mind screamed. There was a certain aspect of physiology to Groathit's magic! How, then, was Farkarrez's brain kept alive with no blood? That was probably where the real magic came in.

A second cadaver shuffled up to Cyrene, and Logan froze. The Reakthi had no sword arm, and the young man remembered the soldier who had given him his own wound upon his left arm. In a blind rage, Logan had wheeled about and severed the man's arm from his shoulder. Thank God only Farkarrez could think, or else a number of the shuffling corpses would seek revenge on the young man.

The one-armed Reakthi handed Cyrene her dagger and ambled off. The corpse holding her let go and also lurched off to one side. The sun gleamed off the girl's hair and flesh as she stood there, legs spread slightly as she stanced herself for battle. Her blue eyes hungrily peered at the blade she held tightly in her hand.

Farkarrez withdrew a bundle and unwrapped a number of daggers. Once again Logan thought he saw emotion flicker in those dead eyes as the Reakmor glanced up at the nude blonde stanced before him.

"I think you'll find this game quite entertaining," he rasped, picking up one of his daggers. "You see, what you did just before you slit my throat was something I've never seen anyone do before, and Reakmor Farkarrez never makes the same mistake twice. So, as a bit of education for both of us, we'll just have to see where your weaknesses are in that little dagger-deflecting trick of yours."

Apprehension grew as Logan watched the Reakmor's blade glint in the sunlight. Cyrene's deep blue eyes were flashing from side to side, attempting to formulate an escape plan. They had given her back her dagger, and, by Brolark, she was going to use it!

The mountain air shrieked as Farkarrez's dagger hurled out at the blonde. Still looking for a route to freedom, Cyrene knocked the whizzing blade aside. Logan smirked in sympathetic triumph, but Farkarrez readied another dagger. Cyrene easily batted the second weapon away as well.

"You're quite good," Farkarrez complimented her. "You'd have to be—you killed me. But I have the feeling you can't keep this up forever."

Helplessness and fear filled Logan with a mixture equalling dread. Farkarrez, he knew, was right, and the Reakmor was no longer alive, so he would never tire. Cyrene, however, had had three days of torturous riding plus one day of narrow escapes. She wouldn't be able to last long in the Reakmor's game.

The next dagger nicked Cyrene on the finger as she knocked it to her right, and the fourth she had to dodge. The half-circle of silent corpses unnerved her, and she was concentrating more on escape than on immediate survival.

Farkarrez's fifth dagger creased her hip, and the blonde staggered. She barely deflected the sixth blade that screeched for her head, and the seventh knife's hilt struck her knee, knocking her to the ground.

Logan's muscles instinctively tensed as he watched the blonde go down, his mind fiercely trying to think of a rescue. Farkarrez held an eighth dagger ready, smirking at Cyrene as she slowly pulled herself to her feet.

"If this had been combat," the dead Reakmor said with a grin, "I would not have hesitated, but this is, after all, only a game." The knife wavered in his yellowish hand. "Are you ready?"

"Bastard," gritted Cyrene.

Farkarrez chuckled at the insult, and his slit throat quivered in delight. "Good, you're ready."

The dagger sailed from the Reakmor's bloodless fingers, and Logan decided a direct charge at the living corpse would do no good. Neither would attacking any of his men. Farkarrez already had the Jewel in his possession, and his soldiers had enclosed Logan and Cyrene in their half-circle. Still, they had to wait for Vaugen . . .

Sweat dribbled down Cyrene's face as she turned the eighth dagger aside, but the ninth blade skimmed her shoulder, filling her right arm with searing pain. She could feel the warm touch of her life fluid as it trickled down her bare skin, and, exhausted, she waited for Farkarrez's final throw.

"Farkarrez!" a sudden voice cried out, and Cyrene opened her eyes in wonder.

Both blonde and animated corpse saw the figure stanced upon the cliff, its feet precariously close to the edge. It took a moment before the weariness and pain lifted the fog from Cyrene's eyes and she recognized the form as Logan. Farkarrez, meanwhile, had fallen silent, his dead eyes once again hinting at the slightest bit of emotion.

Logan gave the cliff before him a quick glance before turning back to the dead Reakmor. "You don't have everything you came to get," the young man declared. "And you never thought to guard our backs—after all, who would try to escape by leaping to their death?" Logan's blue eyes flashed. "It's my turn to call the shots, Farkarrez, and I say let her go."

The Reakmor got to his feet, his pale fists clenched at his sides. "You are a fool, Matthew Logan," he gargled. "We have the Jewel."

A powerful force of terror built itself up inside the young man as he gambled with the corpse. "You only have the Jewel," he corrected, "but your leader wants more. If you don't let Cyrene go, you'll only have half of what you came to collect."

The terror started to subside as Logan watched the deceased Reakmor stop and think. One of Farkarrez's soldiers took a shambling step toward the young man, and Logan inched nearer to the cliff.

"I swear it!" he yelled. "I'll jump! Then where will you be?" He chanced a snide smirk. "Your leader won't like what you've caused."

A swift hand halted the dead soldier starting toward Logan, and Farkarrez turned his emotionless gaze on Cyrene. There was silence in the Hills as the Reakmor glanced back at Logan.

"You are fortunate you are no use to Vaugen as an animated corpse," Farkarrez scowled. He waved a yellow-green hand toward Cyrene. "You heard your lover," he spat. "You are free."

Cyrene remained where she was, staring at the young man and dead Reakmor. Somehow, Logan was important enough to the Reakthi that he had to be kept alive, but did the blonde dare leave? Vaugen himself was coming here! Vaugen! The man who murdered her father! The man Cyrene swore vengeance on! She could have her chance to strike back for her father—

or Farkarrez might kill her before the Imperator even got within three leagues of the Hills. She, unlike Logan, was of no importance to the Reakthi.

Hastily, the blonde sprinted through the half-circle of dead soldiers, bundled her provisions in her arms, and hurried down the hillside. She hesitated a moment, giving Logan a swift glance before she raced around a boulder and was lost from sight.

"And none of your men leave this camp tonight," Logan ordered. "Not until she's far away."

Farkarrez ground his chipped teeth. "As you command," he grated. "Now kindly step away from that cliff."

"Not until tonight," he retorted, "when I know Cyrene's safely away."

The Reakmor released an animallike snarl as he turned away and started retrieving his daggers. Certain Farkarrez was not going to rush him, Logan peered down at the mountains below him. Sparrill was stretched out before him, green and beautiful, yet that insistent buzz of disharmony hung in the clean air. The Sea of Hedelva glittered to the young man's left, and, questing, his eyes scanned the south. Moknay and Thromar were somewhere in that direction, probably heading toward Prifrane. Hopefully, Cyrene could get there in time and tell the two men where he was. He had only won a small skirmish against Farkarrez—the real battle would start when Vaugen arrived . . .

Matthew Logan stared as shadows splashed themselves across the greenery of Sparrill, reaching out dark tendrils toward the Hills and his perch. The ring of dead soldiers waited silently behind him, their putrid odor spoiling the freshness of the mountains. Farkarrez reclined against a nearby boulder.

"Surely the girl is a safe distance by now," the Reakmor said. "Why don't you come away from there?"

Logan tore his eyes away from the encroaching darkness and peered down at his bare feet. "Give me back my clothes," he answered.

Farkarrez waved to one of his warriors and the corpse shuffled over to the pile of provisions. As it went to move aside the Jewel, there was a brilliant flare of light and the animated corpse crumpled to the ground, dead once more.

Quietly, Logan cursed. If only Farkarrez had been the one to get his clothes, then the other corpses would have been left here leaderless and escape would have been much easier.

Reakmor Farkarrez scrambled to his feet, his dead eyes narrowing. "You have odd fortune," he said to Logan. "I had no idea the Jewel was capable of doing such things. Fortune, however, is also on my side—for I have the Jewel." He turned to the skeletal thief. "You, bring him his clothes, and do not touch the Jewel."

The magically intact skeleton clattered over to the supplies and pulled free the already half-exposed clothing. Obediently, it tossed them in Logan's direction and returned to its place in the half-circle.

Leaving the protective bargaining of his perch, Logan hastily jumped back into his garments. When he finished tugging on his sweat suit, Farkarrez had already stationed two men at the cliff, expressionless eyes and faces staring dumbly at Logan.

"You must not be one for sport," Farkarrez rasped. "Why did you make me release the girl? I had such things in store for her."

Logan felt the warmth of his clothing joined by the heat of rage. "You're sick!" he spat.

Farkarrez chuckled his hideous chuckle. "Far from sick," he quipped. "I'm dead."

While the Reakmor's garbled laughter echoed out across the Hills of Sadroia, Logan's experiences of the past few weeks returned. Perhaps there was another way of tricking the dead warrior.

"Why don't you make yourself alive again?" the young man questioned.

Farkarrez's eyes sparked briefly. "How?"

Logan shrugged, hiding his grin. "The Jewel is all-powerful, isn't it? It kept that Zackaron guy alive for years—why can't it bring you back?"

The Reakmor laughed harshly. "I am not stupid," he declared. "We just saw what the Jewel did to one of my men. Greed will not overcome my caution concerning *that* gemstone."

"But your man wasn't touching the Jewel," argued Logan. "It just kind of flared up. It might have been nothing more than an accident."

"Your suicidal threat technique worked much better,"

Farkarrez gloated, smirking in two places. "Next time, stay with that."

Logan frowned and turned to the south again. If he wanted to get out of this mess, he'd probably have to wait for Moknay and the others. Hopefully, they'd rescue him before Vaugen got here. If they didn't, Logan wouldn't be here when his friends finally did come for him.

Stars soon flickered into sight as the sky turned black, and Logan lay on his back, staring up at the pinpoints of light. Farkarrez and his zombies stood motionless about him, and some appeared to be asleep . . . or at least shut down. There were still far too many to run from, and, even if Logan did escape, he couldn't leave the Jewel to fall into Vaugen's hands. The Jewel! If only it would flare up again and knock out some more men.

The young man paused, gazing at the night sky. It was odd that the soldier had been felled by such a small flare-up of light. During the last disaster, the thief had been burned, but not entirely disintegrated. The corpse toppled as if it had been instantly snuffed out. Why would the Jewel instantly down one of Farkarrez's warriors?

Silently, the young man rose up on one elbow, scanning the corpses guarding him. If only he could get to his supplies!

Logan crept forward, attempting to hide himself in the darkness. One of the dead Reakthi guarding his supplies was inactive, and the others all moved rather sluggishly. If Logan suddenly burst through the ring of cadavers, he should be able to grab his weapons before any of the corpses reached him. Abruptly, he could feel Farkarrez's eyes upon him, confident the young man would fail, unarmed or otherwise. But Logan knew better. He wasn't going to use his weapons . . . he just wanted it to look like that. Let Farkarrez think this was nothing more than another one of his sick "games."

As Logan shot forward, Farkarrez called out, "Your weapons cannot harm us. We're already dead."

The young man grinned to himself—he had judged the sadist Reakmor perfectly. Farkarrez had purposely allowed Logan to attain his supplies probably to have his men subdue him and crush his last hope of escape. Logan, however, knew his escape was imminent.

At least, he hoped it was.

Rolling past outstretched arms of decaying flesh, Logan halted beside his provisions. Dead warriors shuffled toward him, and, just for good measure, Logan tucked Moknay's dagger into his belt. The Jewel glittered beside him, but he ignored the gleaming gem and pulled out the small bulb of stone that lay beneath it.

Blood-red light bathed the hillock as two corpses crashed to the earth, their magical life pulled from their decaying shells. There was a startled shout from Farkarrez as Logan spun the talisman over his head, striking another zombie across the face. The Reakthi collapsed, portions of his body immediately shriveling up. Whirling the glaring talisman out before him, Logan gathered up the Jewel and his sword.

"Pull back!" Farkarrez was screaming. "Get away from him!"

Logan smirked to himself as the remaining cadavers stumbled backwards, glazed eyes reflecting the bloody glare of the talisman. Hastily, Logan snatched up Druid Launce's staff—everything else had been taken by Cyrene. He then took a cautious step down the hill, watching the troop of animated dead cluster before him. He realized something was missing from the horde of corpses, and bony fingers suddenly clamped around his throat. Damn! The only swift soldier had been the skeletal thief, and Logan had allowed himself to be captured by it once again!

Fluttering down from where it always lingered about the young man, the disturbing buzz of mismatchment resounded in Logan's ears. This time, however, there was a certain tone about it—an odd sense of benevolence. It was not accusing Logan of being an intruder, and Logan felt as if the sensation disliked the animated Reakthi more than it did the young man; it wanted to help.

Logan agreed.

The buzz strengthened in Logan's mind and the red flare of the talisman suddenly snaked its way up Logan's arm. The thief's fingers shattered into dust as the red glow reached Logan's neck and continued to entirely consume the young man. He could barely hear Farkarrez's voice as the buzz increased, and red light obscured his vision. With a sudden charge, Logan hurled himself into the middle of the Reakthi zombies, and corpses fell about him, lifeless once more. The buzz in his head became almost painful as the glowing young man forced his way toward Farkarrez and drove the flaming talisman into the Reakmor's magically beating heart. Fear exploded in the dead man's eyes as the red glare vanished from around Logan and extinguished the sorcery flowing in Farkarrez's veins.

Reakmor Farkarrez died a second time.

The persistent buzz stopped as the stone talisman splintered into fragments. Hurriedly, Logan looked over his shoulder at the remaining cadavers and bolted into the Hills. Although he was lost, on foot, and had no food, a feeling of pride filled the young man as he ran down the mountainside. He had escaped on his own power—through his own intelligence—and had not depended on anyone else to come to his rescue. Only trouble now was—where was Prifrane?

Lost

The stars and moon dimly lit the rocky terrain as Matthew Logan jogged down a slanting hillside. His left arm grasped the Jewel, throwing his balance off somewhat. Many times Druid Launce's staff saved him from falling, its sturdy wood supporting the young man as he scrambled through the mountains. He threw anxious glances over his shoulder, expecting to see Farkarrez's dead warriors shuffling after him, but he knew he had left them far behind. The night and mountains only surrounded him, and one hillside looked very much like another as Logan slid to level ground.

The pride that had swelled within him had faded, and a gnawing doubt had replaced it. Exhaling, Logan sat down upon a large rock, his blue eyes scanning the darkness. He was alone, he mused. Alone and lost in this lousy place. The first time he had been lost, at least he had had a horse to do the trekking. Now he was on foot, trailed by alive and dead Reakthi alike, and he had no idea where he was. Oh, how he longed to be back in his apartment!

An odd thought popped into Logan's mind. Back home! How was this affecting things back home? Did time travel at the same rate on Earth as it did in Sparrill? If it did, how much strife had he caused? His parents, his friends, all of them would be worried sick about him. They'd probably report him as missing and there'd be a big huge search for Matthew Logan all throughout Santa Monica! And, with his luck, his job was no longer his, and his landlady had probably rented his apartment to somebody else already. Jesus H. Christ! Logan wanted to get back home, but would there really be anything to come back to? No job, no apartment, no explanation for the cops, his family, or his friends. Damn this stupid place! he cursed. It

throws me inside out, upside down, and completely messes up
my life in both worlds! Damn it to hell, I want to go home!

Depression set in as Logan looked at the night-filled mountain range. He wanted to go home, all right, but he couldn't do
that right now. He was lost. At this point he couldn't tell his ass
from a hole in the ground! And here he was, grumbling about
his previous world and how grand it used to be before that
goddamn wind picked him up and spit him out in Denzil!

Logan's eyes brightened. When he and Cyrene had first
entered the Hills, he had reminisced about the hills he had
climbed back home. Backpacking had not been unfamiliar to
Logan, and he had learned quite a few helpful hints should he
ever get lost.

The stars twinkled down at the young man and he cursed.
Confound it! he exclaimed to himself. The damn stars aren't
the same here! There isn't any North Star here so I can fix my
position!

Immediately, he calmed himself down. His anger could give
way to frustration or panic, and he knew well that people who
got lost usually wound up running in circles. The first thing
to do was stay calm. So there's no North Star; there are other
techniques to determine direction. Fortunately, the night sky
was clear, and Logan knew he would not have to rely on moss
or darker tree trunks to decipher east from west. There was
another trick he had learned to tell direction.

Yeah, he thought, wait 'til the sun comes up.

The young man kicked himself for being so pessimistic and
searched out a small stick. He poked the twig into the dirt at his
feet and moved out of the light. With the moon behind it, the
stick cast a pale shadow on the ground, which Logan marked
with a pebble. Humming to himself, Logan turned and started
pacing, glancing at his glowing watch every now and then.
Although the face of his watch still glimmered red and silver,
Logan could tell when a few minutes were up and looked back
down at the stick. The shadow had shifted slightly to the right
of the first pebble, and Logan now knew that the east was to
his right. Remembering that his friends had told him Prifrane
lay to the west, the young man left the twig sticking up from
the ground and headed to his left. That little method had come
in handy, he observed, but he still had to find his way out of
the Hills if he expected to find the town.

Logan suddenly halted, anger seeping into his blue eyes. The most important thing in the rest of his survival tactics was to travel in a straight line, which, according to Earthly rules, would, sooner or later, come to a road, a railroad line, or a stream. Here, of course, a railroad or a road were quite unlikely. Aw, shit! Logan swore to himself. Why does everything have to happen to me?

Murmuring about his foul luck, Logan found another boulder and sat down. In about five hours the sun would rise behind him, marking the morning of the sixth day, and he knew he would never make it to the town in a day. Not only that, the fact that he had no food caused his stomach to rumble furiously, and his feet hurt from slipping and sliding down angling hillsides. Gently, he rubbed at his sore ankles, and weariness pounced upon him like a vicious predator. You need to rest, the fatigue whispered. Find your bearings, head west, then spot the town. All that needed to be done in the morning, so sleep.

The exhaustion's logic agreed with Logan's, and his eyelids closed: He was soon asleep.

"You should not be here."

The voice arose from the eddying tidepools of red and silver light, piercing the stillness with its echoing, authoritative tone.

"You hold sway to the entire multiverse. You are an Outsider. You should not be here."

Matthew Logan's eyes flickered open, staring at the spiraling vortex of blood and metal that drenched the Hills with its blinding glare. A familiar sensation of wrongness swelled up around and within him, and a manlike shape composed of complete blackness stepped toward him.

"I am a Being of the Megacosmos—you are an infectious microorganism to this world. You do not belong here. You are intruding. You upset the natural Balance of things and cause much havoc to be spread throughout the Macrocosm. Even the land senses your difference. Can you not hear its damnations?"

The reverberating, powerful voice of the Blackbody gradually faded into the vacuum of lights and colors, and a wheezing chorus of whispering voices replaced it. The sense of mismatchment expanded, rippling as the whispers grew louder, and Logan could tell the chorus belonged to the feeling itself.

Get out. Outsider. Get out. Outsider. Get out. Outsider. Get out.

The sensation became overpowering, knocking Logan to his knees as it tried to pry apart his skull. The damning whispers slowly receded, but the wrongness inside him remained. Helplessly, the young man looked up into the red-and-silver illumination and saw hazy forms encircling him. Only their faces were detailed—all else was out of focus. They were his friends, people he had known in Sparrill and on Earth; they were his foes, from Sparrill and Earth alike. All gazed down at him, unaccepting scowls drawn across their faces.

"Get out, Outsider," Moknay snarled.

"You should not be here," spat Cyrene.

"You do not belong," his parents condemned.

"Parasite," Groathit cursed.

"Murdering stranger," Druid Launce accused.

"You are not one of us," Priestess Mara charged.

"Defiler of the land," growled Thromar.

"Intruder," his coworkers sneered.

From face to face the unfriendly scowl was the same. All of these people told the truth! Logan cried to himself. He was an Outsider; he was a stranger! But they had no right to blame him! No right! Was it his fault every way he tried to get home loused things up even more? He was different here, he knew that—why was that such a crime?

"You are capable of causing the destruction of the entire Macrocosm if you stay," the Blackbody answered his unspoken question. *"You also cause great unrest in the natural Balance of things."*

The feeling of disharmony gained more power, its agonizing buzz drilling into Logan's brain. The whispering chorus returned and the hazy forms chanted along. Teeth clenched as if to battle the pain, Logan clamped his hands over his ears in a feeble attempt to block out the words. But the chanting was inside him as well, and he could not force the voices out. Screaming, the young man shut his eyes and curled into a fetal position. Chants and buzz strengthened until Logan's skull felt as if it would explode . . .

* * *

Sunlight seeped into the Hills as Logan's eyes popped open. Stupid dreams, he grumbled. Stupid red-and-silver dreams! Just what the hell was that one supposed to prove? Oh, well, I've got other things to do than sit around and interpret dreams.

Logan got up from his rocky bed, stretching, and scanned the quiet hillsides. The dirt and stones were lit by the yellow rays of the sun, and the cool mountain air seemed to restore Logan's strength. There was something astonishing about the very air of Sparrill, the young man noted. It seemed to perk him up— return strength he would have thought lost forever. The past week had consisted of three days of harsh horseback riding, one day of escaping earthquakes, and one day of capture. Not to mention his night with Cyrene and his previous night running. Not only that, he hadn't eaten since his capture; and yet, the air of Sparrill lifted him—gave him the strength he needed to go on. Maybe it didn't affect just him either, he mused. Most of the people he had seen had been in pretty good shape. Something in the air enhanced people's health, he guessed, and his was included.

Get out.

Logan froze. Streams of sunlight cascaded into the Hills, blazing down upon him like a spotlight as the whispering dissipated. A familiar buzz boiled upward from the earth, sinking into Logan with the sensation of misplacement. Bewildered, the young man leaned against Launce's staff, eyes wide as he searched for the astral choir.

Outsider, you do not belong. Get out.

His dream! Logan recalled. The sensation in his dream had spoken, and now, it truly *had* found its voice! The feeling of disharmony itself was communicating with the young man! Jesus Christ! That was even worse than before!

Intruder, the disunity said.

"Shut up!" roared Logan, wheeling around in an attempt to find the speaker. "I am *not* intruding! This is your fault!"

The rasping chorus did not reply, and, somehow, Logan knew he was right. The very feeling that disturbed him so much had had a hand in his transportation from Earth to Sparrill. At first Logan had assumed the sensation to be an exaggerated version of unfamiliarity—like the feeling one gets going to someplace new and different—but it was more. It was the very essence of the land, that aspect that made the enhanced health possible, the law that made women infertile until marriage. Somehow, this god-awful sensation tied in with all that, and, while continually accusing Logan of intruding, it had been a major cause in bringing him here. But why? And just what was so damn important that interested Vaugen so much?

Gathering the Jewel under one arm, Logan started westward, ideas running through his mind. Why was he so important to Vaugen? Because he came from Earth? Possibly . . . he had been addressed as "man from another world" by two of Vaugen's men. But why was a "man from another world" so damn important that he had to be taken alive? Did it somehow have to do with his being different? Perhaps. No one else Logan had met had been plagued by the infernal buzz that, even now, remained hovering about him. But just how did being different make him important? It hindered him more than helped him. A few times the sensation had gotten so bad Logan had almost passed out—Shit! When the Blackbody had attacked, Logan had almost been knocked clear out of his saddle! If Vaugen wanted to be different, let him! Logan was getting downright sick and tired of Sparrill and of being different!

Then leave, the disagreement demanded.

I am trying to leave! Logan shot back, grimacing as the buzz increased. Why don't you leave me alone? Look, I helped you with the zombies.

The whispering chorus of voices had no reply, but the infernal hum strengthened. If only it was a bug, wished Logan. I'd squash that sucker flat! Unfortunately, the ever-present feeling was not physical and could not be stamped out. Grumbling, Logan continued his trek through the Hills, turning, once again, to the mystery of his importance.

It can't be my knowledge of weapons, he thought. I mean, I know what they look like and how to use a lot of them, but I can't make them. Christ, if Vaugen wants someone to engineer him a catapult, he's chasing after the wrong guy! Boy, wouldn't that just be great if that's what he wants? As soon as he found out I don't know beans about building things, he'd wipe me out! Or maybe he wants to go to Earth? Naw, that's a comic-book plot. The bad guy wants to conquer all known dimensions! I don't think Vaugen wants to rule Santa Monica—if he does, he'll have another disappointment.

Like a swarm of bees, the sensation of mismatchment converged on Logan, momentarily deafening the young man with its obnoxious buzzing. Logan snarled at the feeling. Ever since it had aided him in destroying Farkarrez, the feeling had gotten nastier. The young man sneered: That's gratitude!

A low gurgle sounded from Logan's empty stomach as the young man skidded down an incline. A bizarre duet resounded in his ears as his grumbling stomach and the infernal buzz simultaneously barked their displeasure. This was becoming too much!

"Shut the fuck up!" Logan thundered, and his voice bounced off the mountains to sound over and over again.

As his curse faded across the Hills, the perturbed rumbling of his belly ceased; the discordance did not.

Bastard! Bastard! Bastard! Bastard! The young man fumed, storming over a rocky ledge, Launce's staff stabbing into the hard-packed ground. This sensation was really getting to be a bother! If it was going to remain this persistent, Logan would have to do something about it.

His blue eyes turned away from the hillsides and fixed on the golden Jewel under his arm. I'm lost, he told himself. Stuck in a mountain range trying to find Prifrane. I've got the Jewel, however, and I *am* in the Hills. Since I don't have a good shot at finding the town, why don't I search for the Smythe myself? Then I can get the hell out of here and this goddamn feeling will *leave me alone!*

His anger and frustration agreed, and Logan surveyed the Hills. Then, deciding upon his route, he continued westward, searching for the Smythe.

"My feet are sore, I don't have any food or water, I'm lost, and there's this buzz which is driving me insane!" Logan told the Hills his problems.

Groaning, he sat down, placing the Jewel in his lap. The sun was directly above him, warming the mountains so that sweat dribbled down his face. The brownish yellow soil was like snow, reflecting the rays of the sun and spitting them back into Logan's face. Sunglasses would be so handy right now, the young man thought wistfully.

A fumbling footstep kicked some pebbles free as Logan twirled around. He could sense someone behind a slope of rocks, probably attracted to him by his earlier comments to the Hills. The clumsy step he had caught made Farkarrez's dead warriors a possible choice, but none had been fast enough to have caught up with him already. His heartbeat quickened as his mind suggested Cyrene, but instant depression set in as he knew the girl would be out of the Hills by now—and the blonde had not been as loud and as unskilled as whoever lurked behind those stones.

Cautiously, Logan withdrew Moknay's dagger and slid off his seat. "All right!" he called. "I know you're there! Come out!"

Through the glare of the yellow-brown earth, Logan saw the squarish head poke up from behind the rocks, stringy black hair falling into the blue-skinned face.

"Foooooood!" the ogre bellowed, hurriedly stomping toward Logan.

The young man plopped back down to the ground, staring up at the happy ogre with distaste. "Boy, did you pick the wrong time to come back!" he stated. "I don't have any food at all! Not even for me!"

The light blue creature stopped before Logan, its wide smile vanishing. "No foooooood?" it questioned.

Logan shook his head. "None at all," he replied. "Not even a little bit."

The huge beast cocked its massive head to one side. "Nooooooo?" it asked again.

Logan cast his gaze to the ground. "No," he agreed.

Oddly, the ogre's smile returned as it plopped down beside Logan, causing a few rocks to shudder in the minor tremor. Wonderingly, Logan watched as thick fingers reached into a pocket of the tattered pants around the light blue waist and extracted some of the fruit Launce had given Logan.

A gigantic hand thrust itself under Logan's nose. "Foooooooood!" the ogre boomed cheerfully.

Logan's eyebrows shot up. "You sneak!" he exclaimed. "You saved that last handful I gave you!"

The ogre grinned crookedly. "Gave yooooooou!" it replied, dumping the food in Logan's lap.

The young man peered at the fruit for a moment, contemplating. It wasn't really fair to take something the ogre had so carefully saved, he thought. Then the ogre wouldn't have anything to eat. "I—I can't take this," he protested.

The light blue ogre blinked.

Logan handed the fruit back. "This is yours," he explained. "I can't take it."

The light blue creature frowned when Logan tried to dump the food back into its lap. Huge hands stopped the young man before he could finish ridding himself of the fruit.

"Fooooooood!" the ogre bellowed, giving Logan back what he had returned. "Yooooooou!"

You're the one who lost his horse; you're the one who doesn't have any provisions, Logan's mind blamed him. You can't go and take someone else's.

Logan faced the blue creature. "I can't," he started. "It's not . . ."

Contorting its face into a hideous grimace of rage and indignation, the ogre released a furious growl, raising its brawny arms high above its head in a threatening gesture.

"All right! All right!" Logan hastily said. "I'll eat it!"

The crooked smile reappeared across the light blue face.

Logan devoured the fruit. Even after the weeks that had passed, the food remained ripe and the succulent juices soothed Logan's dry throat. While he ate, the young man laughed at his own eagerness, realizing it was usually the light blue ogre who wolfed down his food.

An idea formed in Logan's brain as he finished a fruit. "I happen to be lost," he told the ogre in between mouthfuls of another piece. "Have you seen my friends?"

"Frrrrrrrriends?" the ogre asked back.

Logan nodded. "Yeah, especially Cyrene. Blonde, a girl, in a white dress? She might still be in the Hills."

"Whiiiiiite huuuuuumaaaaaan?" queried the ogre.

"No, she's not the white human," Logan responded, although, in the ogre's terms, the white-dressed blonde could have been. "Say, where is the white human? Is he still following me?"

The grin on the squarish face widened. "Deeeeeead!" it answered. "Yooooooou!"

For a moment, Logan hesitated, then the realization sunk in. "Farkarrez!" he cried. "He wore a white chestplate! And he had been brought back by magic! That was what you had meant, wasn't it?"

"Maaaaaagic!" the creature agreed.

"What about Pembroke? The mad human? Is he still far?"

The light blue beast paused before booming, "Faaaar."

Logan threw away the core of the second fruit and started on a third. "What about Prifrane?" he wondered. "Can you show me where the town is?"

Puzzlement entered the ogre's eyes, and its smile diminished.

"Lots of people," Logan tried again, bringing his hands together as if to indicate a lot. "You know, a village?"

Titanic shoulders heaved as the ogre shrugged.

"You don't know where it is either?" Logan muttered. "Welcome to the club."

"Cluuuuuuuub?" the huge creature repeated.

A small smile crossed Logan's lips at the ogre's ignorance. "Never mind," he told it.

The ogre screwed up its face. "Neverrrrrmind?" it echoed. Its grin widened as it tapped the side of its huge head. "Meeeeee got!" it declared proudly.

The sun dangled just above the mountaintops as Logan and his light blue companion trudged onward. With hills on either side of him, Logan was not sure exactly where he was in the mountain range, but he had figured the Smythe would be somewhere in the very center. That way it would be difficult to find him, but not impossible.

With Druid Launce's staff lending support, Logan started up a grade. The heavy footsteps of the ogre did not sound beside him, and Logan turned around.

The light blue beast was staring at the dirt, pointing. "Feeeeeeet," it said.

Logan scrambled back down and inspected the soil. As the ogre had noted, a number of prints decorated the earth. Most were booted feet but, here and there, the upside-down U of horseshoes marked the ground. A twinge of hope rose in Logan as he guessed this must be the path to the Smythe, but then he noticed the military order of the horses' hooves and the precision marching of those on foot. And, caught in the midst, was one set of smaller prints—markings that were almost feminine.

"Cyrene!" Logan cried out loud, and the ogre stared at him in confusion.

Frantically, Logan tried to follow the tracks, but hooves and feet branched off, sweeping away Cyrene's dainty footprints. Fearing the Reakthi had caught up with the girl, Logan traced the footprints farther into the mountains, the blue ogre trailing behind him in silent puzzlement.

Logan halted, pointing toward the horses' tracks. "You go that way," he instructed the ogre. "Follow those prints. We've got to find Cyrene." He hesitated a moment, knowing the beast would not understand personal names. "She's a white girl. Can you find her?"

"Whiiiiiite girrrrrrl?" the ogre repeated.

"Yes! Yes! She might be in danger! We've got to help her!"

Worriedly, Logan hurried after the tracks, leaving the ogre to follow the others. Cyrene! His mind raced. Alone, on foot, against at least two troops of men! She'd never be able to outrun them or defeat them. She was helpless. Logan knew that. He had been with her, slept with her—he knew how soft and fragile she was. She couldn't face two troops of soldiers! Oh, God! Don't let her die! Let her be all right!

As the sun dropped lower into the west, shadows began to invade the Hills. All sense of direction fled the young man as he pursued the prints, and all that mattered was rescuing Cyrene from the death the Reakthi would give her.

Scrabbling madly around a corner, Logan let out a shout as a horse suddenly blocked his path. The horse released its own startled snort, skittering backwards as it eyed the young man. A hint of recognition sparked in the green eyes. Slowly, Logan approached the stallion, smiling as sunlight gleamed off its yellow hide and green mane.

"I don't believe it," he murmured, patting the horse's nose. "You picked the exact time to come back!"

The young man swiftly replaced the Jewel in a saddlebag and climbed into the saddle. The yellow-and-green horse tossed its head happily, eagerly obeying Logan's command to follow the tracks. Clouds of dirt spewed into the air behind the stallion as it charged across level ground, following the military footprints. The sun had almost completely disappeared as Logan and his horse rounded a gigantic boulder, their hoofbeats resounding about them. Unexpectedly, the yellow-and-green mount halted, barred by a squadron of uniformed men awaiting them. Hoofbeats which Logan had thought were his horse's own sounded, and two mounted men blocked any hope of retreat.

One of the Guardsmen on foot smiled. "Outsider, you are hereby under arrest by order of His Ultimate Paramount, King Mediyan, for presenting a danger to Sparrill and her Ruler. Sentence may be reduced if you agree to work for the King— if not, you shall be slain."

Great! Logan thought. They weren't Reakthi, they were Guardsmen! And now Mediyan wanted Logan as badly as Vaugen! Where the hell are Moknay and Thromar when I need them?

And, as if the lead Guardsman could read Logan's mind, his sardonic smile widened.

· 12 ·

Guard

"Excuse me?" Logan inquired innocently. "'Outsider'? Just what do you mean? I'm a perfectly harmless traveler on my way to see the Smythe."

The lead Guardsman sneered in response, menacingly fingering his sword hilt. "'Harmless traveler,' eh?" he repeated. "On your way to see the Smythe, are you?" His eyebrows knitted across his brow. "Then what do you call these clothes you're wearing?"

Logan wished he could sneer back but kept up his charade. "Clothes," he retorted. "Why? What do you call them here?"

A few of the Guards sniggered, but a sharp glare from their commander silenced them. "Your clothing is definitely not of Sparrill, Denzil, or Magdelon. Where did they come from?"

Suddenly Logan loved all those people who had mistaken him as from somewhere else. "Droth," he replied immediately.

Guardsmen and commander were quiet. His ego taken down a few pegs, the leader waved three of his men forward. "Search him and his horse," he ordered.

Logan was going to protest yet did not. So far he had them doubting if he was the "Outsider" they were searching for. There really wasn't anything on him or his horse that would incriminate him—at least, he hoped not.

The trio of Guards emptied his saddlebags and motioned for him to dismount. Complying, Logan leapt off his horse and let one man search his body. The remaining two inspected the items of his leather pouches.

"Sir," one of the Guards called, "there is only one item of any value. All the rest is meaningless."

The commander had obviously been struggling with his anger as he gritted, "What does he carry?"

"About ten pieces of gold, a tin of snuff or something, some rations, and a large jewel," the Guard reported. "Nothing else is on his horse."

"His only weapons are a Reakthi sword, a dagger, and a large staff," another soldier declared.

The commanding Guard held out a hand. "Let me see the gemstone," he ordered.

The glittering Jewel was placed in his extended palm, and Logan held his breath. If Moknay and Thromar had told him the truth about Mediyan's Guards, they wouldn't be all that bright; and certainly not up on Cosmic Jewels . . . unless some of them were religious freaks, then they might know something. According to his companions, the Guards were only concerned about carrying out Mediyan's orders and getting some goodies in the process—really not much better than the Reakthi in that sense. Logan could understand the people's hatred toward their ruler and his soldiers.

The Guards' leader tossed the Jewel back to his men. "Replace it," he said uncaringly. He had suffered quite a blow from Logan's act and was determined to make up for it. "You say you come from Droth?" he interrogated. "Tell me, who rules there?"

Gulp! Logan swallowed hard. Now he's getting tricky! But . . . wait a minute. Thromar told you Droth was an island past some Dragon's Neck. Obviously, anyone from Droth would have had to have sailed over. "I really couldn't tell you," Logan answered. "I sailed from Droth quite a while ago, before the four Imperators became three."

Logan smirked; that should convince 'em!

The menace radiating from the uniformed Guardsmen started to diminish, but the inimical glow remained in the commander's eyes. Coldly he approached, his eyes boring into Logan's. "You said you were going to the Smythe," he sneered. "Why?"

"That gemstone is magical," Logan admitted. "I would like to give it to the Smythe since I'm certainly no spellcaster."

The Guardsman rubbed his chin. "Did you happen to see anyone else as you came through the Hills?" he questioned. "There's a number of Guards searching for three fugitives."

"Three fugitives?" repeated Logan.

"Yes," the Guard replied, "Moknay the Murderer, Thromar the Rebel, and an Outsider with black hair and wearing an odd blue uniform. Squads of Guardsmen are spread as far as Frelars and Wailvye searching for them once we received word they were heading westward. Funny, but you have black hair and a blue uniform."

Logan shrugged. "I'm sure I'm not the only one."

"No, true," the commander replied, "but how odd that you should be moving west as well, hmmmmm? It seems there's a lot of people traveling westward through the Hills recently— like that girl we ran into."

Logan jerked to attention, and a confident smirk crossed the Guard's lips. "Is something wrong?" he mocked.

Logan clenched his teeth. His sudden move had alerted the other Guardsman as well as their leader. He had to think fast or else they would know he had been with Cyrene. "Uh . . . no, nothing's wrong," he lied. "It's just that . . . I met a girl just before I entered the Hills myself. A real pretty blonde."

The commander grinned. "Yes, that was her. How odd that you saw her and nobody else. Reports have it she was traveling with the three."

"Well, I didn't see anybody else."

"Funny," sneered the Guard, "that's exactly what she said before we killed her."

The shock was obvious on Logan's face. So stunned by loss, the young man was unconscious of the Guardsmen that surrounded him, weapons drawn. Their commander stood off to one side, his past embarrassment erased and replaced by conquest.

"I thought so," he jeered. "You *are* the Outsider. Now kindly come with us or we shall drag you by your private parts."

One of the soldiers flanking Logan asked, "Should we take his weapons, sir?"

The lead Guardsman waved him off. "No, let him keep them—there's more than enough of us to detain him should he decide to be heroic." The Guard turned and started toward some men carrying supplies. "Oh, one other thing," he called arrogantly over his shoulder to Logan. "The blonde isn't dead. She's faster than a bearded peakgoat in these Hills."

Twice in a row Logan lost the use of his expressions. Tricked! he moaned inwardly. Just like he had been conning the Guardsmen! Damn!

Triumphantly, the commanding Guard scribbled a message

and released a small batlike bird into the air, the note strapped to its leg. Its tiny wings flapping, the bird soared northward and headed out to sea.

"We'll be taking you to Frelars," the Guardsman remarked, watching the bird vanish. "From there we'll take a ship back to Magdelon and to King Mediyan. As I told you before, if you cooperate, your punishment will be less severe—if not, you will be slain." He raised a scepter and the squadron of Guardsmen began northward, the unfortunate Logan among them.

Torches crackled in the night as the Guardsmen went about sorting provisions and sharpening weapons. A group had gathered near Logan, telling dirty tales and singing rowdy songs, but he paid them little attention. The commander sat upon a large boulder, grinning down at his troop and his captive in haughty success. The hillsides were bathed in the light of the dancing flames, and the noises of the night remained still, silenced by the ruckus of the Guardsmen. Logan sat on the ground, staring longingly at some men eating meat. Small growls of hunger sounded from the young man's stomach as he sat there, and he frowned at the aura of foul luck that entombed him. Captured twice—and in the same mountain range, yet! His cliff tactics might not work here, since the horses required level ground, and, besides, Logan had no idea how desperate Mediyan was. Vaugen, he knew, wanted him alive. Mediyan, from what the Guards had implied, might kill him even after his capture.

A peculiar breeze brushed over Logan, and the young man trained his blue eyes on the Hills. A wind that was not truly a wind had passed over him, touching him with its sense of unbalance. Curiously, Logan peered into the darkness of the mountains as the unsettling breeze caressed him once more. It wasn't the blatant disharmony. No, that was still the same as ever. This feeling was more unnatural, like a very distortion of the air around it.

It was gone as suddenly as it had appeared.

A footstep nearby pulled Logan out of his wonderings and he glanced up to see a young Guardsman step beside him. The sandy-haired youth set himself down near the young man and held out some food, a friendly smile on his face.

"I don't like to see people go hungry," he stated. "Makes the monsters in their bellies restless."

Logan patted his own grumbling stomach. "Tell me about it," he muttered. He gave the food a skeptical glance. "You didn't poison this, did you?"

The young Guard barked a laugh, taking back a piece of meat and stuffing it into his mouth. "Convince you?" he asked back.

Tilting his head to one side, Logan shrugged and began eating the cooked meat. The taste was immediately recognizable as chicken, and Logan eagerly wolfed down the familiar meat. The Guard watched him, stroking his thin blond beard about his chin.

Cramming the last bit of chicken into his mouth, Logan turned back to the young Guardsman. He was eating like the ogre again, he realized. A pity the light blue beast wasn't there now.

"How long have you gone hungry?" the Guardsman questioned.

"Too long," Logan returned. "I've been busy."

Interest burst into life in the Guardsman's eyes. "No doubt. Doing what?"

"Getting lost," Logan answered. Then, "Getting captured."

The youthful Guard could not mistake the anger in the young man's voice but his smile did not diminish. "My name's Aelkyne," he continued. "I'm from Scrydaen. What about yourself?"

Logan sneered at the uniformed man beside him. "What's it to you?" he scowled.

"Let's just say I'm curious," the young Aelkyne responded. "We've been looking for you since that first report came in near Eadarus."

Logan hesitated, his eyebrows lifting in surprise. "Then that march into Eadarus wasn't a coincidence!"

Aelkyne chuckled. "No, of course not. That troop was, however, fortunate they were so close by."

"But why?" queried Logan. "Why is everyone chasing me?"

Aelkyne held out empty hands. "We don't know that," he admitted. He nodded toward his commander. "I don't even think Eldath knows—only Mediyan and his spellcasters."

Logan's caution of the young Guard dispersed as confusion

mingled with frustration overwhelmed him. Why? Why? *Why?* his mind screamed. Was it his difference? If so, what was so damn great about it?

Aelkyne noted the perplexed expression on Logan's features. "Something wrong?" he wondered.

Useless! Logan told himself. There was no way on Heaven or on Earth—or on any other world, for that matter—that Logan would be able to decipher the mystery of his importance! And that fact was absolutely maddening!

". . . haven't been a Guard for long," Aelkyne was saying, "but I would like to know something about you or your world."

The words struck something deep within Logan, and he realized how close they were to the words uttered by Mara. Mara, the young man sighed. She had been so lovely, so determined to keep him from harm that she had been hurt in his stead. This world was not fair, he concluded. It was a brutal place of injury, pain, death, and mysteries. His world had been so much easier.

"My world was a much simpler place," Logan said softly, lost in his own memories. "We had machines and devices that did all the nasty jobs for us, and most people didn't even have to live with themselves if they didn't want to. They just wrapped themselves up in their own little world of lies and automation and could blame their faults on others. Some of us didn't mind our place in society: we worked, we slept, we lived. Life was relatively uncomplicated for the Everyman. There were things to do, and people to do them with, but they never resulted in injury or death. Sometimes I wish I had never left my world, other times . . ."

Logan went silent, and Aelkyne watched him closely. The carousing of the other Guards went on around them, but the two were wrapped up in their own discussion, oblivious of the men singing and drinking about them.

Logan turned on the sandy-haired Guard beside him, despair and grief mirrored on his face. "I was on my way to find the Smythe," he whispered, "to go back home. I never wanted to come here, get involved, do what I've done. But now it's too late. I'm stuck again and your whole world is going to blow." The young man stared off into the Hills. "I've done what I can, and it wasn't good enough."

There was compassion in Aelkyne's eyes as he gave a swift glance over his shoulder and saw Eldath was glaring directly at the two. The young Guardsman backed away for his own safety. Logan didn't notice the Guard depart; his eyes remained locked on the blackness around him . . . Blackness that resembled his own failure.

The following morning was overcast, troubled with black clouds like Logan's emotions. The buzz of misplacement circled above the young man yet he was unaware. Blindly, he walked on after the Guardsmen, fear, failure, and dread raining from the dark clouds and soaking him. At times, a spark of hope sputtered in his gloom, remembering his many companions out in the Hills. Surely one of them might recall him and seek him out. But then the sorrow would regain ascendancy and drown out that flickering tongue of hope.

As the squad of Guardsmen made their way through the Hills, Logan spied a small waterfall some distance to his right. Odd, he mused, he had seen no river or stream while he had been traveling. True, his captors were taking him in a northeasterly line, but Logan had heard no water at all while lost. In fact, the only time he had seen water in the Hills had been that first day with Cyrene.

Fond thoughts of the girl began to skip through Logan's mind, blinding him to the danger. The waterfall he saw was indeed from the very same spring he and the blonde had bathed in as it wound its way through the Hills. In the course of a few days it had journeyed some distance from its original starting point, but the clear water had not been the only thing moving from that grassy knoll.

Logan was daydreaming of Cyrene when the dead Reakthi attacked.

The Guardsmen's horses reared and startled shouts went up from the band of uniformed men. Disbelief filled their eyes as the chestplated corpses advanced, and two men went down before their comrades could even bring themselves to trust their eyesight. Instantly, swords were drawn, but no Reakthi blood stained the ground. Stabbed, impaled, or dismembered, the cadavers continued forward, breaking through the lines of Guards in their steady advance toward Logan. Even decapitated the lifeless Reakthi fought, their one purpose to recapture Matthew Logan. Eldath, his mount surrounded by dead Reakthi, did not even think to turn toward his captive. He and his troop were being attacked by corpses and none of them would fall. Logan was the very last thing on his mind.

A snort pulled Logan free of his initial surprise and he turned to find his horse at his elbow. Throughout the confusing tide of Reakthi and Guardsmen, the young man saw the bearded face of Aelkyne before he was swept up in the battle.

The white flare of hope roared to life in Logan's breast, and he leapt astride his stallion. Hooves beat the hard-packed earth as the yellow-and-green mount galloped free of the battle. Mindlessly, the Reakthi corpses tried to follow, but the squad of Guards blocked their path. Swords and axes clanged, and blades cleaved into dead flesh, yet the chestplated dead kept struggling. Concerned only with the animated cadavers, Eldath urged his men onward.

Logan escaped in the chaos.

The black clouds became friendly, protecting Logan from eyes hidden in the heavens, and the almost identical hillsides also grew amicable, hiding Logan from his captors. The blazing white spark within him strengthened, swelling the young man with good fortune. Twice he had been captured; twice he had escaped—both times with Jewel intact. Abruptly, the friendliness of the Hills increased, and the abnormal breeze touched him from its subterfuge in the west. Acting on instinct, Logan directed his mount that way, trailing the wind of unbalance deeper into the mountain range.

The Guards and Reakthi were some two miles behind him when Logan finally brought his horse to a stop. Perched atop a ledge, the young man peered out toward the south. Hills stretched before him, but that odd, unnatural feeling was somewhere close by. Curiously, Logan looked east, then west. Each time he was greeted by more hills. To the north, however, the bizarre unbalance crouched among the hills, and Logan suddenly saw the cavern hidden in the crook of a mountain.

"Smell anything?" he asked his horse as he directed it toward the cave.

The green-and-yellow horse hesitated a moment, sensed no danger, then halted again. Quizzically, it cocked its head to one side, and Logan thought perhaps it too had sensed the strange, abnormal wind blowing from within.

"You think there's anything in there?" he questioned his mount.

As if in response, the stallion snorted and shook its green mane. Slowly, Logan urged the horse in, and an unearthly green light illuminated the cavern walls. Like the corridor of a house, the stone widened out to reveal a tall figure leaning over a glimmering orb of color. Dark brown hair streaked with grey crowned the head, and a trim beard and mustache decorated the lean face. Wild, dark brown eyes flicked up from the glowing ball and fixed on Logan. A strange smile spread across the face.

"You've come back?" the tall figure inquired. "I didn't think you'd find me. Isn't that right? Oh, no? Perhaps not. Then again . . . Sit! Sit! Make my home comfortable."

Logan blinked in confusion, his blue eyes transfixed on the robed form facing him. The rocky chamber was filled with miscellaneous devices, and the ever-present buzz increased as Logan scanned the room. A sudden thought exploded into his mind and he turned on the lean figure.

"Are you the Smythe?" he questioned.

A lean but strong hand stroked the trim beard. "Hmmmmm? The Smythe? Oh, me? Why, yes. I suppose so! You are who?"

"I'm Matthew Logan," the young man returned, smiling as he dismounted. "Jesus Christ, I never thought I'd find you!"

"Jesus Christ, yes!" the gaunt spellcaster echoed. "Find me you have! Or did I find you?" He paused a moment as if to puzzle out the question; then, curtly, he turned back to Logan. "Did you come here to give me more girls? If you did, I really don't need them. I'd much rather want clay. Clay, you know? Have you ever built with clay?"

Logan threw his horse a questioning look, but his mount's green eyes gave no indication of danger. Shrugging, the young man withdrew the gleaming Jewel and handed it to the eccentric wizard.

"Actually," Logan said, "I came to give you this."

The Smythe inspected the massive gem closely, his dark eyes flashing. "This? This?" he quipped. "What's this, then? An egg?"

"It's the Jewel of Equilibrant," explained Logan.

"No, it's an egg," the Smythe insisted. "A giant Cosmic egg

that will hatch and give birth to a whole universe."

"You mean it's capable of doing that?" the young man exclaimed, hoping he had interpreted the wizard's allegory correctly.

The gaunt Smythe began to flap his arms about in birdlike fashion. "It must have come from the huge Star Gull, a bird that nests in the suns themselves." An odd expression suddenly screwed up the spellcaster's face. "No, no, that's not right. This is the Jewel! That's it! The Jewel! Oh, the powers inside this egg—Jewel! *No!* It's a woman's breast! Yes! Feel how smooth it is, how round and firm. But she has no nipple! Yaaaaagh! Deformity! Freak! Outcast! Unclean!"

Spellcasters were strange, Logan decided, eyeing the Smythe with uncertainty. No wonder the man liked to hide in the Hills—he reminded Logan of men like Salvador Dalí on his own world.

"It seems to be leaking energy," Logan went on. "My friends suggested I bring it to you."

The gaunt Smythe stopped his wild prancing and screaming and glared at the young man. "Leaking?" he repeated. "Leaking? Oh, yes, this is very serious. Very serious indeed. What makes you do that?"

"Excuse me?"

"What makes you dance around in circles while you have intercourse with the moons?" the magician queried.

What the hell did he mean by that? Logan thought, trying to decipher the spellcaster's odd choice of words. Oh, wait a minute! Replace "dancing in circles" with "being lost," and "intercourse with the moons" with "fucking things up," and the phrase made a little bit more sense.

"I'm not a spellcaster," Logan answered. "I can't stop it from leaking."

"I see," nodded the lean wizard. "I see. I am seeing. I shall see. I saw. I have seen. I had saw. Look out! Deformity! Freak! Outcast! Unclean!" He paused a moment, squinting at Logan. "What do you want?" he suddenly demanded.

Looks like you can't hide anything from this guy, Logan noted. "I want to go back to my world."

The sorcerer's eyes flared. "You have a world? So have I. What is yours?"

"Earth," declared Logan. "I want to go back to Earth."

"My world is Grobolobo. Your world is Earth. Our world is GroboloboEarth."

"Do you think you can send me back?"

The Smythe stroked his beard. "Did you create your world?"

"Huh?" Logan wondered. "I'm sorry, but . . ."

"I created mine. Do you know where Grobolobo is? It's under that rock, and death comes every nightfall." The wizard abruptly shook his head violently, as if clearing the cobwebs from his brain. "Sorry, sorry. Check Jewel; send back. Yes, I have it. You must understand, I find it quite difficult to grow Bloodpetals." He handed the golden Jewel back to Logan. "Do you comprehend?"

The young man ran a hand through his hair, trying to formulate an answer. Unexpectedly, the spellcaster wheeled on the shimmering orb behind him. "Girl!" he yelled. "A girl is without!" He ran his hands lovingly over the orb. "Ooooooh, soft! So soft. But no nipple! Yaaaaaaagh! Deformity! Freak! Outcast! Unclean!"

"Girl?" echoed Logan. "There's a girl outside?"

The hope still ablaze inside him, Logan scrambled out of the cavern. Rounding a corner, glinting silver almost tore into his neck and a fist rammed into his jaw. Logan fell to the ground, stunned, the Hills spiraling around him. Someone was saying his name, but he could not tell who. It wasn't until soft hands helped him off the ground that Logan stared into Cyrene's deep blue eyes.

"Matthew," the blonde smiled brightly, "I didn't think I'd see you again. I tried so hard to think of a way to free you from Farkarrez, then I ran into Mediyan's Guards, and . . ."

"I know! I know!" Logan interrupted, regaining his senses and his excitement. "But I did it! I found him! I found the Smythe!" Eagerly, he pulled the blonde into the cavern, a grin drawn across his features. When they entered the stone chamber, Logan could not help but grin wider as the gaunt spellcaster looked up at them. His smile faltered when he noticed the terror in Cyrene's lovely eyes.

"Matthew!" she cried. "That's not the Smythe! It's Zack-aron!"

· 13 ·

Mistakes

"Matthew!" Cyrene cried. "That's not the Smythe! It's Zackaron!"

Logan's initial reaction was to run . . . to simply turn about and rush out of the narrow corridor of stone. But the wildness in Zackaron's dark eyes also flared with a power beyond comprehension—a power that had driven even its user insane. How could Logan hope to flee a man who could destroy then recreate him on the spot? Zackaron reigned over nature itself with his madness, and Logan began to understand the abnormal wind of unbalance flowing from the spellcaster's home. The magician had the energies of his world at his fingertips, yet his mind was incapable of using them correctly.

Trying to shrug off the terror Cyrene radiated beside him, Logan faced the gaunt sorcerer. "I'm sorry," he apologized. "I've made a terrible mistake. I didn't mean to give you this egg. I was going to bring you clay."

Zackaron's eyes expanded in excitement. "Clay? Clay?" he parroted. "Excellent! Have you ever built with clay?"

Logan casually replaced the Jewel in his horse's saddlebag and took hold of the reins. "Actually, I have," he answered the wizard. "It's quite good. Especially for making things."

The lean magic-user nodded his head enthusiastically. "Yes! Yes! Make things, I do! Make things! But pity! Pity me! So many are wrong! So many mistakes!"

Logan was almost intrigued to stay and listen to the rantings of the wizard. What kind of things did Zackaron attempt to make from clay? the young man wondered. His powers made anything possible, but his mind would cause major drawbacks in any creation. No wonder Zackaron was so opposed to deformity!

The mindless spellcaster stepped toward Logan, and Cyrene stiffened as the dark eyes locked upon her. "Did you make her?" the sorcerer queried, his eyes aglow with appreciation.

"No, I didn't," responded Logan, "but I can get you some clay so you can make something like her."

Zackaron's face lit up. "Can you?" he cried, almost child-like. "Do so! So do!"

Nodding in reply, Logan backed out of the cavern, taking Cyrene and his horse with him. He could still hear Zackaron chortling from inside as he mounted up and pulled Cyrene behind him. Fear had stolen Cyrene's voice from her as Logan started his horse forward, thanking whatever had caused Zackaron to return the Jewel to him.

Darker clouds began to populate the sky as the yellow-and-green horse trekked through the Hills. Logan was slightly unsettled by Cyrene's silence—wishing their reunion could have been a little bit more romantic—but remained quiet himself as his horse rode on. The blonde's arms locked tightly about his waist served to quell some of the desires boiling within, but Logan felt cheated that the girl had not even praised him for his marvelous escapes. She did like him, didn't she? Why wasn't she as giddy over his good fortune as he was? Oh, well, the shock of bumping into a man with enough power to reconstruct the universe and with hardly enough common sense to feed himself might send anybody into a state of silence.

A confident smirk drawn on his face, Logan glanced down at the saddlebag hiding the Jewel. His heart almost leapt into his throat as he saw the golden rays leaking from the leather sack. The persistent mismatchment had gotten so strong it no longer warned him when the Jewel was acting up. It probably would not have triggered any warning in Logan until after the Jewel's glare signaled the danger itself.

"Cyrene," Logan whispered, "I think we're in trouble."

The blonde behind him moved to peer over his shoulder but still said nothing.

"The Jewel's glowing," he explained, and her arms tightened about his waist. "It might be about to discharge again."

Logan gazed up at the darkening clouds apprehensively and a knot formed in his stomach. The increased buzz of dishar-mony had really torn away his usual defenses, he realized. He had no idea if those black clouds looming above him were natural or unnatural—but the yellowish light seeping from his saddlebags indicated it was the latter.

A stifled shriek ripped through Cyrene's lips, and Logan pulled his eyes away from the clouds. A blur of pink caught his attention, but whatever had made it had swerved out of sight. Logan questioningly glanced over his shoulder at Cyrene, but the blonde still refused to speak. Her eyes were wide, fixed in the direction of the pinkish flash, yet no explanation came from her lips.

There was a hellish screech from the mountains, and a throng of creatures swarmed down the hillsides. Their distorted limbs flailed in the air, and bleary eyes reflected the Jewel's golden glare. Logan was so horrified he accidentally drew in the reins, and the stallion stood where it was while the cluster of monsters rushed closer.

Humanlike in shape, the creatures loped down the sloping hillsides. Gnarled limbs—some too short, others too long—sent dirt spraying into the air, and thick streams of saliva oozed from the contorted mouths and misshapen teeth. One of the beasts scuttling down the mountainside was nothing more than a deformed head perched atop an outstretched hand, while another was the upper torso of a man that gradually turned serpentine. Another monstrosity flailed four arms at the cloudy sky, its many disproportioned fingers clenching into warped fists.

Somewhere, from maybe a million miles away, there was a voice calling to Logan.

"Matthew! *Matthew!* Get us out of here!"

Fingers shook Logan awake as the perversions of nature neared. Drawing himself away from the terror charging him, Logan blinked his eyes and felt Cyrene's breath upon his neck.

"*Matthew!*" she screamed. "Let's go! *Please!*"

With a silent glimpse back at the nearing deformities, Logan rammed his Nikes into his horse's flanks and bolted forward. Enraged screams pursued the pair, their horse galloping headlong across the mountains. A growl of thunder exploded from the black clouds above as the aureate flame of the Jewel brightened. The Jewel! Logan's mind shouted. Those things sensed the Jewel—like that Demon did! They wanted it!

Cyrene screamed and Logan almost pitched off his horse as the green-and-yellow stallion skidded to a halt, stopping precariously close to a cliff. A sheer drop angled before them, and boulders cracked and fragmented like egg shells lined the bottom. The earthquake must have utterly destroyed this hillside, Logan mused. What must have been a level path around the mountain was now interrupted by a fearful drop of some hundred feet. Frantically, Logan looked right, then left. The right offered a level route yet betrayed an aura of possible rockslides or unexpected drops. The left, however, slanted upward, and Logan knew his horse would be unable to make the climb carrying two riders.

Swiftly, he dismounted and motioned for Cyrene to do the same.

"Take the horse up," he commanded, withdrawing his sword. "I'll cover our backs."

The blonde paused a moment before snatching up the reins and beginning the difficult ascent. Logan trailed, dangerously scaling the mountain backwards as he went. It did not take long before the screeching distortions of men burst into sight, their malformed limbs slashing the mountain air. Cyrene's breathing quickened as fear coursed through her slim frame, and her climbing became erratic, making her stumble more as she fought the slanting hillside. Like fluid, Cyrene's fear flowed down to Logan, and beads of perspiration dotted his brow as he gazed down at the mockeries below him.

Scuttling like twisted crabs of flesh, the swarm of deformities followed after the couple. Lust burned in their blurry eyes. Perhaps they thought the Jewel would return them to normal, like Logan had tried to persuade Farkarrez into believing, but what in the world could have mutated people into the crawling monsters that shrieked beneath him?

Logan paled and almost swooned as the realization struck him. Zackaron had not been mindlessly rambling when he had mentioned his creations. The things scrabbling and clawing their way toward Logan were Zackaron's. These were the wizard's deformities, his freaks and outcasts. And now they had come out of hiding in the hopes of attaining the Jewel.

Blue-white lightning ripped through the clouds, bathing the Hills with its electrical glare. The man-things cowered in the bluish flash but then their greed returned, and their twisted limbs helped them scrabble higher.

Breathing heavily, Logan reached a small, level cliff and directed Cyrene to run eastward along the narrow ledge. There was a sudden snarl from above him, and Logan toppled. Pain raked the young man's back as he somersaulted down the sloping hill, a hideously large, doglike beast snapping at his neck. Disgust swirled in Logan's belly as he completed his roll halfway down the hill and gripped the muzzle of the monster facing him. It was a hairless dog, he saw, and his stomach heaved in revulsion at the misshapen canine eagerly slobbering for his blood. Fear accompanied that sickness as Logan noted the sudden shock of the attack had knocked his sword out of his hand.

"Cyrene!" he choked, struggling to keep the disfigured snout and teeth away from his neck.

The herd of "mistakes" climbed nearer, their gibberish ringing in Logan's ears.

The winds picked up as the black clouds roiled and churned like angry waves. Cyrene stopped upon the ledge, glancing back down at the struggling forms. Her skirt billowed about her legs as the moaning gale whipped around her, and quick fingers pulled free the dagger at her thigh. The turbulent air shrieked as the blade rocketed forward and lodged in the dog-thing's neck. Black, putrid blood splattered Logan's face as the monster he battled jerked, a warbling howl tearing through its throat. With a violent heave, Logan sent the quivering monstrosity down the slope, knocking the twitching corpse into the cluster of misproportioned beings. Desperately, the young man pulled himself to his feet and resumed his hurried climb up the rocky face. The winds sent dirt spiraling into the darkened sky, and Logan's contacts ached as he struggled to reach the ledge once again. Another quarrel of blue-white lightning split the sky, and thunder shook the mountains. A tremendous voice unexpectedly tore through the clouds, and, so deafened by the noise, Logan was almost sent tumbling down the hillside once more.

"*MY JEWEL!*" the firmament boomed.

Oh, great, Logan sneered. Zackaron finally recognized the Jewel for what it was!

Helped onto the ledge by Cyrene, Logan noticed the thunderous voice had proven some good. So terrified by their creator's cry, the hideous man-things charged recklessly back down the mountainside and ducked into concealment, forgetting all about Logan and the hope his cargo had ignited.

Nervous that the insane spellcaster may appear, Logan leapt onto his horse and pulled up Cyrene. The ledge they were on was narrow, and possibly weak, yet the enraged cry of Zackaron had even sent waves of terror rushing through Logan's mount.

The yellow-and-green horse swiftly skirted the edge of the mountain path and galloped across the rim. To Logan's right was the dizzying drop that awaited them should the horse falter or stumble; to their left was the mountain wall with its jutting rocks that threatened to extend too far and knock both horse and riders from its face. Fortune, however, no matter how fickle she was, decided to accompany Logan, and the stallion soon reached a wider path that sloped between this mountain and a second one. It was not long before the threat of falling diminished, but the possibility of other earthquake-made drops lingered in Logan's mind.

"What in Agellic's name were those things?" breathed Cyrene, the fear still coating her voice.

"Zackaron's 'mistakes,' " the young man replied. "At least my mistakes aren't that bad!" he added, sarcastically. "I only steal Cosmic Jewels and mistake insane wizards for the Smythe! Some mistakes, huh?"

Cyrene saw nothing funny in Logan's humor and went silent once more. If they aren't Reakthi, Cyrene became somewhat timid in battle, Logan noted. Like Moknay, she showed a certain fear toward magic. She was no warrior-woman—thank God! Macho females were as bad as macho males! Although she did tend to take on such tendencies when their foes were Reakthi, a smile suddenly crossed Logan's lips; she did, he recalled, let me be on top!

No sun dangled in the black, foreboding sky, yet the clouds continued to darken. Logan cursed his glimmering watch when he wondered what time it was but guessed it was nearing late evening. Zackaron's "mistakes" were some two miles behind perhaps, if not directly, then in a roundabout way, and that made Farkarrez's men and Eldath's troop a good four miles back. Still, Zackaron, Logan worried, was a spellcaster, and he could be anywhere he wanted to be in mere seconds. Hopefully, his insanity would keep him from tracking down the couple and disposing of them.

Skidding down a somewhat treacherous slope, Logan and
Cyrene led the yellow-and-green mount to a stone-encircled
plateau. Sparse patches of grass sprang up from between broken stones, and two gnarled trees leaned in the strengthen-
ing gale. The purple-black clouds overhead roiled eastward,
flickering tongues of blue-white electricity crackling within.
Pursued by Reakthi, Guards, and Zackaron, Logan still found
his eyes straying to Cyrene's flapping dress and billowing dark
blonde hair as she stood upon the clearing.

"Where are we?" she questioned, looking out at the darkened Hills.

"Beats me," Logan replied, wishing he hadn't phrased it in
quite such a manner. "I haven't known where I was since I first
entered these stupid Hills! I figure we can rest here, though."

"Not all night!" the blonde cried.

Logan frowned at her fear. "Of course all night!" he
answered. "It's too damn dangerous to travel these mountains
at night. We're riding a horse, not a . . ." He fumbled for what
Eldath had said. " . . . bearded peakgoat."

Disheveled by the wind, Cyrene nodded and sat down.
Logan sat across from her as the darkness crept in, almost
hiding the young blonde in its black tendrils.

Hooves rent the stillness, and Logan grasped Moknay's dagger protectively. Cyrene's own hand went to her sheath, but her
dagger was gone, lodged in the throat of Zackaron's dog. She
watched Logan as the resounding hoofbeats grew louder, and
dark horses crested the rim of their plateau. A whispered curse
escaped Logan's lips as he made out the Guardsmen's uniforms
of the pair seated upon their mounts.

Logan readied his dagger. Christ knows how many men are
on the other side of the hill! he muttered to himself.

When a dark arm pointed in his direction and at the Jewel's
escaping glare, the silver dagger hissed from Logan's hand
and sailed through the cloudy night. The young man's heart
stopped beating, and Cyrene gasped, as the glinting metal
streaked for its target . . . and was snatched out of mid-air.

"Does this mean you don't want to keep it?" the cloud-
ridden night asked.

Logan let out a cheerful whoop. "Moknay?"

The Murderer leaped off his grey horse and slid down the
incline to join the young man. "Certainly," he said with a

smirk, handing back the dagger. "I do wish you'd stop trying to return my gift—or at least find another way of doing it."

The other Guardsmen lost his balance on the slope and slid the rest of the way down on his backside. "Brolark, that smarts!" Thromar grumbled indignantly.

"How . . . ? What . . . ? When . . . ?" Logan stuttered, futilely grasping for words.

Moknay clamped a friendly hand upon Logan's shoulder. "That's what I always liked about you, friend," he quipped. "You come right out and say what you mean."

The gibe made ease and gratitude stream throughout the young man. "How in the world did you find us?" he finally sputtered. "And what are you doing in Guardsmen uniforms?"

"Obviously," Thromar declared, tugging at the ill-fitting costume, "you don't know who it was who gave Moknay the name of Murderer, friend-Logan!"

Logan shook his head.

"Mediyan, who else?" Moknay grinned, his teeth glinting in the dim light of the Jewel. "I've taken out more of his commanders and leaders than Vaugen, old age, and Brolark himself! And what better way to find you, friend, than by disguising ourselves as Guards and joining in the search? If you haven't learned by now, there's quite a number of troops looking for you."

"I've learned," the young man retorted, "but how did you get those uniforms?"

"A squad of goons tried to arrest us!" Thromar laughed. "We showed them a thing or three!"

"They didn't name me Murderer for nothing," Moknay added.

"I know," put in Thromar. "You have to pay them."

Logan threw his arms about his companions, thanking whatever gods existed in his world and theirs. They were together again, and things never went badly when Thromar and Moknay were on hand. The two were unbeatable, and Thromar held the knowledge Logan so desperately needed.

As darkness settled beneath the blanket of storm clouds, the group retold their tales. Moknay and Thromar, each continuously interrupting the other to tell his point of view, explained how they had escaped from the first squadron of Guards and had disguised themselves so as to join another troop. When messages arrived that Logan had been spotted in the Hills, Murderer and Rebel broke ranks and charged northward. It had been a combination of pure luck and Thromar's excellent tracking ability that had allowed them to find Logan so swiftly.

Logan then recounted his adventures, leaving out only his night with Cyrene. Moknay and Thromor applauded the young man's skill and intelligence in destroying Farkarrez and his almost successful attempt to trick the Guards. They cheered as Logan told of his escape from the soldiers and congratulated him on his exit from Zackaron's chamber. Moknay shivered, though, when Logan pointed out the gleaming Jewel and the gathering black clouds.

"I fear if we were to talk to Barthol, he'd tell us we had about four more days," the Murderer mused. His grey eyes scanned the foreboding sky. "Whatever the Jewel's about to unleash, it certainly is building up quite a store of it."

Logan fixed his own blue eyes on the nefarious heavens, brushing his black hair out of his face as the winds shrieked past him. "How far are we from the Smythe?" he asked Thromar.

The fighter stroked his reddish brown beard. "Moknay and I flew like the *Deils* to get here, but I do believe it's slightly west of here."

"No, it's south."

The quartet froze as the disembodied voice wafted across the plateau and vanished upon the gale. Lightning broke through the darkness, but the clearing remained empty of all else but themselves. The sudden flash of blue-white light suggested that no one had made that rasping whisper of direction.

"Pardon me," called Moknay, "but I think it's west."

"No, no," the whisper corrected, "it's south."

Amid the increasing wind, the gleaming Jewel, and the land itself, Logan felt the disharmony of the world slacken. For the first time since he had been in Sparrill, the sensation of mismatchment—the accusing buzz of wrongness—faded entirely. Blind in the darkness, Logan acquired new senses and warned Moknay with a faint tap on his shoulder. Questioningly, the Murderer stared at where Logan pointed, yet neither man saw a thing. It was only after another crackle of lightning that the four saw the robed figure standing by the edge of their clearing.

Thromar's huge sword slid free of its sheath.

"Replace your sword, Thromar," a whispering, asthmatic voice advised. "I come as a friend, not as an enemy, albeit you have enough of those."

Free of the disturbing sense of disunity, another feeling plagued Logan's mind. That voice! he thought. That voice was infuriatingly familiar! The young man knew he had heard it once before . . . but he could not think of where. It eluded him like a dream eluded a waking man.

A dream! Logan's mind exclaimed. The voice of his first dreams! The whispering tone of the businessman/monk!

The third crack of blue-white light revealed the smile on the lean face as the mysterious newcomer approached. "I see Matthew knows who I am," he stated pleasantly. "And I wish to congratulate you, young man. You certainly didn't make as many mistakes as you think you did."

Moknay's hand was on Logan's shoulder in unspoken puzzlement, but the joy of meeting up with his companions and the release from both danger and misplacement stunned Logan to the point of speechlessness. Valiantly, the young man battled the happiness clogging his throat but could not speak.

There was a sudden eruption of color, and what Logan thought was another flash of lightning was actually a teleportation spell that unloaded its passengers and their horses in an elegant room of oaken furniture and smooth stone flooring.

"Brolark's backside!" Thromar roared. "Where are we?"

"My home," the robed stranger replied, and, in the light of the room, his features were immediately recognized by Logan.

The domed head was bald on top, yet long strands of pale blond hair streamed to the stranger's robed shoulders. His eyes held the friendly glow they had sparked with in Logan's second dream, and none of the threatening, ghastly tones lingered in the whispering, raspy voice. Standing before Logan—in the flesh and not in a dream—was the businessman/monk himself!

Moknay had a dagger out, his distaste for magic obvious in his grey eyes. "And just where is your home?" he queried. "I don't like being sucked out to nowhere."

The businessman/monk smiled. "You were already standing on my rooftop," he said. "I only thought I should pop you down. You would have never have found the front door from where you were standing! That's why I suggested going south. You know, down?"

"You still haven't told us who you are," Cyrene snarled, her hand reaching for her dagger that was no longer there.

"Oh, but it's so much fun playing guessing games, Cyrene," the businessman replied. "For example, I know who you are, and, let me say this, I don't necessarily agree with your methods or your actions. You're not what you appear to be, my dear, and, frankly, I don't like what I see. And you, Moknay. I must thank you and Thromar for seeing my friend here safely." He turned on Logan. "And you, Matthew. You have questions to ask me and tasks that need completing, don't you? Well, let's see how good you are at my games. This is the sixty-four-thousand-dollar question, Matthew: Who am I?"

Timidly, Logan found his voice: "The Smythe?"

Surprise exploded in the young man's mind.

The long-haired businessman/monk placed a pair of glasses on the bridge of his nose. "Jonathan Smith to be exact," he replied, "and, yes, Matthew, I come from Earth."

· 14 ·

Smythe

Logan blinked in astoundment. "You?" was all he could make out.

The long-haired businessman nodded his head, a smile on his lips. "Of course, Matthew. I was once Jonathan Smith, a mild-mannered businessman for a rather large corporation until this odd wind picked me up and spit me out here. Since then I've become the Smythe—spellcaster par excellence!"

Logan's companions were silent as the young man struggled to speak. The shock on his face was obvious, and wonder swirled in his blue eyes. He finally asked, "Why?"

The Smythe looked at him. "Why what?"

"Why me?"

"Why not?" The Smythe took a seat at a large oaken table and steepled his fingers. "You were probably on hand. That's the way things worked out for me. I just happened to be there."

"But you're the one who warned me!" protested Logan. "In the dream. How did you know I would be the one out of millions of other people?"

The spellcaster grinned. "Ah! That! Try and follow what I say." He cleared his throat. "Before you arrived, you had a dream in which a nasty, bald-headed fellow—me—warned you not to misinterpret, as it were, dreams from truth. Later, when you got 'zapped'—as you so quaintly put it—to Sparrill, that warning came in handy. While in Debarnian, you had a second dream. Only this time that nasty bald-headed man wasn't quite so nasty . . . in fact, he was a little bit confused. He looked you over curiously, muttered something about it must have worked because you were still alive, and then vanished. Do you remember?"

"Yes," Logan nodded, "but I don't see . . ."

"That second dream was, in all truth, the first dream," the Smythe went on. "I had to first wait until you had arrived in Sparrill, see who you were, and then go back in time and warn you. That was what I meant by it must have worked. Is all this understandable?"

"The second dream was the first?" Logan repeated unsteadily. "Like in a time warp or something?"

"Crudely put, but yes. I couldn't do anything until after the wind had picked someone up and I learned who that someone was. All right?"

The young man rubbed at his forehead, the astonishment in his eyes replaced by puzzlement. "So there's no special reason?"

"None whatsoever," replied the magician. "For any of us."

"Any of us?" Logan echoed. "It certainly made a good choice with you! You became the Smythe!"

"My being the Smythe has hardly anything to do with who I am," the businessman answered. "It's not some inner calm that allows me to be a spellcaster here, it's where I'm from. Matthew, you and I are very different here—we don't belong. Because of that, the land senses our difference. What makes this land so different is its magic. The two differences then—us and the magic—clash, and yet, also merge. It was no accident you stumbled upon the Jewel, my boy. You are attracted to magic just like magic is attracted to you."

"What am I, some kind of magnet?" the young man retorted.

"In a sense, yes," the Smythe responded. "Because we are not of Sparrill—not of this world—all magic and magical items attract—and are attracted to—us. It's the strangest twist on 'opposites attract' that I've ever heard of!"

"But I don't want to be a spellcaster," Logan cried. "I want to go home."

Jonathan Smith stroked his chin. "Not me, my boy," he said. "I wanted to stay. I was sick and tired of my life on Earth and was quite glad for the change of pace. Of course, you're not a spellcaster the first day you set foot in Sparrill—it's a slow, lengthy build-up—but I muddled through. I survived. And now"— he motioned about him— "now I am the Smythe, second only to Zackaron."

"Is Zackaron from Earth too?" Logan wondered.

"Good heavens, no!" the wizard declared. "Zackaron has the gem in your saddlebag to thank for his powers."

"What you're saying," Moknay said from one corner, "is that Logan is capable of becoming the next Smythe."

The Smythe turned on the Murderer. "Quite so. Quite so. In fact, that's the whole reason for the wind. Sparrill's magic knows it must have a vessel in order to be used—for the good of the land, of course. Still, once Logan's here, it's up to him who he sides with."

"I don't want to side with anybody!" the young man shouted. "I just want to leave this place. That's why I came here—not to be your bloody replacement!"

The Smythe sighed somewhat and leaned forward in his seat. "Yes, yes," he said, "that's your choice as well. But these 'mistakes' are vital to the land. That, my boy, is something I've come to learn since being here. Mistakes are a vital part of anyone's life . . . even to something as vast as Sparrill itself.

"You and I, Matthew, are mistakes. And we ourselves suffer from a number of odd accidents. Like the Jewel. As I said before, your leaping astride Pembroke's horse was not accidental, and yet, it was. It was no accident that the Blackbody blamed you first for upsetting the natural Balance of things, and, then again, it was. And it certainly was no accident that you camped by the Ohmmarrious so you could talk to the Sprites, and yet, it was. Is all this understandable?"

"Yeah," muttered Logan, "my life here's nothing but one big contradiction."

The Smythe chuckled at the quip. "Hardly, dear boy, Hardly. Can you remember what Groathit said to you the first time he faced you? You denied he was there, saying Sparrill was a dream and everyone in it was created by you. Groathit then said, 'I should think not . . . although . . . we may become so later.' He was referring to the power you could hold. The power that could, indeed, make Sparrill . . . or unmake it."

"Is that why the Reakthi-scum are hounding friend-Logan?" Thromar queried.

"Partially," the Smythe answered. "True, if Logan stayed he would be as great as—if not greater than—I am. However, our difference to the world makes both magic *and* magical items easy to find. Think what Vaugen—or Mediyan—could do with a man who could gather together every single magical force in the land."

"Destroy anyone who dared stand in their way," gulped Moknay.

"Or else Matthew could help us," Cyrene remarked. "He could help the people destroy both Reakthi and Mediyan."

"I told you before I don't like that attitude of yours, Cyrene," the Smythe barked at her.

"I'm not going to work for anyone," Logan said. "I had guessed that everyone wanted me because I was different, and I was right. Well, I'm sick and tired of being so different, and I want to go back to my world where I can just fit back in with all the others like myself."

Thunder boomed from outside.

"Uh . . . perhaps we had better hand over the Jewel?" Moknay nervously suggested.

"Ah, yes, the Jewel," the Smythe responded. "You know, Matthew, I'm really ashamed of you. You've had the ability to halt the Jewel all along."

Logan's anger exploded at the wizard. "What do you mean? Am I a spellcaster already? Can I do more than take out my fucking eye?"

The sorcerer winced at the foul language. "No, no. Attaining the magic takes a long period of time, as I mentioned previously. Of course, being in the areas of great magical concentration speeds up the process, but, even your close proximity to the Jewel hasn't transferred any magic to you. The nearest time you used any force was when you took in the powers of that talisman. But, as for the Jewel, you must remember, Pembroke was Zackaron's servant-boy. He was no spellcaster."

"Stop talking in riddles, damn you!" Logan spat. "Answer me this: Can you send me back home?"

The stone chamber was silent.

"Yes," the Smythe finally whispered.

Another clap of thunder resounded from outside.

"Answer this, then: *Will* you send me back home?" Logan demanded.

The Smythe got up from his chair. "If you so wish it."

The fury boiling inside Logan gradually subsided and relief washed over him. This "mistake" would be cleared up—Logan would be free to return to his world and his way of life. After all that time of uncertainty, ignorance, and fear, Logan had finally found his way home.

The young man cast his gaze on the three behind him and his guilt crept back into his brain. Druid Launce died to get you here, it told him. Mara was injured trying to save your life. Moknay and Thromar risked their necks to find you. Cyrene gave herself to you in thanks. And now you are just going to leave them? What if your reversal of the wind's "mistake" causes some major calamity worse than the Jewel?

"It won't unbalance anything if I go back, will it?" he questioned the Smythe.

The spellcaster waved him off. "No. The wind will probably pick someone else up once it realizes you're gone . . . hopefully. I'm afraid my time as the Smythe is about up. I'm getting old—even here."

There seemed to be an aura of despair radiating from the long-haired businessman, and Logan felt the guilt grow. The Smythe had come to love his new world and had hoped to pass on his position to someone with similar feelings. Logan, however, had only tolerated this land. True, he had admitted to himself it had good points, but he still longed to return home. A pity he couldn't pop back to Sparrill whenever his own world grew monotonous.

The Smythe turned away from a bookcase and eyed Logan. "You're sure you want to go back?" he inquired.

The young man gave his companions one last glance. "Positive," he replied.

"Very well, then," the wizard sighed. He took a few steps toward a corridor. "We'll have to go into my workroom. These are my living quarters. Can't have any magical smoke seeping into the bedcovers, now can we?"

Although the magician resumed his usual jesting, the gloom still hovered above him. Logan's guilt caused sorrow to twinge in his heart, but he refused to be persuaded by remorse. Not even tears from Cyrene would stop him from going back to his rightful world.

I'll never be able to say good-bye to Mara and Barthol, he thought sadly.

"Now, if all of you would step into next room," the Smythe instructed. "Oh, bring your horses too."

Plagued by his thoughts, Logan took his stallion's reins and followed the robed businessman into another room. The Smythe's workroom was cluttered with devices and artifacts like Zackaron's cavern had been, but in much neater array. Down another corridor the four could see the opening to the Smythe's home, and cold winds howled into the workroom from the orifice. Double doors towered behind them, and a single door was to their left, closer to the actual opening in the mountainside.

"That leads to a back exit." Smith explained the double doors, noting Logan's gaze. "The other door is another passage in from down the hillside. Sometimes the people who come to see me can't make it up the mountain to the main entrance."

The spellcaster busily glanced through a few volumes and pulled a couple of items down from some shelves. As he did, the dark sky became obscured by rain—harsh, violent sheets of water that poured from the black clouds. Ominously, the Jewel glimmered brighter in Logan's saddlebag, and thunder accompanied the glow. Toward the main entrance, shifting shadows of the rain crept into the cavern, bringing with them the musty odor of rainfalls.

"Oh, my," the Smythe breathed, peering toward the main opening. "Perhaps we should check the Jewel before sending you back."

"Perhaps," Moknay agreed, and the word caught in his throat.

Why not? Logan decided. That way he could leave knowing the Smythe had saved this world from destruction. That would relieve some of the guilt.

The young man stepped up to his horse and pulled the glaring Jewel free of its leather encasement. His companions clustered before the double doors as they watched, their eyes reflecting the golden flames lapping up around the facets of the Jewel.

Lightning shrieked across the sky, leaking blue-white light into the workroom. There was a second shriek of severed air and the Smythe stumbled backwards, an arrow lodged in his chest. In shock, Logan rushed to the downed man, the Jewel casting a ghastly shine over the spellcaster.

"Sorry, Matthew," the wizard gasped. "Other . . . ways of sending you . . . back. Told you . . . my time was . . . up."

Dancing shadows played across Logan's face and he glanced up toward the main entrance. The single door nearby had opened, and a number of silhouetted forms had stepped out. The golden fire of the Jewel glistened upon their faces and scintillated off their metal chestplates. A muffled growl came from Thromar as the leading figure approached, his white scars tinted a disgusting yellow in the Jewel's emanation. A gnarled form stood beside him, and both were flanked by archers.

"You've led a merry chase, Matthew Logan," Vaugen snarled, "but I'm afraid our little game has come to an end."

Groathit's good eye gleamed as he peered at the coruscating Jewel in the young man's hands.

Logan remained kneeling, staring back down at the corpse beside him. Blood pooled about him but the young man was beyond sickness or disgust. His rage played up inside him: screaming, vengeful. Just like Launce! His mind raced. *Just like Launce!*

"You bastard," Logan cursed venomously, his eyes ablaze with a fire not of the Jewel.

"Save your petty name-calling for later, whelp," Groathit snapped. "Hand over the Jewel or your friends die."

More Reakthi were filing into the chamber, the archers still in front. There only seemed to be the remaining men of that troop that had pursued them near the Roana, but, in such confined quarters, they were more than enough to slay them. One volley of arrows and Logan and his friends would be pincushions!

"Yes," Vaugen hissed in triumph, "think it over. Weigh the odds carefully. You have nowhere to run—no way to escape. Before you had a whole forest to hide in; now you have absolutely nothing!"

The anger in the Imperator's voice was unmistakable, but Logan turned away and glanced back at his companions. The back door! he recalled, fixing his blue eyes on the double doors. Somehow the Smythe had known what would happen and he had purposely explained the passages around them. Still, unless Logan could send an unspoken command to his friends, any move by any of them would send a wave of arrows twanging throughout the workroom.

Grey eyes locked on blue and the rapport was established. Good old Moknay! the young man thought. He understands!

The twin portals can act like a shield. The only problem is: How can I get to them before I get shot full of holes?

A teasing tingle scurried through Logan's brain, and the buzz of disagreement was back. Now, however, it was once again tolerating the young man. In fact, it held that almost friendly tone as it had once before. An impending sense of urgency flowed with it.

Logan stared down at the Jewel, and the patter of rain resounded in his ears. The Wheel was tilting again, and more than one discharge seemed probable. Barthol had warned them the disasters would increase in magnitude as the Wheel tilted further. The build-up of clouds had definitely indicated a more cataclysmic eruption. In fact, the Wheel could have been going over on its side! Which meant if it was not checked now, Sparrill—and Logan—were lost!

Help me, Logan pleaded with the disunity of magic. If you want to keep zapping people from Earth to become spellcasters, help me!

The disturbing sense strengthened, yet it was focused in Logan's hands. Unexpectedly, a blinding flare went up from the Jewel, and lightning streaked across the heavens. Thunder so loud it shook the Hills reverberated around them, and startled shouts went up from Reakthi and Logan's companions.

Searing heat lashed into Logan's palms, and, obeying an instinctive reaction, he jerked his hands away. A few of the archers shot blindly, and their bolts whizzed dangerously about the workroom. Moknay, however, had taken the opportunity to fling open the double doors, using the leftward portal as a wooden shield against the shafts. Thromar and Cyrene were swiftly leading the horses into the passage beyond, yet Moknay lingered behind, his grey eyes trained on Logan.

"Come on, friend!" he coaxed. "Their sight's returning!"

Logan hastily scrambled to his feet and started for the Murderer. His mind suddenly panicked, and the young man scrambled back toward the Smythe. In his haste, he had left behind the Jewel!

"*Kill!*" Groathit's voice screeched, and the order was echoed by Vaugen.

The Jewel was still hot to the touch and Logan's fingers were reluctant to entwine about it. Out of the corner of his eye he glimpsed an archer steady himself and nock an arrow into his bow. The sudden flare-up had only temporarily blinded them, and some indeed had their vision back.

Swearing, Logan lifted the sizzling Jewel and almost dropped it again as he turned to run. He staggered like a drunken football player, trying desperately to cling to the burning gemstone as he scurried for the back door. All the while he knew full well an archer was aiming at his back.

There was a sudden "thwunk" and Logan crashed to the floor, his balance deserting him at last. In astonishment, he turned to see the archer collapse, a dagger lodged in his solar plexus. Pivoting about in the opposite direction, the young man saw Moknay spring out from behind the protection of the door and hurl another gleaming blade. In reply, two archers fired, and the grey-clad Murderer spilled backwards.

"NO!" Logan screamed, and the Jewel's centerless interior exploded with the young man's rage.

A vengeful lightning bolt forked into the main entrance of the cave and disintegrated the handful of Reakthi standing near the opening. The crackle of electrified air filled the chamber, and Vaugen and Groathit both wheeled around in stupefaction. The remaining soldiers stared dumbly at their charred brethren, then back at the furious young man before them. The rage still smoldered within him, and Logan wished he knew how he had accomplished his previous feat so he could dispose entirely of the murderous lot.

"So, the maggot wants to try magic?" Groathit sneered, his good eye flickering with hatred. "Like a babe trying to swim, you shall drown!"

Gloved hands pulled Logan out of the way of Groathit's warbling blast of sorcery and into the safety of the back exit. "Keep this up and I'll start to get used to that magical blather!" Moknay informed him, shoving him up the pathway.

For a few moments, nothing registered in Logan's mind. It was as if the past seconds had been so alarmingly swift and deadly that he needed a minute to catch up on what had happened. Moknay, he noticed, had only been struck by one of the arrows, but it protruded painfully from his left shoulder; streams of blood were trickling down his chest. Their horses had disappeared, and it took Logan a second before he guessed Thromar and Cyrene had escorted them to safety. Behind him he could hear the Reakthi in pursuit, and he feared another arrow may permanently end Moknay's life. And they were so damn unprotected! There had to be a way to stop the Reakthi!

Logan looked down at the Jewel again but shook his head. First of all, he had no real idea how he had used the powers either time. Secondly, a third usage of the energies could trigger off an almost uncontrollable discharge and really send the Wheel on its way over. The young man had felt such a tremor building the second time he had linked with the gem.

Screaming winds sent raindrops stinging into the young man's face as he clambered free of the back exit. Moknay followed close behind, his face reflecting the pain in his shoulder. Thromar and Cyrene were some distance ahead of them, pulling Moknay's horse onto a ledge that led to a somewhat level path. The heavy rainfall had already plastered their clothing and their hair to their bodies, and the howling gale whipped viciously at their sodden frames. Thromar waved to them as he finished guiding Moknay's stallion up and suddenly jerked a huge finger behind them.

Logan glimpsed over his shoulder to see Vaugen and his men racing after them, also leading horses out of the exitway. Of course they had been riding horses! The young man kicked himself. They must have kept them in the corridor beyond the door.

The ground beneath their feet already sucked and slipped around their shoes while the chestplated soldiers mounted up behind them. Logan and Moknay scrabbled up a muddy incline, muck giving way beneath their weight. Hooves sloshed into the saturated Hills, and Logan feared his death was near at hand. A recognizable "twang" pierced his ears, and the young man wondered where the Reakthi archer had aimed. There was an abrupt, high-pitched wail as Vaugen's horse crashed to the mud, knocking the black-chestplated Imperator across the soggy earth. Puzzled, Logan looked up the incline to see Thromar nock another arrow into the same bow the young man had first used when he had arrived in Denzil. That same self bow one could find in early English times! It was keeping the chestplated soldiers from reaching their prey!

"Whoops!" Thromar boomed. "Friend-Logan! Heads down!"

In blind response, Logan pulled his head down and heard an arrow shaft splinter against the stone above his skull. Labored breathing sounded through the downpour, and Logan saw Moknay straining to keep his grip as more blood stained his clothing.

"Cyrene!" the young man barked the order. "Help Moknay up!"

The soaked blonde failed to hear the young man, her deep blue eyes set on the scarred Imperator below her.

"Cyrene!" Logan shouted again.

The blonde glanced down at him.

"Help Moknay up!" he ordered once more.

Somewhat reluctantly, the girl obeyed as Logan heaved himself onto the ledge and rolled to his feet. A sorcerous shaft of energy burst close to his head, dazzling him with its brilliance, but Vaugen's voice brought the young man out of his daze.

"Groathit!" the Imperator thundered. "Not Logan! We can still use him!"

I'd sooner die than work for you, you heartless bastard! the young man fumed. Vaugen had been the sole cause of Launce's death and the Smythe's death. And by that second act he had destroyed Logan's surest way home.

Moknay stifled a cry as Thromar hastily jerked the arrow free of the Murderer's shoulder. "Sorry about that," the fighter apologized, "but we can't hope for painless bindings at a time like this."

"I'm not disagreeing," the Murderer said, swiftly covering the wound with a strip of cloth.

"Do we ride?" Logan queried.

"Treacherous but necessary," Thromar answered, leaping astride Smeea.

Logan kept the Jewel cradled in one arm as he clambered into his mount's rain-drenched saddle and looked back. Thromar and Moknay readied themselves beside him, but Cyrene was still glaring in Vaugen's direction.

"Cyrene!" the young man screamed. "Goddamn it! Get up here!"

Once again the blonde was reluctant to tear her gaze away from Vaugen, but she finally obeyed Logan's frenzied shout and mounted up behind him. The rainfall increased and lightning split the black sky. Mud and water splashed under the hooves of the three brightly colored horses as they forged their way through the downpour and sludge. The splattering hoofbeats of pursuit forced their way through the noise of the rain, and Logan gave a quick glance over his shoulder. Beyond Cyrene's own dripping face, the young man could see only a wind-beaten wall of raindrops.

"Pull up! Pull up!" Moknay's cry shattered Logan's thoughts. "We're coming to a turn! Don't let your horse slip!"

Immediately, Logan responded, slowing his mount down as the horses came to the curve. In normal weather the slight bank would have required little slowing, but in the muddy, unpredictable torrent of rain the mounts had to slow down or else pitch over the side.

"Brolark!" Thromar cursed. "How in the name of Harmeer's War Axe can they see us, let alone trail us? I can hardly see the twists in the Hills!"

Moknay gave the landscape behind them a useless glance. "I'm afraid Logan's carrying a rather obvious piece of cargo," he stated. "More than once that Jewel's acted like a beacon."

While the trio of horses galloped on, Logan shifted the Jewel to his center, trying to shield its glare with his body. The gem was still warm, but no longer painful to the touch; however, its constant flame refused to be blotted out by Logan's frame.

"Kill them, Matthew," Cyrene hissed in his ear. "Blast Vaugen and his troop to Gangrorz's Tomb!"

"How the bloody hell am I supposed to do that?" the young man shouted back.

"The Jewel," the drenched blonde replied. "You did it before. Kill them."

Violently, Logan shook his head. "Too dangerous," he explained. "Even if I knew how I wouldn't do it."

"Not even for me?" she cooed sweetly.

Logan clenched his teeth. "No! It's too dangerous!"

The amorousness drained out of Cyrene's voice. "You bastard," she spat. "After what I let you do?"

Emotional pain struck Logan to the very center of his being. She hadn't meant anything she had implied? he contemplated. It had all been an elaborate game? She had, after all this time, only been using him? Using him as a tool to vent her anger on Vaugen? After he had finally given his trust and affection to her, she was just using him, like the golden-haired Riva had attempted to do?

It suddenly all became clear to the young man. Cyrene's dislike of Moknay and Thromar, her fear of Zackaron and the Blackbody, her heartless indifference toward Logan's escapes, and her supposed love for the young man. All had only been concerned with her revenge. Moknay, Thromar, Zackaron, and the Blackbody all could have kept the young man from her, and, of course she wouldn't compliment his escapes: she didn't feel the pride he had felt. And her love . . . ! It was nothing but her desire to use him . . . just like Vaugen and Mediyan wanted to. *That* was the attitude that the Smythe disapproved of so greatly in the girl.

Logan sneered furiously to himself. No wonder! he growled mentally.

"Logan! Logan! In Agellic's name, wake up!"

The blonde behind him let out a scream that pulled the young man from his thoughts so that he finally heard Moknay's cries. Another curve sloped before them, and Logan had not reined in his horse. The yellow-and-green mount started to slow itself down, but it struck Smeea with a jolt that knocked the black-and-red horse into the slush. To avoid having his legs crushed, Thromar heaved himself out of the saddle, hit the muddy path, and slid clear off the edge.

"Dung!" the fighter swore as he disappeared over the cliff.

Half-running, half-staggering, Moknay dismounted and charged through the muck to the ledge. In shock and horror at what he had done, Logan joined the Murderer. Smeea indignantly climbed to her feet, shaking slime and mud from her mane. Cyrene's deep blue eyes remained on the men as she dismounted; then she turned and faced the sheets of rain behind them.

Logan was greatly relieved when he saw the massive hand clamping a wet stone at the rim of the cliff.

"Give me your other hand," Moknay called down to the fighter, removing his gloves.

The Murderer clamped the fighter's meaty hand in his and tried to pull him up. The swampy soil forbade traction of any kind, and Moknay himself almost slipped over the edge as he struggled. At last the Murderer found some well-anchored rocks and set himself behind the stones, straining to lift his war-sibling. Blood began to soak through the bandage at his shoulder, and pain etched itself into the lines of Moknay's face.

"Agellic, you're heavy!" he grunted.

"What do you want me to do?" Thromar retorted. "Lose some weight while I dangle here?"

Moknay turned his pain-ridden face on Logan. "I need some help!" he called. "Give me a hand! Careful you don't slip!"

Logan hesitated a moment and turned to the girl behind him. Drenched by the constant downpour, Cyrene's clothing was practically transparent, and her dark blonde hair was a shade of brown as it clung to her scalp. The wet dress and bodice gripped her every curve, and Logan fought back the desire to kick her in the butt. Instead, he handed her the Jewel and went back to Thromar.

Cautiously and strenuously, the pair grappled to pull the Rebel to safety. Twice they almost had him up, but the undependable ground would suddenly reject their footing and send one of them sprawling—and send Thromar dangling. The pair would then try again, both of them suffering—one from a shoulder wound, the other from burned hands.

Blue-white lightning slashed through the tempest as Thromar clawed his way through the mud and reached the path. His stolen uniform was smeared with runny brown muck, and rainwater dribbled down his face and made tiny cascades through his beard. His beady eyes went wide as he struggled and squirmed through the mire to lay on level ground.

"What in Imogen's Blaze is she doing?" he wondered once he was safe.

Logan and Moknay turned to see Cyrene facing the dark forms that rode toward them through the cloudburst. The girl's hand slipped under her clinging dress, but her dagger's sheath was empty. Vengeance burned in her eyes as the Reakthi drew nearer and the blonde peered down at the Jewel in her grasp. Another quarrel of electricity shrieked through the heavens as Cyrene raised the gleaming gem over her head.

Riding a horse taken from one of his men, Vaugen's eyes went wide as he thundered out of the unnatural storm. Groathit reined in beside him, his spiky blue-grey hair seemingly untouched by the rain. The chestplated warriors all brought their mounts to sloppy halts, eyes fixed on the blonde wielding the mystical gem.

Lightning cracked as the Jewel's glare increased.

"You killed my father," Cyrene snarled through the downpour. "I'm going to kill you."

The golden Jewel flared like a miniature sun.

"Cyrene!" Logan yelled. "Don't!"

A vengeful smile drew across the blonde's lips as the Jewel's flame strengthened and surrounded her. An agonizing shriek suddenly tore through her as the Jewel erupted, its blinding glare intensifying. Soaking-wet clothing instantly cindered, and cosmic fire obscenely caressed the blonde as she dropped to her knees. The foul odor of burning hair wafted across the strong winds as Cyrene collapsed to the muddy ground and lay sizzling in the mire.

Anticipation sparked in the spellcaster's one good eye as Groathit eagerly leapt from his horse and grabbed the fulgurant Jewel, ignoring the flickering tongues of fire licking at its side.

"Mine!" he cackled victoriously. "I have it! It's mine!"

His face streaked with mud and rain, Logan turned mutely on Moknay and Thromar. His companions stared back, Logan's own shock and horror mirrored on their faces. The silver-chestplated Reakthi spellcaster held the incandescent Jewel in his bony hands, and Vaugen was grinning behind him in like triumph.

Thunder shattered the firmament and the entire earth trembled below them. Fearful glances came from both Reakthi and Logan's party. Groathit looked up at the grumbling sky, a frown on his face as he wondered what dared interrupt his success.

Logan caught his breath.

"What is it?" Moknay questioned, his fear of the Jewel glinting in his cold, grey eyes.

"The Wheel," the young man replied. "Cyrene's triggered off another discharge. I sensed an unbalance in the Jewel when I used it myself. Cyrene's managed to set it off. I think the Wheel might very well be tipping over on its side."

The marshy ground shifted again beneath their feet, and a blazing white bolt of electricity screeched through the darkness. Moknay fought back his misgivings concerning magic as the gleam of the Jewel did not die down but increased.

"Groathit!" Vaugen barked. "What's going on?"

"The Jewel has been leaking energy," the wizard snorted back. "All I need is a little time and I can get the powers under *my* control."

Marvelous, Logan grumbled to himself. The only man on hand who can halt the Jewel is the Reakthi spellcaster, but they can't let him keep it! And yet, if they attempt to steal it back, the Wheel could tip on its side and then there would be no reversing it!

"Friend-Logan!" bellowed Thromar. "What can we do?"

"I don't know," the young man truthfully answered. "We're stuck between a rock and a hard place!"

"Looks more like a lot of mud and a mountainside," the fighter mumbled in confusion.

Groathit's thin lips began to utter some inaudible incantation, but the Jewel persisted in flaring brilliantly. Wailing bolts of lightning arced across the sky more frequently as more and more energy seeped free of its prison and wreaked havoc with the natural Balance. "There will be nothing to stabilize the forces of the Wheel and act as equilibrant!" Barthol had informed them. "The Wheel will have no means to achieve equilibrium, and it will tilt until it entirely flips over and destroys us all!"

The ground bucked below their feet as streams of golden force ejected from the Jewel.

The mountaintop across from their path exploded, hurling rubble and silt through the clouds. A figure wearing a nimbus of unbelievable energy stood atop the destroyed peak, arms outstretched in a godlike gesture. Dark hair streaked with grey billowed in the gale, and intense fury boiled in the dark eyes.

"You have something that belongs to me!" Zackaron boomed, the aura of power crackling to accent his charge. "I have come to take back what is mine!"

His sunken features highlighted by the Jewel, Groathit jerked his head up to glare at the wrathful wizard. His talonlike hands closed in about the Jewel and his eye glittered his unspoken refusal.

The Hills groaned as the earth heaved once more.

"Friend," Moknay whispered into Logan's ear, "I was told once some very good advice which I think we all should heed: 'Never stand between dueling spellcasters.'"

The rain fell harder.

· 15 ·

Tilting

The Hills were lit by the crackling flame of the Jewel and the sporadic bursts of lightning from above. Logan stared in awe as a third source of illumination walked upon the screaming winds and placed his foot in the rain-bespattered ground of their path. The wildness seemed burned from Zackaron's eyes by the very shield of power roaring about him, but it had been replaced by a boiling anger that made Logan cringe as the sorcerer neared. This one time, the young man was glad someone had stolen the Jewel from him.

"You have something that is mine, Reakthi," the dark-eyed spellcaster snarled. "Return it at once."

Groathit cocked his head to one side, and his bad eye glinted dully in Zackaron's fire. "It is mine now, madman!" he spat back. "I have labored too long for this trinket to suddenly hand it over to you!"

The nimbus of magical force surrounding Zackaron sparkled, and furious pinpricks of energy popped in the dark air. "Are you challenging me?" he asked, a hideously confident smirk on his face.

Groathit's fingers tightened about the Jewel.

"Do you know who you are dealing with, Reakthi?" Zackaron asked, taking a bold step forward. "I am Zackaron. I am Master."

The gnarled Groathit responded by flinging deathly black rays at the dark-eyed sorcerer. Zackaron threw up an arm and deflected the crackling bolt, causing it to explode against the mountainside.

Thromar leaned toward his two companions. "Who do we root for?" he wondered.

"We don't," retorted Moknay. The Murderer frowned as the

muddy Hills bucked underneath them. "The longer those fools fight, the more energy escapes from the Jewel."

Silenced, Logan turned back to the battling wizards. Howling quarrels of thaumaturgy cast eerie shadows across the Hills. Groathit was stumbling back, holding the glimmering Jewel in one arm while dazzling blasts of magic sprang from the other. Zackaron casually advanced, his face set in a grin of certainty. Blistering streams of enchantment shrieked from his fingers, and his aura of force blazed in happy compliance. One of the beams yowled through Groathit's defenses and knocked the chestplated wizard into the ooze.

Vaugen and his men pulled their horses back, the Imperator raging at his warriors. He was directly in front, and the cluster of horses at his back denied him the chance of safely backing away from the blinding display of magicks before him.

His good eye flashed his fury as Groathit pulled himself from the quag and released sanguine bolts from his palm. Zackaron's protective screen flickered as the blood-red rays struck, yet he retaliated with ruby beams of his own.

Logan's eyes fell upon the Jewel Groathit had left within the slime. The glaring golden tongues of energy continued to waver and dance across the facets but practically went unnoticed. The wailing streaks of sorcery rocketing from the wizards' fingers nearly drowned out the constant flare of the gem.

Those wizards were so busy fighting they probably wouldn't notice if someone crept in and took the Jewel from them, Logan mused.

"Don't try it," Moknay advised, reading Logan's thoughts. "It would be folly to try and creep in there with those two hammering the mountainsides with their magical claptrap! Besides, if one of us could do it, we'd probably have both sorcerers on our backs!"

"What the hell can we do?" Logan wanted to know. "The longer we wait, the more the Wheel tips!"

"It's no use trying to explain it to those two," Thromar snorted. "Battling wizards are like drunken men: Neither wants to be disturbed and both are very indignant when they are. They'll fight one another for that Jewel until the Wheel *does* tilt and we all blow up!"

Moknay gave the dueling sorcerers a glance and then turned

back to Logan. "Any idea what the Smythe meant about you being able to stop the Jewel?" he questioned.

Logan sneered. "I think he was being sarcastic," he replied. "Remember all that crap about how powerful I could be if I stayed? He was probably referring to what I'd be able to do once I was as powerful as he was."

"Fat lot of good that'll do us!" grunted Thromar. "The Wheel isn't going to wait until you're a spellcaster."

"It would have had a long wait 'cause I'm not going to be a spellcaster!" Logan answered. He swung his gaze to the battling magicians. "No one's going to be anything unless that Jewel isn't stopped soon."

The horses behind the three men neighed uneasily, pawing the mud with their front hooves. The barrage of theurgy must have been unnerving them, Logan surmised. *I know it's bothering the hell out of me! That stupid buzz hasn't let up once!*

"Groathit!" Vaugen shouted. "Not toward me, you fool!"

The Reakthi spellcaster glared over his shoulder as he was forced to retreat. Vaugen frantically fought to pull his horse away while the men behind him struggled likewise. The cluster of hooves and unstableness of the ground worked against the Reakthi, and Vaugen remained exactly where he was, Groathit stanced in front of him.

"Have you had enough, Reakthi?" Zackaron jeered.

Groathit kept one foot near the glaring Jewel. "You shall rue the day you dared combat me, madman!" he warned.

There was an eruption of flame that almost scorched Vaugen's mount, and Groathit was devoured. In his place stood a grotesque mockery of the human form. It was some hybrid between human and crocodile, and it pointed an iron-clawed hand in Zackaron's direction. Thundering blasts of magic knocked the dark-eyed wizard to one side, and his halo of energy winked out.

A smile drew across the demonic Groathit's face, revealing needle-sharp fangs. His eyes both glistened red, but the right was brighter than the left.

Zackaron pulled himself from the mire and glared at his opponent. "You like to change shapes, do you?" he snarled, and spittle trickled down his chin. "You face one who *is* the Macrocosm! And I would like to see you change again!"

Intricate patterns of light formed in the dark air before Zackaron as lightning speared the black clouds. The marshy ground continued to groan, tilting sympathetically with the unseen Wheel. As if suddenly unbalanced by the shifting hills, Groathit toppled to his knees, a scream tearing from his throat. His demonic form was forcibly ripped from him by Zackaron's dazzling conjurations, and the Reakthi spellcaster could feel his very flesh churn and bubble under the dark-eyed wizard's commands. His gnarled limbs fused together, and folds of flesh covered the magician's mouth and eyes. When the sparks of light diminished around Zackaron, a titanic maggot writhed through the sludge where Groathit had been.

Revulsion shook Vaugen by the shoulders as he gaped at his mutated spellcaster. There was another flash of fire from Zackaron's hands, and Groathit bulged and shifted like the very Hills themselves. A grotesque hue of brown spread across the disproportioned maggot, and its flesh turned as mucous as the mud around it. Excrement's foul odor stabbed through the gale as Zackaron transformed Groathit into a massive mound of dung, but flickers of magic sprouted from the wizard's hands once more, and Groathit underwent another change.

Amusing himself, Zackaron drew a hand upward, and the pliant blob of protoplasm that was Groathit obeyed. The pink-ish substance bubbled skyward, stretching like what Logan thought resembled Silly Putty. A mouth suddenly materialized in the pulp, and an agonized scream shredded through the mountains. The shriek was answered by a crackling shaft of lightning as the Jewel pulsed brighter.

The mounts of the Reakthi troop nickered, their eyes glazed as they nervously glanced around them.

Zackaron brought his hands together and Groathit re-formed in a bellow of sorcery. Overcome by unbearable pain, the Reakthi spellcaster slumped to the mud, his chest heaving in his effort to breath.

"Next time," Zackaron warned, "do not challenge one who controls the very forces of the multiverse."

The wizard arrogantly strode through the rain and muck to lift the Jewel that lay beside Groathit's twitching foot. Logan's horse suddenly snorted behind the young man, and Moknay's horse also jerked its head up fearfully.

"Wait a minute," Logan whispered to himself. "The horses . . ."

In question, Moknay and Thromar turned to look at the nervous mounts as Zackaron faced Vaugen and his troop. "Do any of you wish to battle me for what is already mine?" he queried smugly.

Even Vaugen's grey eyes were aglow with fear.

Zackaron seemed distraught. "Pity," he sighed as madness trickled into his voice. "Pity me." He swung on Logan and his friends. "Any of you?" he demanded. When neither of the three responded, a sad frown came to Zackaron's lips. "What good is this game unless someone will play, hmmm? If no one will play, I shall take my Jewel and my leave."

How badly can things go? Logan asked himself. The damn Wheel was probably going over on its side and the Jewel still hasn't been placed in check. Not only that, Zackaron had gotten the Jewel away from Groathit but seemed to be slipping into his usual insanity. Pretty soon he'll be more interested in making things from clay rather than checking the Jewel. The whole world will go up in flames while Zackaron tries his hand at making someone!

The flaring Jewel suddenly spiraled out of Zackaron's hands and landed in the slosh, spraying filth as it hit. A thunderclap accented its splash, and twin quarrels of electricity slashed the sky.

Illuminated by the lightning, a wet and bedraggled figure crouched on the hillside, spiderlike. "No," the newcomer informed. "You cannot take what is his! You must not leave with what is Pembroke's!"

A childish smile played upon Zackaron's lean face. "You wish to challenge me for what is mine?" the wizard asked, ignoring the fallen Jewel.

"Pembroke will," Pembroke replied, snarling. "Child is his!"

Thromar jerked his head so sharply that water hurled from his soaked hair. "Brolark!" he cursed. "I don't understand. I thought Pembroke worked for Zackaron!"

"For many years," Moknay replied with a curious grin. "For too many. I'd guess Pembroke thinks the Jewel is his. He doesn't even recognize his master."

Servant-boy, Logan's mind hissed. Servant-boy.

Pembroke scuttled like a lizard down the hill and into the

mud. He eagerly grabbed the blazing Jewel and unsheathed his Triblade, facing his dark-eyed master. Both men ignored the lightning and the shifting earth as they peered at one another through the tempest.

"Who are you?" questioned Zackaron.

"He is Pembroke!" the lithe servant replied. "Pembroke is father of this Child. Infant of Pembroke and the multiverse, she is!"

Logan glanced back at his horse that pawed at the sodden path. Pembroke had been lurking nearby all this time! the young man realized. It had been the servant's radiation of fear that had been affecting the horses—not the magical duel or the unnatural storm.

"I still don't get it," Thromar mumbled beside him.

Logan ignored the fighter and turned his gaze toward the sky. The black clouds were churning and boiling like an angry sea, and lightning constantly pierced the darkness. They were wasting precious time, he noted. The Wheel was tilting farther and farther with each passing second as more and more energy escaped from the Jewel.

"Return what you have taken!" Zackaron commanded Pembroke. "It is mine."

"No! No! Mine!" the servant spat. "*My Jewel!*"

The bedraggled servant's shriek stabbed through Logan's mind, and all the horses skittered backwards nervously. The mountains also quivered in fear as the ground continued its gradual shift.

A yowling bolt of magic vomited from Zackaron's fingertips. Silver glinted in the downpour as Pembroke knocked the mystical blow aside with his Triblade. There was an abrupt shout amidst the chaos and Groathit flung himself at Pembroke. The wiry servant screamed in rage and surprise as they splashed into the mire.

You must remember, a rasping, disembodied voice whispered, *Pembroke was Zackaron's servant-boy.*

Logan wheeled toward the source of the voice, and his blue eyes locked on his yellow-and-green mount shaking its head in the rain. A sudden daze sunk its fangs into the young man's neck, and all the blood drained out of his face.

"Friend," Moknay asked, noticing him go pale, "are you all right?"

Still dazed, Logan's lips said, "We need the Jewel."

Moknay raised an eyebrow at the entranced young man. "Huh?"

Logan broke free of his trance and grabbed Moknay by the front of his shirt. "We need the Jewel!" he shouted frantically. "The Wheel is tilting!"

"We know that, friend-Logan," Thromar said, trying to soothe him, "but we're powerless to prevent it."

Mud squished underfoot as Logan turned on the fighter. "I've had the ability all along!" he yelled. "We need the goddamn Jewel!"

The heavens screamed as if torn apart.

Moknay fixed his steel-grey eyes on the forms struggling through the storm. Cataracts of mud spilled from the mountain peaks, and precariously set boulders began to sway as the Hills shuddered.

"You need the Jewel?" he asked.

Logan nodded his head desperately.

Moknay took a cautious step forward. "I'll do what I can."

Groathit ducked under the jagged point of the Triblade and reached for the mud-concealed Jewel. "The *Deils* take you, Vaugen!" he cursed. "Order your men to help!"

"Order your men to help!" parroted Zackaron, sliding further into his madness as he grappled for the blazing gemstone.

The black-chestplated Imperator swung on his men. "You heard him!" he barked. "You four! Aid the spellcaster! Get that Jewel at all costs!"

As the quartet of warriors dismounted, Moknay slid through the shadows of the mountains toward the battle. His fear of magic swirled in his eyes as he spotted the filth-smeared Jewel and crept forward. A misguided shaft of sorcery exploded behind his head and the Murderer cursed as he dodged forward. Mud, wind, rain, lightning, and tremors all worked against him as Moknay rose into a crouch and started forward again.

Thromar watched apprehensively, gnawing on his lower lip; Logan scrambled to his horse.

The four rain-spattered Reakthi jogged around the struggling forms. One released a cry as Pembroke's Triblade winked silver and neatly severed the soldier's foot from his ankle. In a splatter of blood-mingled mud, the Reakthi pitched forward and fell screaming into the slime. His companions swiftly scampered backwards, pelted by the insistent rainfall.

"The Jewel!" Groathit was cursing them. "Get the Jewel, you fools!"

Moknay gave the storm-torn sky a worried glance and charged headlong for the gleaming Jewel. He glimpsed back at his friends and saw Logan wading through the sludge toward him. A sword almost took off the Murderer's head as he swung back around and narrowly ducked under the blade. The Reakthi who had attacked toppled off balance, deceived by the treacherous mud. Lightning whined through the black stormclouds as Moknay attempted the dive for the Jewel but also lost his traction.

The Hills seemed to crumble beneath them as the tremors intensified.

"Moknay!" Logan was screaming. "The Jewel! Get it!"

One of the remaining Reakthi reached down for the glaring gem when a magnificent funnel of energy spiraled heavenward. The chestplated soldier was knocked backwards by the eruption, and a searing, magical wind tore at Moknay as he inched nearer to the scintillating Jewel.

A boulder rumbled down the hill and crashed over the side; lightning illuminated its route.

The world moaned as if dying.

"Moknay!" came Logan's voice again.

The Murderer gave the flaming Jewel a suspicious stare. His fear was even stronger than back in Plestenah when they had gone across the bridge. And with good reason! The Jewel had not been traitorously spewing columns of Cosmic fire!

Moknay swallowed his fear and lunged.

"Logan! Catch!" he yelled, throwing the Jewel high into the rain-filled air as soon as his fingers clamped around it.

Time was suspended as the glaring Jewel spun through the tempest. Vaugen, Groathit, Pembroke, Zackaron, Thromar, and all the Reakthi stared in hushed awe as the incandescent gem spiraled through the rain on its way toward Logan.

The Hills rumbled and thunder shattered the sky as the Jewel splashed at Logan's feet. Hastily, Logan flipped open the lid of the tin he held in his hand and gathered a handful of the bluish powder inside. A dense fog of blue energy spumed up around the young man as he smothered the blazing Jewel with the foul-smelling dust, and a lightning bolt shrieked in protest.

The Hills dimmed as the golden flame of the Jewel wavered . . . and went out.

The harsh rain slackened as Logan fell to his knees, peering at the docile Jewel. The blue powder had miraculously disappeared on contact with the golden gem, but it had worked as Logan had guessed. That was what the Smythe had implied when he said Logan had had the ability all along. Pembroke, the businessman had reminded them, was no spellcaster, so Zackaron had to have given him a way to keep the Jewel in check himself. The way of doing that was the small tin of foul-smelling snuff, something so trivial it had constantly been overlooked—yet carried by Logan through almost the entire trip.

A portion of sky forced its way through the rainclouds.

"He did it!" Thromar roared cheerfully. "Friend-Logan, you've stopped the Wheel!"

Logan inhaled deeply, wiping rain and sweat from his brow. For some reason, he did not feel like celebrating. He was cold and wet and had lost his hope of returning home. His love had been rejected and misguided, and two more people were lying dead because of him. No, he certainly did not feel like cheering.

Zackaron got up from the mud as the rain let up even more. "That's it?" he inquired, crestfallen. "The game is over?"

Moknay glared at the wizard, wiping muck from his hair. "Looks that way," he responded.

"Oh." The spellcaster glanced back down at Pembroke. "You! Why are you lying there? Quickly, quickly! Get out! Get up! We have so little to do and so much time to do it in!"

The lean servant pulled himself out of the mire, his black eyes trained on the mad sorcerer. "Pembroke, he is. How is it you know of Pembroke?"

"Forgetful," stated Zackaron. "I am Zackaron. I am Master. I shall be Master. I am forevermore Master. I is Master. Agggh! Deformity! Freak! Outcast! Unclean! Make haste! Make haste! We must away!"

The drenched Pembroke shook himself like a dog and sent mud and water flying. "But Child," he argued. "Pembroke cannot leave his Child."

"Child, you want?" Zackaron replied. "I shall build you one from clay."

As Zackaron lifted his arms, Pembroke's ebony eyes locked on Moknay. "Pembroke shall have his Child," he hissed.

There was an implosion of air and spellcaster and his servant were gone.

The rain became a drizzle.

Moknay scrabbled to his feet and glared at the force of Reakthi still confronting them. Dripping muck, Groathit raised himself from the slush, his good eye flickering with fury. There was a plop of disturbed mud and Vaugen leaped off his horse.

"Unfortunately," the Imperator smirked, "you won't be rid of us quite so easily. You're a sensible man, Murderer. Give us Matthew Logan and the Jewel and we may spare you."

"Spare me your lies!" Moknay snapped, reaching for a dagger with slick fingers.

"Come, come," Vaugen answered, "you're in no condition to fight. You have a wounded shoulder, and I'm sure your friends wouldn't want to see you hurt more."

Thromar unsheathed his sword, teeth clenched. "Keep back, Imperator," he rumbled, "or I shall do to you what I did to Agasilaus!"

Groathit hovered behind Vaugen's shoulder like a mud-splattered shadow. "You frighten us," he mocked.

Voicing a war cry, Thromar charged through the mud. Bowstrings drew back and fixed on the huge fighter. Clumsily, Thromar slid to a stop, eyeing the archers from atop their mounts.

The winds died to a breeze.

"Matthew Logan," Vaugen jeeringly called to the young man. "Your friends are to be fodder for the carrion crows unless you have something to say about it. Are you willing to work for us? A simple 'yes' will save your friends' lives."

Silently, Logan raised his head and stared without seeing. Loss upon loss had piled up upon the young man, and he was overwrought with grief. Launce, Cyrene, the Smythe—all of them were dead.

His surest chance of going home was just as dead.

"Well?" the Imperator demanded.

"He'll kill us anyway!" Moknay warned.

Groathit's hand flamed orange. "Silence!"

Logan blinked away some of the sorrow and focused on

Vaugen and his band of Reakthi. They were threatening the lives of his two friends, he realized. They were threatening to kill Thromar and Moknay!

The familiar rage began to swell in Logan's breast as he fixed his eyes on Vaugen.

The archers drew their arrows back even further.

"We're waiting," Vaugen mocked.

An unexpected ruckus exploded behind the Imperator, and half his troop pitched over the side of the cliff. The arrows and bows dropped from the archers' hands as they twirled to see the line of men behind them spill to the soggy ground. One archer careened over the mountainside; another's horse was bodily lifted into the air. In shock, Vaugen jumped away from his troop as they were mercilessly struck down by some unseen foe.

A blue face suddenly surfaced among the mounted warriors.

"Foooooooood!" the ogre bellowed, batting Reakthi away with each swing of his brawny light blue arms.

Just as surprised as Vaugen, Moknay and Thromar cast bewildered looks at Logan, but the young man was not looking at them. His eyes were locked on the black-chestplated Imperator, and the wrath that churned within his pupils was incredible!

Under Logan's direct command, a meteoric fireball exploded from the Jewel and caught Vaugen full in the chest. Battered by the destructive blow, the Imperator jerked like a marionette caught in a windstorm. He slammed into the side of the mountain, his flesh ablaze with Cosmic fire. The last of his men went spinning down the hillside as the light blue ogre halted in the mud, its crooked grin proudly stretched across its face.

Groathit gaped at Logan. Magic! the spellcaster realized. The whelp had purposely reached into the Jewel and had torn free a portion of magic! Beforehand he had only directed the Jewel's discharge, but now he had actually delved into the gem itself and had extracted its magicks!

The wizard turned as Vaugen peeled himself from the mountainside and lurched in his direction. The Imperator's flesh was charred and melted, and wisps of smoke snaked from his burned scalp as he groped for support.

"Groathit," he rasped through seared lungs. "Go."

The gnarled spellcaster whirled on Logan. "The Smythe is dead," he said with a sneer, "and I shall see that you do not take his place! And this time, Vaugen shall not stop me!"

A tongue of flame shot into the drizzling rain and engulfed both spellcaster and Imperator. When it fluttered out of existence, the two were gone.

The rage and sorrow slowly released its hold upon Logan, and he was surrounded by his friends when he looked up.

"Remember what I told you about too much of that blather?" Moknay joked. He glanced over his wounded shoulder at the ogre towering behind him. "I take it this fellow is a friend of yours?"

The ogre grinned. "Friennnnnnnnd!"

Logan placed the last stone on Cyrene's grave and turned to the trio gathered on the path. The slight drizzle of rain had ceased, and early morning light was filling the sky from the east. The hillside, however, was marred with burn marks, and countless prints churned the muddy soil of the ground.

Cleaning any lingering sludge from his sweat suit, Logan headed for his horse. As he lifted the Jewel from the ground, Thromar asked: "What are we going to do with that thing?"

Logan shrugged.

"Give it to Barthol," Moknay suggested. "He'd be so scared of it he'd always remember to keep it in check."

"Would it be safe?" Logan queried.

"Leave your friend here to help guard it," the Murderer advised, pointing at the ogre.

Thromar finished removing his soiled Guard's uniform and chucked it over the cliff. "What about you, friend-Logan?" he wondered. "What are you going to do?"

Logan placed the Jewel in his saddlebag and mounted his horse. "I don't know," he admitted sullenly. "The Smythe said something about other ways home. Maybe I can find one of those."

Moknay jumped into his horse's saddle and winced at his injury. "Well, then I guess it's up to Thromar and I to help you," he declared.

Logan threw the Murderer a quizzical glance, but Moknay's smile told him he was sincere.

The ogre gave all three men a puzzled stare as they started their horses forward, but it eagerly trailed them.

Thromar's yellow teeth shone through his beard. "I've got an idea," he said.

"Holy Agellic!" Moknay exclaimed in mock awe. "Will miracles never cease?"

"Jest if you want, Murderer," Thromar remarked, "but the Smythe said something about Sparrill herself causing friend-Logan's arrival—so she can just as well send him back."

"How?" Moknay and Logan both inquired.

The question was even on the ogre's face.

"The very Heart of the Land," explained the fighter. "The Bloodstone guarded by the Sprites."

Moknay stroked his mustache. "Hmmm, perhaps you're not as stupid as you look, Thromar," he jeered.

"Stuuuuupiiiiid!" the ogre boomed happily.

Logan scratched his head. "Are you sure this Bloodstone exists?" he asked. "I thought it was a myth."

"You saw the Sprites yourself!" Thromar responded. "And with your magic-attracting ability, there shouldn't be any problem finding it!"

Moknay smirked. "Would you care to wager on that remark? Say, five gold pieces?"

"Make it ten!" Thromar retorted.

"So be it! Ten it is!"

Thromar grinned again. "But this time there'll be *no* dancing on corpses!"

Logan felt a smile draw on his lips as he stared into the rising sun, and the warmth of its rays sent hope surging through him. There was still a chance of getting home, he told himself, and his companions would be at his side until then.

He had been right, he thought with a smile. Sparrill *was* a nice place to visit . . .